G000016124

PATRICIA HICKEY was bor
graduate of Trinity Colleg
years with Aer Lingus in sales and publicity. She has also
worked in educational representation and was National
Secretary of the National Parents' Council (Primary).
Patricia has broadcast two short stories on community radio
and had a monologue performed in the City Arts Centre,
Dublin. She is a writer and landscape painter; married, with
three children; and lives in north County Dublin.

GREEN POPPIES

Patricia Hickey

THE
BLACKSTAFF
PRESS

BELFAST

Thanks to Paul, for saving my sanity and endangering his own in cyberspace; to Patsy Horton of Blackstaff Press for her acute literary insight and faith; to Hilary Bell, editor, for her great sensitivity and patience; to Rachel McNicholl for her incisive attention and advice, and to everyone at Blackstaff Press; to my friends in Súil Eile, especially Joan and Nora.

First published in 2004 by
Blackstaff Press Limited
4c Heron Wharf, Sydenham Business Park
Belfast BT3 9LE
with the assistance of
the Arts Council of Northern Ireland

ARTS
COUNCIL
of Northern Ireland

Patricia Hickey has asserted her right under the
Copyright, Designs and Patents Act 1988
to be identified as the author of this work.

Typeset by Techniset Typesetters, Newton-le-Willows, Merseyside

Printed in Great Britain by Cox & Wyman

A CIP catalogue record for this book is available from the British Library

ISBN 0-85640-756-9

www.blackstaffpress.com

for Martin,
Anna, Paul and Eve

It sounded like the slap of rope falling on water, sharp, decisive, just the way I remember it as it fell from the ferry all those years ago. One minute I was reading the newspaper, the next one she slapped me on the hand. The sound rang across the room but nobody stirred. Most of the residents here are deaf. May says that you would need to rap some of them on the head with your knuckles to gain their attention. I heard the nurse say that she had spoken to me already, that I didn't hear, that she was a while trying to attract my attention. But now she is placing her hand down on the back of mine, as if we are beginning a game, like children about to pile their palms one on top of another in turns, faster and faster, each one scrambling not to be the last one on top of the pile. Like me. The last one on top of the pile, the rest of them all dead. How strange to be out in front like this, alone. Sometimes I expect to see them lining up behind me – William and the younger boys and delicate Esmee trailing a tiny Lucinda along at the rear. I have to check myself from glancing backwards at times. And they are children, when I remember my brothers and sisters, always children. It is as if my mind has placed them forever beyond the reach of their individual stories.

I forget what it was that I was reading in the newspaper that had me so absorbed. Oh yes, the ring. They found it on the island – Spike Island they call it now. Ugly name. A prison island. All the old barrack buildings are used to contain those we wish to lock away, a sort of social tidying up. It seems there are work areas there, places where the prisoners can cultivate vegetables. That's where the ring was found, by a prisoner tilling the soil. Eighty years or more lodged there and suddenly the soil is turned over and there it is. Such an inconsequential thing, really, a small piece of mined and polished metal. Did it gleam up at him, I wonder, or did he feel his spade strike it?

'Get back from that sea wall can't ye. Ye'll catch yer feet in the rope.'

They pulled me back from the wall as the rope rasped across the granite pier and fell with a sharp slap onto the water before being dragged on board the small ferry. I stood watching as the boat moved away from the quay, heading out into the channel that would take them on the brief trip to the island. The khaki-green uniforms of the soldiers were like blobs of ocean frozen into peaks on the deck, as the distance dimmed them even to my sharp nine-year-old eyes.

I heard about the ring from my mother. Mrs Durell lost it, although there was some talk about why she took off her wedding ring in the first place. They were good at wondering about things like that. Somebody said that there was a reward for the finder, although nobody seemed to know what that might be. I felt it would have to be something that glistered as much as the ring – a half sovereign perhaps. If I were to search, I would have to take the ferry to the island, even though my father had asked me not to visit while he was on duty. But this was different. This was important. As I watched the ferry make the short crossing and waited for it to return for the next trip, the sound of lapping water seemed to slow down gradually, yet kept up its lap lap lapping against the quay wall, so that I felt anchored there by the slow rhythm as if time would keep me there, forever waiting.

I never did discover what the reward was for the finder of the ring. I suppose that I must have hunted for it in all those unlikely places that a child would look. There were so many excuses for a trip to the island then but somehow I cannot remember the one involving the search. Yet I can remember the disappointment of not finding the ring and failing to earn the reward. But the greatest disappointment of all was being forbidden to go to the island for a month. The water lapped across the stones, shattering in white glassy splinters before being slurped back again into the greener depths. This was serious. The summer stretched before me, an endless invitation to roam free, and my greatest freedom of all had been taken away.

'Helena, you must respect your father's wishes. You must request his permission to visit him when he is on the island. It is not always suitable for you to arrive unannounced all the time.'

'But Mama, I only go when the thought pops into my head. And anyway, he's not always here when I do think of making an arrangement. And why isn't it always suitable?

He only sits at that old desk writing all the time. He always leaves it as soon as he sees me, so it can't be all that important.'

'But of course it's important. They are reports that have to be written. Of course they are important.'

'Reports are stupid things. He's a soldier. Why should he have to write reports?'

'Now, Helena, no need to be rude. Other children don't go over to the island to see their fathers while they are on duty. What would happen if they all decided to visit at the same time? The island would be overrun by children.'

'Better than soldiers.'

'Helena, don't be disrespectful.'

'I'm sorry, Mama.'

'Now, remember, you must not visit for the next month, until you learn to comply with our arrangement.'

'But Mama!'

'Enough, Helena.'

She turned her hands towards me and made a slight movement in the air as if she were shooing geese before her. She wanted me out of the kitchen, an end to the disagreement. Mrs O'Sullivan had gone home early and Mama was busy preparing supper alone. This was something she did twice a week, on Mrs O'Sullivan's early days. On these occasions Mama was transformed from a reserved, slightly distant personality into someone trying very hard to be brusque and efficient but who succeeded instead in merely appearing fussy. She moved about the house in a nervy flow from room to room, picking things up, straightening a picture, placing boots in a row in the back porch, folding a newspaper, opening and closing windows, until finally coming to rest in the kitchen.

Sometimes I thought she was practising what she had seen Mrs O'Sullivan doing. Yet no matter how fast she moved about her home, no matter how brusque her movements, she could never approach the magnificent, sweeping gestures of her housekeeper.

Perhaps it was Mrs O's girth that made the difference. ('Helena, her name is Mrs O'Sullivan,' Mama constantly reminded me, but I only ever called her Mrs O. I think she liked me to call her that.) The slightest swaying of her hips would swivel her around in her arduous dusting routine, and I frequently held my breath, waiting for delicate figurines to fly off the chiffonier or a lamp to go spinning through the air. But she had an inbuilt spatial awareness that was unerring. She could glide her enormous hips past the most fragile piece of furniture without as much as a tremble from the leaves of the parlour palm.

'Light as a fairy,' Papa would laugh, as he watched her run down the garden path and turn along the seafront in the direction of home.

Her early finishings coincided with my father's early homecomings. Mrs O liked to leave before he arrived, or failing that, to be on the way down the garden path as he came through the back kitchen. As soon as she heard the creak of the back porch door and the thump of his boots as he dropped them onto the boot-rack, she was off. 'Just to let you have some time,' she would say, with a brief nod in the direction of the noise, sweeping up her basket, narrowly missing the china hen holding the eggs, swaying down the hallway and out the door without a backward glance. And always at the front steps she would call back to me, with a slight turn of her head, 'Ye can come up and see Benjie if ye wish,' and then she was gone, leaving Mama in the kitchen, transforming herself, tugging at her skirt, as if a change of clothing was required to mark her move into her new role, and settling instead for movement, for the incessant, ineffectual dash around the house until finally returning to the kitchen and commencing the supper preparations.

Perhaps that is why she appeared to be preoccupied so much of the time. She wanted to conclude things, always allowing me to go so that she could devote herself to whatever was preoccupying her thoughts. Her pale skin and white-blond hair shimmered in the kitchen, an incandescent presence that required nurturing, lest it be quenched. At least that is how she appears in hindsight and I think that is how Mrs O saw her then.

'Don't you be bothering your mother, Helena, you hear?'

This admonition was thrown at me frequently out of the blue, as if I alone might be the source of bother for Mama. She thought that as the eldest girl, I might take responsibility for the actions of my younger brothers and young sister (Lucinda was not yet born). But then I was the only one on whom she could bestow her thoughts about my mother, as I was the only one who visited her home, where she could speak without fear of being overheard. My eldest brother, William, was too busy with school (or with avoiding it) and trying to wheedle his way onto a fishing boat to be bothered with visiting, while my sister Esmee and the younger boys, Peter and Gerald, were still too young to travel any distance from home unaccompanied. Benjie, Mrs O's youngest son, who was a year older than me, would grin across her chaotic kitchen, the signal to follow him into the O'Sullivans' back yard, where he busied himself endlessly with mysterious chores associated with his father's fishing boat.

'Her life isn't easy, you know, your mother's,' Mrs O would say, speaking into the vague kitchen spaces, peeling potatoes, chopping onions and cabbage, feeding baby Róisín, putting logs on the huge open fire that blazed away winter and summer to cook the food and dry the clothes. She was given to musing about Mama's life as she worked, a seamless ribbon of talk that wound in and out and around her chores until she made mention of 'the Officer', my father. All her talk seemed to lead to mention of the Officer. When I was older and understood politics a little, I saw this form of naming my father as a distancing of sorts, one that allowed the nebulous Home Rule sympathies of her family remain untainted by her contact with the Officer's family. But then, at nine years of age, what I detected was a story that was spun and spun in the air above my head, changing slightly in detail over time, as I played with Benjie and ran in and out of her kitchen.

'The Officer will be home by now,' she always announced with finality as if this marked the end of something, thumping a large pot of potatoes on the scrubbed table or plopping the baby down onto the floor, where an enormous green and navy woollen rug was spread. That was on the days when I had spent several hours with Benjie. It was the signal for me to leave. We never said goodbye, although I always thanked her for the bread and jam she fed me, and I left the door open as I left, as if I were only slipping in next door, soon to return.

Leaving Benjie's home each time placed me briefly in what I thought of as a topsy-turvy place. The clamour of his world seemed to rise in answer to my leave-taking of this corner at the edge of the town. Everything there gave the impression of being slightly tilted, in keeping with this jutting piece of headland which was raised at a sharp angle to the low road along by the sea. And as if the tilt was insufficient to mark it off from the rest of the town, the paving stopped some distance short of this place, so that the street in summer had a cloud of ochre dust hovering a few inches above the ground, except of course when it rained, and then the street ran with a yellow mud that stained the children's feet the colour of newly dried flax and clogged up the cracks in the rough flagged floors of the fishing families' cottages. I thought that the tilt of the street was deliberate then, to give the fishermen a better view of the sea. And all along the short street the clamour moved in and out of open doors as I passed, as the children clanked broken lobster pots, metal buckets, glass floats and splintered oars, while the smell of decaying fish and soapy water, seaweed and cabbage filled me with a headiness on the downward slope to the seafront and the sedate terrace that was home. I have always associated noise and clamour with happiness since that time.

Strange how I can step back into that funny tilted street as easily as if I were about to step outside the door. May said that I should write down all of my memories, give them a beginning, a middle and an end. But I can't explain to her that this would give them a different shape, a sequence, filling the gaps with slick ironic comments, so that they would appear like some tired Victorian leftovers. No space then for spontaneity and the lovely crabwise movement of my mind that constantly takes me by surprise and moves me so easily from one thing to another in an endless glorious slippage. May said that she understood, when I explained how I like to jump in at any point of my choosing, indulge myself and then leave. But May doesn't believe in memories. She says her family's memories always lead to rows, as their recollections are so 'contrary', and she draws out the last syllable as if all the rancour is captured in that final sighing sound. 'Leave the memories with the dead,' she says frequently. Ah, yes, the dead.

'So, Helena, how is the delightful Mrs O?' That was Papa's standard greeting to me on my return as he hoisted me aloft and then plopped me abruptly on the dark green sofa.

'Mrs O'Sullivan, dear', Mama would say quietly with a sigh, knowing she was wasting her time.

I knew Papa used this form in order to tease Mama. Then he would drop a kiss onto the top of my head as he moved from the sofa to the winged armchair, where he sat each evening rustling the newpaper and looking towards me across the top of it from time to time as I told him about my day. He did not change out of his uniform immediately on returning home, preferring instead to sit a while in his chair, listening to me and reading, his figure encased in heavy wool. In the gaslight his uniform took on the ochre colour of the mud on the street where Benjie lived and which gathered between his toes. Papa gave off a strange sulphuric glow in the fading sunlight that seeped at an angle through the tall windows, so that I remembered him as a beacon after he had gone, an eternal cresset lodged between the high dark wings of the chair.

One by one my brothers and my sister would drift down to where we sat in the drawing room, coming quietly from high up in the house, like dormice who had curled up beneath the eaves, stirring only when he arrived, hoping to avoid any close questioning about their day. Papa always managed to detect, by some means known only to him, the forbidden attractions that enticed each of us daily. Perhaps it was a certain windblown saltiness about William that told him he had once more been out on a trawler, having missed school to do so. And maybe it was the long superficial scratches on Peter's legs that told of his escapades in the gorse searching for larks' eggs. Esmee, too pretty and too timid, would manage to hide behind Gerald as he told of his latest invention – usually something exotically useless, made with mirrors of clouded glass weathered on the beach – until Papa would bend forward and reaching his hand behind him, draw Esmee out of the shadow of his chair and say, 'Did you find the fairies at the bottom of the garden, Esmee?' This always served to infuriate her, much to his glee.

'There are no fairies in the garden, Papa,' she would say with exaggerated patience, her head down, twisting and turning her pinafore in her hand as if she were wringing a fairy's neck. But always she was rescued by Mama bustling in from the kitchen, down the narrow passageway and calling us into the dining room, where she had set out several covered dishes.

'Richard, do stop teasing her,' she would say as we clattered our chairs back and sat down and Mama pushed a froth of frizzy blond curls from her forehead with the back of her hand before serving the meal.

Entering the dining room was to encounter an eternal winter. The sun that angled into the drawing room never penetrated here. The town was too steep for that, backed up as it was at the end of our garden, rising in a sheer sandy cliff at the boundary and leaving our tiny courtyard in permanent shadow. Whenever it rained, which was often, Papa would say in his booming sergeant-major voice,

'Mark my words, it will all slip down on us in the night and push us into the sea, just you wait and see.'

'Oh Richard, stop frightening the children, please,' Mama always said in response, as if she held the expectation that he would always frighten us and what was expected of her was an admonition.

And yet we were never frightened by him. What frightened us then, or what frightened me, was the air of distance that Mama carried about her, a sort of distracted absence, as if whatever it was that had deserted her would be found in her frenzied movements about the house in Mrs O's absence.

'There now,' Mrs O would say each time she returned, 'you managed fine on your own, now, didn't you?'

And Mama would smile wanly, eyes flickering sideways and beyond Mrs O, and then she would retire to her bedroom for a brief period as Mrs O reclaimed the kitchen. I imagined Mama then finding the things she had been searching for as she moved her brushes around her dressing table, the gunmetal sea beyond her window reflecting back at her from the speckled mirror.

'Say grace,' Papa would mutter gruffly, lowering his chin onto his chest as we all fell silent around the table. I cannot remember anyone ever saying grace aloud. It was presumed that we all knew how to say it and that we would all say it silently. But I never knew what to say, remembering only bits of it from school.

'Bless us, oh Lord ... which of thy bounty ... through Christ our Lord ...'

Sometimes I would strain my ears, trying to catch a whisper of someone else's version of grace, but nothing came back to me from the silence, just the occasional creak of a chair or the flicker of an eyelid as we each checked for a sign from the others that grace was over, finished, said. I don't believe that anyone said the actual words, ever. Grace was a prologue to the meal, that was all. Like someone ringing a dinner gong.

Papa's gruffness always disappeared by the time we raised our heads. There was a merriment in his eyes each time he finished whatever it was he did in that brief interlude before we ate, as if he were laughing at some private joke. Mama always appeared slightly fretful as we began our meal, waving her hand vaguely at us to quell our voices, flashing a glance at Papa.

Perhaps Papa declined to say grace aloud in deference to Mama, who was a Protestant.

'Church of Ireland, Richard, *please*,' she would remind him quietly on the odd occasion when he referred to her religion.

Or perhaps he did not want to draw attention to their different religious allegiances, although in the way of children we knew that there was this vague unspecified thing between them. We knew that he went alone to the Catholic church on the hill each Sunday when he was not on duty, and we went occasionally to church with Mama, where we tried to join in the solemn lengthy hymns and listened in awe to her wonderful singing voice. She seemed to be so much a part of what was going on in that tiny church that I felt she did not belong to us in the way that other children's mothers belonged to them. She became transported by the music, the stained glass light smote her hair with slivers of purple and magenta and I felt that everyone in the church must have noticed her and thought her an angel as she floated in that refracted glow.

And then of course there was the house rule — 'Never speak of religion or politics in company'. We were reminded of this frequently from an early age, before we understood what it could possibly mean. Yet I understood that this too came from that indefinable wellspring of difference between them. It seeped out to encompass our lives, so that children in the local school looked on us as something strange and exotic because we had a Protestant mother and a Catholic father. They too seemed to have heard of our house rule, at least until they were older. And in some way it also became linked in my mind with Mrs O's reference to Papa as the Officer and her rapid departures from the house as the hour of his homecoming drew near.

The baptismal roll of the Church of Ireland congregation in Queenstown at that time was dominated by entries of my family's births — every second or third child a Galvin. Once, when I queried this, why we had so many more children than other families, which only seemed to have two or three in comparison to our five, Papa said it was because God had been very generous with our family and given us lots of babies. I found it difficult to understand this picture of a giving God, especially as it was not Mrs O's view of things.

'Your unfortunate mother with all those children', was a frequent saying of hers beneath her breath, accompanied with a long drawn-out sigh as she piled endless white sheets into a large oval tin bath filled with boiling water on top of the range. How could God give Mama five children out of generosity, while Mrs O saw her as unfortunate rather than lucky to be singled out in that way? One day I started to say this to Papa but somehow the thought got twisted when I tried to put it into words and it just ended up in confusion with him laughing, his head thrown back and his black moustache twitching.

'Perhaps we can put the names of our family on the baptismal roll in the new church when it is finished,' I said.

'You mean in the cathedral?' Mama said. 'Helena, that has been forty years under construction and it is still not finished. That it should take almost half a century to build a cathedral, even if it is French gothic, really beggars belief.'

'Now, now, Ally, it'll soon be finished and well worth the wait,' said Papa.

'That level of grandeur is not required to pay homage.'

'Of course not, but it will help raise our thoughts to the Almighty in such magnificent surroundings.'

'Well, you know I don't hold with that ostentatious display of wealth.'

'What is "ostentatious", Mama?'

'Something that is too showy, Helena, a sort of exaggerated display.'

'Hardly an exaggerated display, Ally, to copy the best of French architecture for the house of God.'

'It's not necessary, Richard.'

And so they came once more to silence.

'Helena, have you finished your tea yet? You must be the slowest drinker in the place. Maybe I'll ask the Slapper to put something stronger in it for you. That might make you hurry up and finish it.' May laughs loudly.

'I'm sorry, May, I got absorbed in the newspaper. Here, you may as well take it. It's cold now.'

'Nothing new in this place.'

May always refers to the nursing home as 'this place' or 'the place', as if it had been set down in a vague geographical space without any identifiable landmarks around it, making it the only thing that has a shape or solidity for her. She likes to say that she has been working here forever, which probably explains the vagueness of her role, drifting around in a blur of dusting and cajoling. I imagine her journeys beyond these walls to be equally vague.

Perhaps she knows the surroundings too well, having spent her entire life amongst them — almost fifty years.

Perhaps she can no longer see them, sleepwalking through the familiarity of these streets beneath the brick horizon that has shuttered her life in this corner of Dublin. Street names carried once the potential for a more exotic existence – Dolphin's Barn, Fatima Mansions, Rialto. Dark brewery smells crossing the tops of redbrick terraces caught beneath the canopy of nondescript sycamores along the South Circular Road as it bent around the city. I can see them now, tiny frozen figures, gliding from the limestone walls of the stadium, pausing briefly before merging with the huddled black-clad figures from the synagogue further along the road, moving through a childhood place May cannot rediscover because she never lost it to view.

But it's different for me, knowing the area once as a child, losing it, then finding it again in old age, like reaching into the back of a cupboard and discovering an old photograph. I can map it out in my mind right now – canal, river, river – neat, watery parallels separated by rises and dips in the land. The nursing home sits on its level stretch of ground with water aft and fore, like a barge teetering at a canal lock, poised to descend from one level to another – that is, if I manage to overlook the intervening roads. The South Circular, Mount Brown, Inchicore Road, Conyngham Road, snaking city roads now, sending their noise up the stepped land through the night to the home, like the faint whirring of a tired electric fan.

The windows here are mostly closed at night in deference to our ancient bronchial wheezing. But on windless nights I open my window and listen to the sounds as they float upwards, while along the corridors the residents grunt and groan their old-age regrets. By day the windows are flung wide open and streams of fresh air move through the place in great draughts and push the balls of fluff that May has missed from under the bed across the shiny vinyl squares until they lodge in the corners of the room. Sometimes May will absentmindedly pick one or two of these up and study them, as if she does not know what they are or expects them to yield up a secret, before depositing them in the wastepaper basket.

But for the most part the place is clean, an undisinfected sort of cleanliness, as if to let us know that we are not ill, only old. The squidgy sound of rubber-soled shoes echoes down the timbered passages, and the wheels of my wheelchair – my buggy – make a sound that makes me giggly especially if I turn it too sharply, a noise which always causes my niece Rebecca to wince. And I like the way the sun streams in through the tall arched windows along the corridors. It seems to come from a higher, cleaner place than in Queenstown, where the light appeared to reach us through water. It makes me think of the nuns long gone from here, who might have stood looking out from their convent windows, watching the wretched and the rescued moving about the courtyard below, tending the vegetables in return for shelter and a vague, blurred spiritual sustenance.

May's sweeping brush crashes off my chair legs and sends vibrations up my back. She talks and bangs and pounds around my room, her short body swinging from side to side. These are her aerobic exercises, she likes to joke. Mostly what she exercises is her anger with her family, and the episodes of her domestic wars are shattered into splinters in the air around us as she works and talks.

Sometimes I try to get to the residents' lounge before she begins her daily foray but her routine is never predictable. When I think I have left her to the confines of the first floor, she is capable of sweeping into my room with energy and gossip, ignoring the fact that I am reading, and I am obliged to leave my book aside and listen to her.

'The trouble with you, Helena, is that you read too many of those war books.'

'They're not really war books, May.'

'Ah, call them what you like. Sure, would you take a look at them.' And she picks up a stack of books from the windowsill, collections of war poetry, books about the origins of war, trench warfare and anthologies of letters from dead soldiers. She bangs them back down with a thump. 'Were you in it – the war, I mean?'

'No. I may look old, but even *I* am too young to have been in the war.'

May stands regarding me, then looks away as if she has lost interest in the subject, pursing her mouth and glancing around. I think she is about to resume her dusting.

'So who was in it then?' She sounds so distant that I have to strain to hear what she is saying.

'My father.'

'Really? Was he at Dunkirk?'

'No. That was a different war.'

I sigh, too loudly for politeness and wait for May's resurgence of interest, which I feel will surely follow.

'I remember seeing a film once about all the soldiers trying to leave the beach there and all these little boats that I wouldn't trust to take me from one side of Sandymount strand to the other were bouncing up and down on the waves, waiting to take the soldiers back to England. God, it was awful.'

May continues her ineffectual routine, pushing a waste-paper basket before her brush, ignoring me. She is in one of her indifferent moods, when she loses interest quickly, or she may come back to the topic at an odd moment later, or tomorrow, or the day after. Now she is singing in a strangely determined throaty voice, the disturbing, lying cheeriness of 'It's a long way to Tipperary'.

I am considering how to spend the morning. The newspaper no longer interests me but I could try the crossword until May finishes her diving and swooping here, then get her to push me down to the lounge and chat to the other residents for a while. Rebecca says that I must make more of an effort to be sociable, but today I'd really prefer to stay here.

The tip of the birch has reached up to my window. A few lime green catkins have begun to appear within the last few days, jumping around in an erratic dance when the wind blows, which is most of the time. And then there are the mountains. Rebecca tried really hard to get me a view of the mountains. She was so pleased about this room. She makes such an effort to get things right, frets over so many things that are not really important – a crystal decanter for my bedside table, a tiny radio whose dial is too small for me to read. May says that I shall probably get lead poisoning from the crystal.

'That's something I could never get my head around, Helena, how men can go and fight another man's fight. The war, I mean, the Great War especially.'

May is no longer indifferent. She raises her head as if she is sniffing the air and I drag my eyes away from the horizon.

'Well, it was very different then. They believed in different things to us. They thought it was an honourable thing to do.'

'Oh yeah? King and country, you mean? Well any eejit who believed that deserved to have his head blown off. Oh

God, Helena, I'm sorry. I didn't mean to say that. I wasn't thinking of your father. Did he . . . I mean, was he . . . ?'

'It doesn't matter. It was a long time ago.'

And I want to look at the mountains again and trace the edge of the housing developments at their highest point, pushing like lava flow into Tibradden and Rockbrook and Rathfarnham, where fields folded softly around each other in my childhood but are now cut into patchwork squares, tiny yards for city children to play in beneath kitchen windows.

'Me and my big mouth. "May," they say to me at home, "you're as diplomatic as a gunboat." '

'Really, May, don't worry about it.'

May stands in the centre of the room and it crosses my mind with horror that she may be about to burst into tears. She jerks her head up and grimaces. 'It's just that all my family were republican back then, although I think they called themselves Home-Rulers or something like that. Most of them still are, out of habit. It's a sort of religion in our house, although I manage to steer clear of it, mostly. But it gets into your veins, the way you think, the way you speak. But mostly I don't think about it.'

But May is telling me once more that of course she does think about it, quite a lot, that she has always known this, that it is something she turns over and over in her mind in an attempt to deal with her difficult brothers. And the fine threads of her thoughts almost manifest themselves before me and she grapples them back before I have fully grasped them.

'But I always thought that those who went to war from here did it because . . . because they felt obliged in some way, because of their families, that sort of thing.'

May seems to be offering me something, an excuse of sorts, a way out. And now it is my turn to become listless and I sense the opening of a fissure, a sensory flash, a memory yet unformed, then nothing.

'I suppose it was something like that.' The listlessness is in my voice yet and I feel ungracious, taciturn almost.

'Well, I don't think you should be thinking so much about it. Not at your age. It's not good for you.'

Not good for me. May taking care of me in the way Mrs O did with Mama in Queenstown nearly seventy years ago, with her urgings and coaxings in her low voice at the end of the hall as we waved Papa off to war. A nice cup of tea, she said, that would be good for her. At my age most things are no longer good for me.

'Oh I don't know about that, May. It's easier to remember back that far at my age than to remember what I had for breakfast. I suppose that's why we old ones do so much reminiscing.'

'Yeah, I suppose. How old were you when – you know, when . . . ?'

'When he died? I was twelve. He went to war when I was nine. I can remember it as if it were yesterday.'

But May has lost interest. Her soft round face, with her dry salt-and-pepper hair standing up in tufts around it, is preoccupied once more. Perhaps she is already preparing for her encounter with the occupant of the next room – James – and his list of complaints. I wonder did Rebecca consider if all of this excitement might be good for me when she sought out this place. May likes James and his collection of medical reference books. She has an episode from her neighbourhood she can set alongside each of his complaints, lurid accounts of diseases and conditions – the symptoms, the course of the illness, the degree of pain and suffering, the final agony. These episodes all end in death. 'He died roaring', is her final punctuation in every deathbed scene, each account leaving James white-faced and breathless, as if he is hearing it for the first time. It's a wonder there are any of May's neighbours still living. She spends lengthy periods documenting these events for James as he sits there in riveted attention, his large pale eyes never leaving her face, bony hands resting lightly on his knees, elbows out from his sides, like wings attempting flight. And after she leaves him, he spends hours moving down the index of symptoms at the back of his medical self-help books, checking and cross-checking, his days an endless physical coping.

But I don't suppose James expected to live this long. None of us did. It was really only a slight change of scene for James − a quick sleight-of-hand, a tiny subterfuge. He probably never even noticed the change from columns of figures to columns of symptoms. And the rest of us here, in our efforts to hang on to outmoded refinements, never even mention the word money, as if we never had need of it. We are more comfortable with symptoms somehow.

I wonder will Rebecca remember to bring the box tomorrow? Sometimes I think she is deliberately delaying bringing it to me. Perhaps she thinks that it may upset me. She thinks about these things too much. All this smoothing out of other people's lives, rearranging and tweaking, removing a perceived intrusion here, a barrier to comfort there. How does she know all these things? All those self-help books, I suppose.

The other day she sat with me for a long time and insisted that we look at the tip of the birch tree. 'Really look,' she said. She began to describe it very slowly, in a low voice without any inflexion, as if I couldn't see it for myself. I wanted to remind her that I had my spectacle lenses changed recently but remained silent, as she was so absorbed. I got tired looking at the branches and looked sidewise at her instead. Her eyes had narrowed slightly behind her glasses as she looked at the tree. Her pale blond hair has become finer and fluffier recently, so that at a distance it could be light grey and she could be mistaken for a woman of sixty, whereas she is a quarter of a century younger. And then there's that slightly startled look and apologetic smile that makes me think that she has missed out somehow, has failed to ease herself into an adult place. And as she continued to talk about the tree and how it moves and sighs, I wondered why her voice bears no resemblance to her mother's voice. She has none of the skittishness, none of that enticing, wheedling style that marked Lucinda as the baby of a large family. Sometimes I think that Rebecca's smile is an atonement for her mother's manipulative ways.

Rebecca's voice continued to tell me how one day soon, when the weather improves, she will take me from here for an afternoon and we will go to the Lutyens garden and hug a tree. That's when my eyes snapped back from her face to the birch tree, to see what it was about it that I had missed, what it was that would make me want to cling to it in such an act of intimacy. And then she was talking again, about wholeness and unity with the earth and I wondered why she never hugs me.

If someone were to soar above this place in a balloon and

take time moving across the sky, this garden would look like a flat, green face with two round staring eyes and two protruding ears all surrounded by green fluffy hair. Nobody would guess it is a war memorial, at least not from up there. Circular fountains and circular lawns. Too much symmetry. I suppose it is all meant to mollify us, smooth out our ruffled edges. If I could annihilate the rows of houses that tumble down the slopes between the nursing home and this garden, I could have an uninterrupted view of all of this whenever I wish. Everything here appears to have arrived in an overflow downhill from the canal and with the slightest tilt will continue a headlong watery dash to the river below. Perhaps someday a great high tide will back slowly upriver and drown the lot.

Rebecca seems to have changed her mind about hugging a tree. She is preoccupied. She placed me here in my buggy in the shelter of the fig tree at my request. I like coming here. Once inside the garden I forget about the symmetry and get absorbed in the nooks and crannnies, the shadows lurking in the corners and at the base of things, hinting at a parallel world. This corner feels Mediterranean and it has nothing to do with the fig tree. It's the heat, I think. It bounces off the wall and the paving stones, as if the warmth has been ensnared here all winter, waiting for this moment to spring its trap. And there is something comfortable about these curves – curving walls, curving paths, a sort of wrap-around feel to everything. I suppose that's intentional too. It's difficult to feel alone standing inside these curves.

Rebecca is walking around the rose beds but there is nothing to see yet, it's too early. Not that she is looking. She is far too agitated, but there is nothing unusual in that. She has been anxious for as long as I can remember. It crept up on her in a way, this habitual worrying. Lucinda ill, unable to mother, it was all a bit inevitable. But was she ever able to mother? Maybe she lacked the imagination for it, no more. Maybe if she had learnt how to value the past, she might have developed an imagination. But somehow she never knew how to look back. No, it wasn't that. She was never interested in looking back. The past held nothing for her, there were no lessons there. She liked to say that she had no time for nostalgia, discarding and destroying letters and photographs over the years. I think that she felt pinned down by them, locked into something that she was trying to re-shape. Photos had nothing to tell her about herself, nor about anybody else. Nowadays, I suppose, we would say that she was trying to re-invent herself, but of course back then we knew nothing about such things. Still, it is strange that Rebecca never portrayed even a hint of her mother's fecklessness, as if she took a conscious decision about it. And now she is in therapy. I suppose it is what they do nowadays, all these young people. They seem so confused.

Wolfgang takes it all very seriously, although he never seems to query why she is attending therapy sessions – at least not in front of me. Perhaps he thinks they are a good idea. But he is frequently preoccupied, so I suppose he has problems of his own. 'I just want to be a good European,' he is fond of saying, after he has had a glass or two of Hock. It used to be, 'I just want to be a good husband to Rebecca', but that was some time ago.

This garden commemorates good Europeans and good husbands too, but Wolfgang never comes here. Not that they considered themselves in those terms then. King, country, empire, honour, glory. Guns, noise, thunder, deafness, silence.

'Are you warm enough, Helena?'

'Yes, thank you, Rebecca. The heat is making me doze. It is surprisingly warm for a spring day.'

'I suppose it is. I wasn't really noticing.' Rebecca gazes upwards towards the top of the fig tree, as if to count the tiny fruits, dormant through the winter, beginning their long, slow plumping out.

'*I ndíl-chuimhne . . . Éireannach do thuit . . .*'

'What was that, Helena?'

'I'm just reading the inscription in memory of the war dead on the wall over there. My father could not have understood these Gaelic words. I wouldn't have understood them myself except that they are translated on the opposite wall.'

Rebecca gives a light snort and I wonder about pollen counts, and then realise she is speaking and I may have missed something.

'You have no excuse, you went to a boarding school and studied Irish. You should be fluent.'

'I know. Strange, isn't it? I never felt the need to remember it. I still don't.'

Years spent in a boarding school in the midlands with black-clad nuns and girls with large red hands appear dimly, vague classroom scenes with wall maps and strange objects in sealed jars on tall shelves, yet I cannot recall the sounds of Gaelic in those rooms.

I realise with a start that I am not sure what kind of Irishman my father was. He never learnt to speak or read Gaelic – an Irish Catholic who spent his short life with the British military, as did his father.

'A soldier of the Empire, trained to operate above politics. "A bit like a priest," he used to joke. He never knew another life, you know.'

'Now, Helena, don't get yourself worked up.'

I am filled with an urge to remember that is overpowering.

'I'm not worked up, Rebecca, I'm too old for that.'

We both stare ahead of us as a ripple spreads across the rank water in the fountain trough.

'I've been thinking about it all recently,' I say, 'about the way the war dead have been resurrected in this country, as if they had suddenly been discovered in a mass grave, instead of being dead for the best part of a century.'

'For goodness' sake, Helena, you read too many news reports.' Rebecca sounds tired and reaches out to take my buggy, as if she needs a support, then changes her mind.

'No, Rebecca, I must say this. We package up the whole remembrance act and peddle it as heritage, did you know that? It's part of the tourist trade now.'

'Sshh, people are looking at us.' Rebecca shifts about uneasily.

'Oh don't be so silly, Rebecca. Why would anyone want to look at an old woman gesticulating in a wheelchair?'

And I have a sudden urge to swing my arms above my head like a windmill, to spin my buggy around in some reckless whirl, a manoeuvre I have never mastered.

'Well, at least they are remembered at last. Perhaps coming here was not such a good idea after all.'

'Rubbish, you know I like it here.'

And we remain silent for several minutes, Rebecca standing tautly beside me, while I ponder when it was that I became this petulant old woman.

'Would you like me to take you around the garden now, Helena?'

'Yes, thank you, dear, that would be nice.'

And I settle instantly into that manageable space that Rebecca has prepared for me with a deft appeal to my nice-old-lady self and yield up my garrulous humour for the moment. And down we go, my buggy clunking and bumping down the steps, through the pergolas with their winding, woody climbers, their tough timber resisting the rising sap, showing no hint of leaf. Past the stone bookrooms with their locked-away illuminated volumes naming the war dead. We could have sent their names into space and deposited them on the moon in a sealed tin. *Clunk, clunk, clunk,* on down the gentle slope, down the tree-lined pathway to the river, where it turns its shoulder sidewise to us in a sullen movement towards the weir. My buggy needs oiling but I shall wait for Rebecca to suggest it. It will, no doubt, get on her nerves shortly. I've become accustomed to the crisp, dry sound, like an agitated lizard flicking its tail in the sun.

The river races alongside us, fast and wide at this point, and we walk, moving along in silence, the river-race flashing points of brilliance back at the sky. The buggy slows its pace, until Rebecca brings it to a halt and comes around and stands beside me. We both watch the river.

'Have you looked at it yet, Helena?'

Ah yes, the box. Dear Rebecca, so anxious to tie up loose ends.

'Looked at what? Oh, the box. No, you see I've been rather busy this past week. There seemed to be a lot going on. We had that bridge league – you know, the one that happens every couple of months. And then there are the smaller sessions in between to keep our hands in. And then of course we –'

I hear the stifled sigh and continue to look at the river and wonder when it was we acquired the ability to pry into each other's lives.

'Yes, Helena, I understand that you have been busy, but you must have looked into the box.'

'Well, not really, as I told you, I have not had any time to myself.'

No time to myself. The great lie we use to hide the terror that it is, after all is said and done, only that − time to ourselves.

'But don't you think that you should sort through all that stuff now? It has been moving from attic to attic for so long it is a wonder that it never got lost. There must be important things in there.'

Important things. God knows, she has had the box long enough and it isn't locked. She was in no hurry to bring it to me and now there is this sudden urgency. It is some sort of lightweight, black lacquered material, brought home by somebody in the family from the Far East. A soldier's memento. Clammy degradations of a jungle campaign all crammed into this small lacquered space. Tiny figures on a sampan, coolie hats and a parasol, barely visible on the surface now. War as a river trip beneath hanging vines. Sturdy-looking lock on it but no key. It is light, despite its size − very light. Once when I lifted it, bracing myself against its anticipated weight, it flew up into the air and then crashed down onto the table. The base has the beginnings of a split in the timber since then, like a rift in ageing yellow skin. I suppose it will give with age as it dries out. And it is papers, papers and not things, that are in it. She must know that.

Rebecca moves restlessly at my side.

'Yes, well I should be able to sort through some of it in the next few days. It shouldn't take too much time.'

'If you like, we could do it together on my next visit.'

'Oh I think I'll manage. How is Wolfgang, dear?'

'Wolfie? He's fine. He's off to Brussels tomorrow to a conference. Something to do with immigrants in Europe ... social integration, that sort of thing.'

Rebecca wanders over to the edge of the river and stands on a soggy patch of ground where swans have trampled the grass. The soft mire gives softly beneath her feet and I watch fascinated as it pools with water.

Wolfgang is always going to European conferences, forever saying to Rebecca that he will bring her to the next one in some exciting city or other. But somehow he never does, or it turns out to be in Brussels.

Rebecca has managed to step back from the spongy river bank and pushes my buggy further along to watch the swans feeding from bread thrown to them by some young children. Their mother stands close by, handing them slices from plastic bags, occasionally guiding them away from the edge of the bank. The swans crowd closely around, necks craning, their slate-blue hooded eyes haughtily watching for the source of the next helping of bread.

'Wolfgang works hard, dear. Perhaps he should take things a little easier.'

'You know how it is with him, his work is his life.'

The swans are becoming impatient, their food supply is not coming fast enough as the young children tire of the repetitious feeding, hands dipping in and out of the bag, the birds snatching the bread, their elegant arching necks belying the grasping, clattering gestures and marigold flashes of their beaks.

'Oh, hardly his life, dear. He needs time to consider other things that are important.'

The bread is finished and the swans begin an exaggerated preening, picking beneath their feathers at invisible irritants, and I realise that I do not know what other things might be important for Wolfgang. I have never known him to indulge himself, even briefly, in any light-hearted activity.

'What things? A family? Is that what you mean?' Rebecca asks.

'Well, nothing specific, I don't wish to interfere, but . . .'

'Well, my mother, if she were alive, would certainly interfere, so feel free.'

Rebecca, of course, is right. Lucinda would have interfered, not out of a sense of duty or responsibility, but out of a strange sense of fun. She liked to manipulate events around her, finding it amusing that she could influence lives in this way. And she was feckless enough not to be concerned about that. After all, as she liked to say on occasion, who ever cared about her feelings? It was all a game with her, nothing more.

'Poor Lucinda, she meant well. But perhaps it's not important to you?'

Rebecca has moved towards the swans, looking at the children then at the crumbs and the plastic bags fluttering at their feet as they slump in a jaded aftermath of the feeding frenzy. Her eyes range rapidly across the group as if searching for a sign, a clue. Abruptly she turns and walks back and stands to one side of me so that I cannot see her eyes. 'Oh, come on, Helena, you never married and never seem to regret either that or the lack of children. Why should you wish all the trappings on me?'

'It was different for me, Rebecca.'

And a subject that I never intended to introduce has crept into the carelessness of my old woman's responses, has slowly shaped itself there before me, so that I am left with it, this great lumpen thing. And of course it was different for me. Different because of the war – both wars. Perhaps it was something simple that slowed my life, a slight turning away at some point, maybe on that pier in Queenstown as I waved my father off to war. Or perhaps I was distracted by some shadowy event that is long forgotten, which caused me to hesitate before moving forward again to one side of my earlier path, an undetected loss of direction until it was too late. Perhaps that is all it was. A shadow.

'Mother used to say it wasn't for want of admirers. There was that accountant she used to tease you about, a regular caller she said.' And Rebecca forces a lightness of tone, a jocoseness that carries her voice high, too high, so that I strain to hear.

'Ah yes, my accountant. Poor Tom. Oh Rebecca, if only you knew how very safe he was, how very, very safe. No dear, I'm afraid he never really featured in any serious way. We were just friends.'

'Safe, Helena? Whatever were you hankering after?'

We both laugh, a release. But I suddenly feel tired. I think it has tired Rebecca too. But this new pushiness on her part no longer surprises me. There is an urgency in her dealings with me, and a fretfulness, that I don't understand. But she knows when to let things go, at least for now.

'Perhaps you could take me back now,' I say.

The wind has freshened and we move along beside the river, taking a path that leads to the lower gate. Jagged silvered lines run along the surface of the water, the wide smooth patches in between sending a gunmetal glow skywards. The sound of Rebecca's breathing reaches me now and again as she increases the pace, a shallow sound like a low-level sawing in a distant field. A group of young boys are scuffling together on the coarse grass bordering the river and stop to look at us with pinched, scowling faces, their close-cropped hair making them appear men before their time. One of them gestures and catcalls at us and they all give loud, broken laughs as we move out of earshot.

'Young thugs,' Rebecca mutters uncharacteristically, and I know that later she will apologise and give me an explanation for their behaviour, excusing them, pointing to a dysfunction not of their making.

We are swinging out through the back gates now and past the blocks of flats that hide the war memorial garden at its lower reaches beside the river. The buggy bumps and wobbles on the broken tarmacadam and shards of glass that litter the ground in front of the flats, a reminder of another, more urban war. We emerge onto the main road and begin the steep climb back to the home. Unlike May, Rebecca insists on calling it The Home and I have begun to consider it a prototype, a sort of ideal home from which all other homes derive, like mushrooms spreading out in an ever-increasing circle from the parent fungus.

This is the part of the return trip we both dislike, a dusty, fumy trek up a steep slope that never seems to have any other pedestrians on it, while the city traffic passes us in a continuous, frustrated snarl.

'It wasn't like this in your grandparents' time,' Rebecca puffs as we reach the brow of the hill.

'Nor in my mother's time,' I mutter, making no effort to raise my voice, knowing she cannot hear above the din.

The traffic continues to spew dust and fumes in its mad

dash west, but we savour our arrival on level ground, if only momentarily. We pass the gates of the Royal Hospital, which Rebecca calls 'the museum', now that it houses modern art. I look across at the limestone turrets on either side of the entrance gate, imagining the feathery fossil-flecks in the stone which I cannot detect from this distance, and slowly follow the line of the wall as it enters the narrow coach-road running to one side. Rebecca has speeded up again in anticipation of the approaching downward slope but I catch a quick glimpse of the house, sitting at a slight angle to the rest of the terrace, skewed in a quirky accommodation of a curve in the road. The original redbrick has been plastered over so that it is now grey and gaunt. But its proportions are untouched and its deeply recessed windows give it a brooding authority in the terrace. My grandparents' home. My mother's home, although she never considered it as such for most of her life.

Down, down, faster and faster across the Camac, a brown, turgid river once, when it took its velvety darkness from the paper mill upstream, approaching a passable cleanness now that the mill is no more. These rundown houses of my childhood have been reclaimed by people who have spotted possibilities in this place, who cluster once more where history was made. And up we go again, another steep slope, the final one, and turn left, down the long, straight road to the home.

'Miss the left turn and we could end up in the canal.'

'What's that, Helena?'

'Oh, nothing. Just muttering to myself, that's all.'

Bloated bodies of dead dogs, bluebottles and flies, bales of rancid hay, rusting pram-frames, supermarket trollies. I knew a young woman once who threw herself into the canal in a fit of depression. It took three days to find her — her body was jammed in the canal lock.

'You exaggerate the bleakness of your youth,' Rebecca said once, when I reminded her of the condition of the canal in the past. Sometimes I think that she has no sense of a time before now. But the past, as some infinite blanket beneath which we snuggled and nurtured and struggled and writhed, has never existed for Rebecca.

Faded redbrick houses recede behind dusty hedges along the South Circular Road as Rebecca takes a final energetic run at the sloping ramp that takes us in through a side door.

'Well, look what the wind blew in.' May is coming out of the staff room, pulling on her anorak, the green khaki one that she says makes her look like a terrorist. 'You look tired, Helena, I hope you haven't been overdoing it.' She continues to ignore Rebecca.

'She's fine,' Rebecca says, with uncharacteristic brusqueness.

'I'll pop up with your tea before I go,' May says to me.

I am accustomed to the tight-lipped checks and balances that pass between these two on my behalf and huddle down in my buggy and wait for it to end, too tired to be amused by it right now. In my room my chair is in its usual position at the window and I'm glad to have tea here rather than join the other residents in 'the communal', another of May's epithets.

'She makes the dining room sound like a public toilet,' Rebecca says. But now she remains only long enough to see me settled down with my tea.

She makes these hasty departures frequently after an encounter with May. Sometimes I think that it is in these brief episodes that I glimpse the real Rebecca. Something falls away from her, she develops a momentary stagger, leaving a shadow, a tiny bird glimpsed picking at its feathers in an endless burrowing search. But it is only ever a glimpse. Even old age does not grant the gift of the whole picture.

I can see the scene on the Chinese box more clearly today – someone has dusted it. Perhaps I did and it has slipped my mind. Another gift of old age! Dust is what I associate most with the box, it was always dusty when I was a child. There were four of them, a set, the other three smaller than this one, graded in size, less useful really. They might even have fitted inside each other like Russian dolls. Things tucked inside things. Like life. I wonder what happened to the other three? Maybe they never left Queenstown. There must have been a great shedding of things after the war. Everything done in such haste and confusion. But of course this box already held the letters and diaries by then. Strange how I remember there being four boxes, yet I cannot remember a time when suddenly there was only one.

It never mattered too much that I was banned from the island for a month. Benjie saw to that with his endless plans, his mind teeming with schemes for adventures. We spent entire days scrambling across fields on the edge of town and making our way down perilous inclines to reach quiet stretches of shoreline. This was a world that was ours alone. Only an occasional fishing boat passed by, too distant to see us. It seems difficult to imagine what kept us occupied over such long periods of time but isolated pictures come to me even now.

I remember the rocks covered with tiny limpets, like millions of discarded miniature coolie hats, the conical shapes broken and weathered so that our feet became scratched and later toughened from endless scrambling across the surfaces. We crouched down between the rocks, watching the boats, pretending they were pirates coming to take us away.

'Aw, Helena, we're stupid. They're not pirate boats.'

'But how would you know, Benjie? How could you tell until you were captured and taken on board?'

'Sails, that's how. They have no sails. Pirates would always have a sailing boat. No noise, you see. They can sail in when it's dark and nobody hears them. They anchor in a quiet bay and come ashore in rowboats. They even know how to muffle their oars.'

'Well, what are these boats then?'

'Soldiers. They are British ships. They must be bringing their soldiers back home.' Benjie shifted awkwardly and took on a stubborn look, the way he used to when he expected me to disagree with some plan or outing he proposed, a look which always served to steel my opposition.

'But my father's a soldier. He is at home. Why would these ships want to bring them home when they are already at home?'

'Oh I don't know. I suppose some of them must live somewhere else. In England, maybe. Didn't your father live in England?'

And the strangeness of that place that was England, a place that teemed with a different life which I had seen once in a photograph album of Mama's, full of carriages in vast, wide streets and shady squares and busy people in elegant city clothes, struck me as the opposite of a place that Papa could call home, with no island smells and salt winds, no narrow streets leaning into the hills, no Mrs O.

'No,' I said. 'Why do you think that?'

'Well, he's in the British army, isn't he?'

'I don't know. He's a soldier, that's all. Anyway, I'm not allowed talk about it.'

'Why not?'

'Because . . . because . . .'

Benjie sent some small, flat stones skimming along the surface of the water, tiny grey–black missiles passing unerringly above the wave tips then sinking suddenly from view.

'My father says there will be a war in Europe,' he said then.

'But Europe is a long way from here, isn't it?'

Distance from my centre in Queenstown was what fascinated me, every place was distant for me, I had not yet been able to establish a scale on which to locate things. The maps that hung on the schoolroom wall were patterns of colour, that was all. The island in the harbour was my horizon. That was all I needed as a reference point. And if war was happening beyond that horizon, then it was unlikely to be real, something that emerged briefly from Benjie's imaginings, that skimmed before me, then was gone, like one of his stones.

'I suppose it is a long way. My father says the war will clear the soldiers out of here for good and all.'

Benjie seldom mentioned his father. He certainly was not an authority to whom he appealed, ever. That was more likely to be his brother Sean. I felt my horizon beginning to blur, so that beyond the island I thought the sea was stirring.

'What do you mean, Benjie?'

'Oh nothing.'

'Does your father not like the soldiers?'

Benjie continued to skim stones and I watched the large grey shape across the bay and wondered if they had rowboats on it they could lower into the water at night like the pirate ships and knew that would not be necessary. Sure didn't everybody know that the soldiers were here already?

'Would you like to come to Rosscarbery on Saturday?' Benjie asked.

I ignored him, concentrating on the island and the slow upward heave of the distant waveless sea, aftermath of a previous storm.

'Oh don't be so grumpy, Helena.'

'I'm not grumpy. How would you know whether I'm grumpy or not?'

'Yes you are grumpy.'

'Well, you don't like the soldiers.'

'I didn't say that.'

'Well, your father doesn't like them.'

'It's not that. It's just that he says that this is not their country. They shouldn't be here, that's all.'

'But it is my father's country.'

'If it's his country, why does he speak in that funny way?'

'What funny way?'

'It's not the way everybody speaks, you know, it's sort of lah-de-dah.'

'It's not lah-de-dah. How should I know? Maybe he learnt it in Dublin. My parents used to live there before they came here.'

And the ping-pong of childish responses had me suddenly exhausted and left me feeling that I wanted to run from Benjie and this place which suddenly felt strange.

'Oh well, it doesn't matter,' said Benjie. 'So, are you coming to Rosscarbery or not?'

'I don't know. I'll have to ask Mama.'

'She'll say no, you'll see. Why don't you say you are coming to my house for the day? That'll be fine with her.'

'I don't know, Benjie.'

'Oh come on, Helena, it'll be fine. My brother Sean will take us in the train. He has business there. He said we can come.'

Sean was nine years older than Benjie, which made him nineteen years old. Even now I am not sure what he did for a living. He said he was a fisherman, working the boats in and around Queenstown, yet he was often in the town when the boats were out at the fishing grounds. He was to be seen coming and going, like a man with urgent business. Benjie would wheedle his way along on some of his trips, now and again including me when he thought I needed some cheering up or when Sean was sufficiently absorbed in his life not to notice my presence. Also, Benjie said that taking us along kept his mother happy, although why that was so, I did not understand.

I gave in to his pleadings and because Papa was on the island and Mrs O was working hard with Mama, starching and ironing the clothes for Sunday, I was free to take off with Benjie and Sean.

The journey was more complicated than I expected. We drove in the cart to the train station, along roads lined with hawthorn and brambles already covered with red berries, several weeks of ripening still ahead of them. From time to time we had to duck our heads to avoid being scratched by a wayward branch. Sean sat on the cross-board, hunkered down into himself as if to escape attention, wrestling with the pony reins, while Benjie and I tumbled around behind him, surrendering ourselves to the swaying of the cart.

We were hurried through the white-painted timber gate of a small railway station and into the train which sat puffing at a platform. We climbed into a carriage of Sean's choosing.

A strange, prickly, short-tufted fabric covered the seats, forcing us to sit still, as it dug into the backs of our knees. The seats were springy and high and my feet did not reach the ground. And then we were off, noisily chugging out of the tiny station, locked between the tall hedgerows along the edge of the track, shading us from view. Sean sat in a huddle in the corner of the carriage, his dark clothes and cloth cap out of keeping with the heat of the day. He never spoke to us, his eyes flickering along the field edges in an endless search, unaware of our existence. But that suited us fine as we chattered and fantasised about the magic lantern show that passed beyond the window in a haze of colour and movement.

The day is indistinct now, but one thing looms out of the haze, a brief refraction of light that originated somewhere out of my line of vision and momentarily illuminated the day. I must make an effort and try to re-create it as it happened.

I suppose that we were met at the station, otherwise how could we have made the trip into the hills lying behind the deep rugged inlets of the coast. But the square farmhouse stands out in my mind, at the end of a narrow overgrown lane. It looked as if the landscape had been arranged around it, so snug was the fit in that out-of-the-way place. Even the moss growing between the rough flagstones in front of the house looked as if it had been cut to size and I wanted to reach down and stroke its velvety surface. And on all of this lush growth glistened a faint moist film, causing everything to ripple imperceptibly as the light shifted across the valley.

Inside the house all was orderliness and scrubbed-down comfort. No colour emerges from memory here, but sounds, of dishes and voices. There was the sound of dishes as the farmer's wife prepared tea and buttered bread for us. We sat around the table with Sean and listened to polite exchanges over our heads, while we eyed the thick slices of bread and jam and waited to be invited to take some. We were waiting for someone or something – that much we could discern from the adult talk. Our patience would last as long as the bread and jam, which nobody else was eating. Sean and the farmer had fallen silent and we ate carefully, thinking they were attending closely to our actions.

Suddenly the farmer rose. 'Here he is,' he said. 'Out ye go now.' He pointed to the door as he spoke. 'There's more to interest the pair of ye outside.'

As we turned towards the door the light was suddenly blocked by an enormous bulk of a man, bending his head as he entered the house. He swept his hat off and a lick of hair fell forward onto his forehead. He noticed us gazing in awe at his great height and grinned.

'So where did this pair of leprechauns spring from?' His voice was low and melodious, yet filled the room with waves of sound as if he were aiming it at some distant place.

'How are ya, Mick? 'Tis great to have ya back amongst us. Go on now children, out ye go and play. We'll call ye in shortly.' The farmer pushed us towards the door and we backed out as the large grinning man watched us. Behind him Sean was ramrod straight beside the table, his cloth cap clutched tightly in one hand.

'Who is that, Benjie?' I asked as soon as the door closed.

Benjie remained silent, looking sulky, and I knew he did not like being excluded from the farmhouse.

'But you must know who he is. Your brother knows him.'

'Sean never tells me anything.'

And this too was new, for Benjie liked to create the impression that Sean told him everything.

'Did you see Sean?' I continued to speak, even though I could tell Benjie was still sulking. We had moved into this new place together, since talking on the beach about the soldiers and the war, where we picked at each other's discomfort as if trying to dislodge the limpets from the rocks where we played.

'What do you mean? Sure, wasn't he in the room with us?'

'But did you see the way he looked just then? He seemed afraid.'

'Ah, don't be stupid, Helena.'

'Well, he was afraid.'

And I knew it was because he thought that man called Mick was important, because he was big, very big. And I didn't tell Benjie this, but thought instead about Papa, who sometimes went to meetings and told us that the speaker could 'bounce his words off the back wall of the hall' if he was a good speaker, and 'couldn't be heard behind a newspaper' if he was bad.

'Oh come on, let's explore, let's see what's in the barn,' Benjie said, his sulky mood vanishing as it usually did after a few minutes.

And we spent our time scrambling into all the secret places of a barn in the golden, scratchy hay and the animal smells that had accumulated in the flaky timbers and channelled floor. And when we were called into the farmhouse again, the big man had gone and Sean was sitting at the table alone, his face serene, his shoulders thrown back.

In the train Benjie asked him who the big man was.

'You'll find out someday, Benjie', was all Sean said, sounding suddenly very grown-up, with a look on his face like Papa when I asked him why the people in the town didn't all like the soldiers and he smiled and patted me on the head and remained silent.

William liked Sean. It was the boats, really, the fact that Sean worked on the fishing boats. William at eleven loved the boats with a passion and always annoyed Papa by saying that he would join the navy as soon as he was old enough, and Papa never said anything, but I knew by the way his moustache moved each time William talked about boats.

'A rig monkey on one of those damned boats you are always gazing at, that's all you will be,' Papa would say if William was feigning illness in order to get time off school.

'Richard, your language, please!' And Mama would sigh as she reached for the Pear's encyclopaedia to check on yet another of William's vague set of symptoms, squinting slightly at the tiny print on the yellowing page.

'A good dose of syrup of figs is all the lad needs. That'll take care of his malingering.'

Papa thought that regularity of the bowels solved all problems and frequently enquired of us as to our daily performances. We quickly learnt to give the correct answer and avoid the weekly dose of syrup. But William's deception was more complex. It was not about missing school for the sake of it. It centred around his passion for boats and the need to be in their presence at every opportunity, even if only to gaze from the quayside. And in a way that I only sensed, it had to do with being on the edge of an energy and excitement that was exclusive to the world of men and which he had begun to experience in the proximity of the fisherfolk. It was the beginning of a distancing in William that I envied and resented at the same time.

He spent all his waking moments planning his next trip. It required the rigour and discipline and eye for detail of a fleet commander to avoid school, avoid Papa and Mama, and anyone who might recognise him or connect him with the rest of the family. Then it required the helping hand of someone among the fishing community who would be willing to take him along on a trip. And as he became a little better known, so his circle of contacts among that community grew. And then Sean took an interest in him and began to take him along, so that William's sea trips became associated exclusively with Sean and his erratic seafaring schedule.

I knew this at the time because William confided in me in order to get my help in organising his forays. I still had my uses. Sometimes this meant helping him to pack a lunch – a big one, because, as he explained, 'You get a ferocious hunger on you when you're at sea.' He had taken to speaking like the fishermen when he related these episodes to me and I tried to understand why it should be a bigger hunger at sea than on land and packed thick slices of ham, as bidden by William, bread, some currant brack made by Mrs O and a tightly corked bottle of ginger ale. Sometimes William sought my help in drying his clothes when he came home. That was more difficult. The water-laden clothes were heavy and he left me alone to drape them over the clothesline that hung above the range, which meant that I had to creep downstairs after Mama and Papa were in bed and rise early the following morning before anybody entered the kitchen.

In return for my help, he told me about his fishing trips with Sean and the fishermen, and a picture was carefully built up in my mind of William's slight, boyish figure huddled among the older men, hauling in nets from the waves as their fragile boats thrashed about in mountainous seas. (As William told it, they never went to sea in other than the most appalling conditions.) Or slithering about among the flapping bodies of the fish as they skittered across the deck in a silvered cascade from the bulging nets. Everything was extreme in those stories, the sense of danger in every account exaggerated with each telling. I sat at the foot of his bed, the iron whorls of the bedstead digging into my back, afraid to move lest he might end the story, remembering that I was there.

And slowly the arc of his story would swing around to Sean. His sullen figure hunched over the reins as he drove the trap to the station on our trip into the hills had remained vivid, to be replaced later by the taut shoulders and distant expression on the return journey. But in William's stories Sean had become transformed, as if he knew that a heroic act would be required of him and that all that went before was merely a preparation. Sean coped with the demanding work on the fishing boats by talking. And William listened.

'They say things are not looking too good in Europe. The trouble lies in German militarism, or so the English papers say. But sure, they have no right to talk.'

'Why not, Sean?'

'Well, look at the situation here in Queenstown. They're stretching things a bit by keeping the yoke around our necks. Isn't self-government the right of any people?'

'My father says this country would collapse if England wasn't there at our backs, that we'd starve without the wealth of the Empire. He says there is many a young man would have gone to the bad if he did not have a job in the army.'

'That's a load of rubbish. They stay here because they are afraid of what an Ireland with a language and identity of its own might get up to behind England's back. They don't understand, or maybe they don't want to. They're afraid of what they might find out. Anyway, I shouldn't even be talking to you, what with your father an officer in the British army.'

'Yes, well I'm not in the army.'

'Lucky you. But one of these days things will change, mark my words. Things are starting to move around here.'

'What things?'

'Oh nothing I can talk about. But you'll see.'

William related these cryptic, verbatim reports to me as I crouched on his bed in the lowered gaslight, lest Mama or Papa might see, an unease sapping the strength from my limbs like a cramped swimmer fighting the current. But of course I did not understand then what lay behind this talk, nor, I suspect, did William, although he liked to pretend that he did. He considered himself indispensable as a crew member and hinted that somehow Sean's position on the boat was enhanced by bringing him along. And perhaps he was right about that last part but in ways that William did not understand then. It was this failure of understanding that brought him into so many confrontations with Papa at this time.

'Helena, you look subdued,' Papa said one evening at the

dinner table. 'What have you been up to today?'

'Nothing, Papa.'

'Come, now, tell your father what you have been up to.'

And so I recounted how I sat in the drawing room and picked the flocking off one section of the fleur-de-lis on the wallpaper, so that only a faint outline of the pattern was left. Papa laughed uproariously, much to Mama's annoyance.

'Richard, you know how expensive it was to cover the walls. It's not as if we can afford to re-paper it for some years.'

'Oh come now, Ally, it's not too noticeable.'

'Well, it would be nice to afford to replace or add to what we have now and again. It really is difficult managing the housekeeping finances these days.'

'Yes, Ally, love, I know. It's the reason I refused the commission, as you know. Too many mess expenses. It's just not worth it. We are better off as we are. I hear this from other men. It's difficult for everybody. But never mind, we can always place the print of Queen Victoria over the bald patch and nobody need ever know the flocking was meticulously removed by our very own Helena.'

'Why does it have to be Queen Victoria?' William ventured.

'And why not, young man?' Papa's voice was tetchy.

'Well, she wasn't an Irish queen.'

'What on earth are you trying to say? Out with it, boy.'

'She shouldn't have had anything to do with us. Or King George, for that matter. We should govern ourselves, that's what I mean.'

The room was very quiet. We did not understand what William was saying but we knew that Mama was the one with whom we could question those sort of things, the things that had to do with the army, England, the sovereign. These were the accepted pivots on which Papa's life revolved and we understood that there was no distinction between what ordered his life and ours. And suddenly one of us was questioning this ordered existence and we grasped it in only the vaguest way.

Papa carefully laid his knife and fork on his plate. I remember noticing that the prongs of his fork were turned upwards and thinking how strange that was, as he had not finished his meal, in fact he had only started it.

'What a preposterous notion. Where did you get this from, William?' Papa was carefully folding his napkin as he spoke, and flashed a glance at Mama, which I did not understand.

'William, is this something which you heard at school? Richard, you know that I have never been happy to send them to the local school. Now look at what has happened.'

'It's all right, Mama, I didn't hear it in school.'

'Then where did you hear it?'

'Oh, around. It is just some talk I heard.'

'Well, young man, I am deeply hurt by your sentiment,' said Papa. 'Self-government would be unlikely to put a decent meal on this table or shoes on your feet. We are part of something greater than this country, an Empire that exists for a better life for all of us and for the honour of God. And furthermore, I see it as an honour to serve that Empire. It offers opportunities for trade and commerce that put tea in your cup and spices in the kitchen. But you, William, need to think long and hard about what you just said and the consequences for you if you continue to pursue that line of thought. You'll find yourself lining up with the Home-Rulers, dashing from parish hall to village pump for their trumped-up little meetings in the hills beyond. No-hopers, all of them, is all I can say, strutting in self-importance, hiding beneath those cloth caps they wear pulled low. This country would be nothing if it were not part of something greater. It can never stand alone, never feed its own.'

Papa tugged down his jacket and trimmed his moustache with the upper side of his forefinger, a slow, deliberate movement. I watched his finger carefully and as it reached the corner of his moustache I felt it was safe to speak.

'Father, Benjie does not always wear shoes, but he is not what you said – a no-hoper.'

'No, Helena, of course he's not. Richard, I really do think that we should rethink the local schooling arrangement for the children. They hear such strange things there.'

'We have discussed it at length, Ally dear, there really is no more to be said. And William, one more thing. You will take your supper alone in the kitchen for the remainder of the week and think about what I have said. It is for your own good. Do you understand?'

'But Papa!'

'Enough, William. Now finish your meal, all of you.'

We returned quickly to our eating, but Papa excused himself and left the room.

Mama stood and turned up the gas in the wall brackets, as the evenings were getting progressively darker now that August had arrived. She returned to the table and ate a little more then quietly asked us to finish our meals and left the room. We could hear her and Papa murmuring in the drawing room beyond the sliding doors. Snatches of their conversation drifted in as their voices rose and fell and I thought of the bell from Mama's church with its sound reaching us sporadically on the wind.

'. . . Things are changing fast, Ally . . . may happen sooner than we think . . . opportunism evident at home . . . a deal may be done . . . the Redmondites will muster . . . a Catholic school is what we agreed . . . I know, love, I know.'

I sat there wondering who the Redmondites were and what was the meaning of 'muster' and could it have anything to do with the yellow stuff Papa sometimes put on his ham and which burnt my tongue and made my eyes turn pink and watery when he let me taste it once. And then Mama entered the room again and I sneaked a glance at her and saw that her eyes were very bright and slightly pink on the lids. But she sat down and ate dessert with us, checking each of us with her shy, sideways glance.

'Has Papa told you that Shackleton – you know, the great explorer – has got enough money at last to undertake his expedition and is due to sail off any day for the Antarctic?'

'I'd give anything to go on a ship like that,' said William, and heaving a sigh, continued, 'but he might not be allowed to go because the navy might need him.'

'Why, William?' said Peter, who tried to remain close to his older brother by asking questions he thought would meet with approval.

'Because there is going to be a war,' said William, head thrown back, peering down his nose at us as if he had assumed the role of the head of the household, conveying portentous news.

A tumultuous chattering began around the table as we demanded to know why and where and what would happen.

'Sure a war is nothing,' said Peter, loudly, still trying to be part of William's drama. 'Anyone can be in a war.'

Esmee and Gerald huddled wide-eyed, chins barely

clearing the edge of the table, the white cloth making their faces pale, their eyes smudged.

Mama removed a hairpin from her hair, tucked in a tiny blond curl like a twist of the hazel that grew in the bottom of the garden. Her head was bent forward slightly and her pale neck gleamed briefly in the flickering gaslight, like a shadow moving on taffeta. She straightened and looked around the table before speaking slowly to us, her eyes fixed beyond us, so that I thought that she could see through the timber of the door.

'Of course there is not going to be a war. William and Peter, you are being alarmist, both of you. War is not something to be treated lightly. But anyway, you don't need to worry. Now, what were we saying about Mr Shackleton? Oh, yes, the money, he has finally got the money he needs and the ship he required and he is stocking up on supplies for the long journey from London to the Atlantic and then south to the Antarctic.'

And we talked of ice and snow and why we never saw much of either in Queenstown, as the girls cleared the dishes and the boys carried hot water to the kitchen sink and coal to the range. And secretly we sighed because we could not afford a live-in kitchen maid like other officers' families and I wished for the umpteenth time that my father was not a Catholic and that Mama had been given a dowry by her stepfather.

Those two weeks in August, before Papa embarked for war, were filled with a quiet light that came off the hills as they slowly took on the colours of bladderwrack and the old amethyst ring that lay on Mama's dressing table. Somehow, in the knowing way of children, we never really accepted Mama's reassurances that war was not imminent. It was much too exciting for us to let go of the idea and we spent our outdoor playtime drilling on the sandy cliff-top behind our house or down on the seashore. We spent hours lying flat on our stomachs behind rocks, with long sticks for guns, pointing across the bay at the great naval ships at anchor. It was Benjie who told us which sticks were suitable as guns and how we should carry them and aim them. When we questioned him, he could not tell us what type of guns they were. What little knowledge he had was gleaned from Sean, who knew about these things, he said, although we never asked how he came to know these things. But when Benjie said that, I thought about the 'trumped-up little meetings' in the hills behind the town that Papa had referred to and the big man with the lick of hair on his forehead whom we had met in the farmhouse with Sean. We made lookouts and dugouts and heaped brambles and gorse around them, scratching our legs and arms and tearing our clothes. And somehow the tiny hedge-tears escaped Mama's attention in those early August days.

Sean brought William game-shooting on a few occasions, but Benjie and I were left to our own devices. That was something especially thrilling for us, because we knew when we saw them from our dugout, carrying a sack, that they must have used real guns if they had caught real animals. William had read somewhere that huntsmen kept a game-book and that they entered the spoils of the hunt in the book, but Sean had scoffed at this, saying it was only target practice for the real thing and I wondered what the real thing might be and I thought that perhaps he meant the war. But I remained silent in case William told me not to be silly. He had told me how Sean had gone shooting in the hills the previous winter, in the snow, and how he shot a wild goose, some golden brown birds he thought were plover, some snipe and a wild hare. He said the goose was large and that Sean's mother cooked it for the family with wild spinach and onions.

William continued to tell me these stories late at night, but if I pressed him for more detail, he became secretive, his face darkening as he feigned impatience or tiredness. Sometimes he talked obliquely about Sean, a strange, meandering form of hero worship showing through, wanting to let me know more about Sean's doings in order to enhance his own standing, yet reluctant to divulge anything of significance because of some greater, unspoken loyalty. But Sean remained a mysterious figure in the background of William's imagination, an exaggerated swagger that steered his life and was visible on the surface for a couple of years.

It was during this period that William began listening at doors.

'You never know what sort of useful information you might hear,' he whispered to me, leaning back on his pillows, his hands linked behind his head in what had become a customary pose, one I had seen Sean adopt when he sat outside his house at the end of the town, idly watching the naval ships in the bay. Useful for what? I wanted to ask, but, as usual, I said nothing. And I knew that he did more than listen at doors, that he also looked in drawers and presses. He had such a wealth of detail on Papa's and Mama's lives, that looking back now, I think that he must have read the letters and diaries too.

It was William who told me about Mama's family. Not a real family, he said, except, that is, for her mother, as the rest of them were stepfamily. He had to explain to me what a stepfamily was and the sudden revelation of a different sort of family associated with Mama made me feel dizzy. She swam before me as someone floundering, trying to cling on to something that had never been truly hers.

Her father died when she was a very young child. (William seemed to think that she was about five years of age.) He had travelled to India on some errand for the British administration and had contracted typhoid on board ship on his return journey and was buried at sea. William said that he was a kind man but I never knew if he had discovered this or imagined it out of kindness for someone who died young or because he believed, as I did, that all natural parents are kind and step-parents are wicked. The discovery of a real grandfather, whom I felt I loved instantly, who might have been an older version of Papa with white hair (for how could he be an older version of Mama, a woman), who might have told stories of how things were when he was young and brought us treats and taken us on outings, was instantly blurred, then wiped from my future with the announcement of his death. The bleakness that opened up then seemed to be all mine, had nothing to do with Mama or any understanding of her grief, as William continued with the story of her mother's re-marriage to an authoritarian freemason. They had five children, Sarah, Melissa, June, Elise and a boy called Bart. Mama found herself living on the edge of another family, where the children, with the exception of Bart, quickly lined up against her as they grew, in a subtle act of permanent exclusion. Bart, the eldest, adored Mama and watched helplessly as his father found time for his own daughters, reminding his stepdaughter, that as she was the eldest child, she must help her mother with the sewing repairs or other necessary chores. Always he seemed to discover a reason why she should not be taken on a walk to the park or on a special trip into the city.

This picture of Mama as someone unloved was shocking to me. It came to me each night when I lay down and every morning as soon as the light crept in through the lace curtains. She was so caught up in an endless activity of fretting about each of us and our needs that the only way of understanding what her childhood was like was to reverse her every consideration and gesture of kindness to us and try to see how that might have been. My mind slowly drew a picture of a life where her clothes were never washed for her unless she did them herself, her breakfast was never prepared, a place never set at the table, her hair never plaited, her shoes never given to the boot-maker's boy when he called to collect the shoes for repairing, no one ever put hot water into the corked water-crock to place in her bed on a cold winter's night. William even hinted that her stepfather forbade her mother from hugging her unless she had hugged all her other children first.

The more I thought about her life, the more confused I became, until my dreams were a whirl of scenes of Mama handing back her breakfast, replacing her unused dishes on the dresser, unplaiting her hair that had been plaited by her mother once when they were alone and removing her broken shoes from the boot-maker's basket and saying, 'No thank you, they will do fine as they are.' My mind became so tangled with trying to cope with all these reversals and dreams that some of my brothers began to ask me what was the matter with me, why was I looking so strange and frowning all the time. And when I tried to explain what I was imagining to William, he became cross and said that if I didn't stop all of this reversal rubbish, he would never tell me anything again. But of course he continued to tell me things. After all, I was the only audience he had, as the others were too young to be interested in what he had to say.

And then he told me the worst part of all, about why Mama had never received a dowry.

'It was all to do with religion, because Papa was a Catholic.'

'But what had that to do with Mama's dowry?'

'Well, you see Mama's stepfather wanted Mama to marry

a Protestant. But Mama fell in love with a Catholic and said that she would never change her mind, that she loved Papa and that was the end of it. And then her stepfather said that was the end of it to be sure, that she would never get another penny out of him. And so she got no dowry.'

I never stopped to consider how William knew what Mama and all the people around her had said to each other. Shining out at me from the darkness of this story was the fact that Mama and Papa had loved each other enough to marry without a dowry. At nine years of age, the fairytale formula was firmly in my head and somewhere further into Mama's story I expected a happy ending. But William spoiled it by insisting that her stepfather never, ever changed his mind.

'But William, maybe he would change his mind if we had lived in Dublin where Mama could be near him, instead of here in Queenstown. Mama really is a very long way from her family, isn't she?'

'Oh don't be silly, Helena, distance has nothing to do with it. I told you, he's a freemason.'

'What's a freemason?'

'It's a . . . it's a . . . sort of a secret thing, where people do things for each other.'

'What sort of things?'

'You know. Helping each other.'

'Well then, why wouldn't he do things to help Mama?'

'I don't know. Stop asking me all these questions, all right?' William never liked to be seen not to have the answer to a question.

Sometimes I would lie awake at night and think of ways of forcing my stepgrandfather to give my mother her dowry. I thought about taking the train to Dublin, perhaps enlisting Benjie's help (anything seemed possible with Benjie involved). It seemed to me that Mama had this extra entitlement, for all the loneliness and isolation she had suffered as a child. And it went without saying that her own father, had he lived, would have given her a very generous dowry. I thought of asking for William's help, but only briefly, and quickly discarded the idea. He was too absorbed in his activities on the boats to be bothered with such a trip.

Night after night I lay in bed thinking about the journey to Dublin, planning in meticulous detail the preparations, all of which would have to be done in secret. Yet try as I might, the plan came to an abrupt halt at the point where we disembarked from the train, its great engine lost in a cloud of steam, hissing and sighing as it settled down after the long hours pulling us along in its wake. The seeping steam was like an impenetrable mesh covering everything, with tiny flashes of colour breaking through the grey. But my imaginings could never take me beyond the station, never permit me to rise above it to see the large city, and I knew that we would never find our way to my mother's home and her stepfather.

Throughout all of this planning I found a shadowy figure in the background with a constancy that drew me towards imagining what he might have been like. This was Mama's father, my grandfather, who died long before I was born and about whom I knew very little. Perhaps it was due to the fact that Mama never spoke about him directly, referring to him only obliquely, with a hesitancy, as if she was afraid any forthright statement might frighten a gentle presence away. And yet I had a vague image of the man, enough to build on in the night as I lay awake thinking about Dublin. Rotund, I decided, and definitely short in stature, shorter than Mama, yet he carried a certain air of authority about him, which probably came from his position on the military staff in the Royal Hospital. I glossed over his burial at sea, which was something I could not comfortably think about at night, or indeed by day, and the sound of the wind whipping across the harbour I drowned out with the bedclothes over my head when the reality of it tried to break through. Instead, I concentrated on the little I knew, on this affable, avuncular, courteous man. As the night wore on, one of the very occasional details of his life moved to take over my imaginings. He had taken Mama to a cricket game once, in a small seaside village on the coast north of the city. Mama's memory of it was vague, yet it had stayed with her in the way of child-hood memories, as a day filled with blue skies, sunshine and everywhere the glimmering whites of the cricketers, and the parasols and long elegant dresses of the ladies sweeping to and fro across the pavilion terrace. Her account had been brief but it remained vivid for me and became even more so in my nightly musings. And to my image of her father I added a cricket ball, which he constantly tossed in the air, inviting me to catch it and intervening at the last second to whisk it away with an uproarious shout of laughter. The repetition of this midair movement went on, sometimes vanishing from sight, as it became interwoven with the sequence of the steam engine at rest in the station and was obliterated by the eddies of smoke, so that all I could see was the hand emerging from the smoke, throwing the ball in the air and catching it, over and over again.

This was the figure that occupied my thoughts in association with the planned trip to Mama's home, not the man who then occupied the position of head of the house and whom I hoped to meet. The comfort and warmth that I constructed around the image of my grandfather is what held it in place for so long. It offered a counterpoint to the exclusion and cruelty of Mama's stepfather's household that sought to shrivel the person she had become.

Queenstown slowly turned toward the sea in that August and came to resemble a honeycomb both in colour and activity. We had been playing in the fields behind the town for several weeks, spying and drilling and building dugouts, returning home late in the afternoon, barely in time to clean up for dinner. One day, while on an errand for my mother, I looked up from the stone I had been kicking along the footpath and stopped in astonishment. The golden haze that had hung over the town in recent days seemed to have solidified, trapping a giant, living, strutting mass beneath it, not busy like ants or worker bees, but a mass of strollers, moving slowly or lolling against walls, chatting to each other or to local women. Slowly they took on individual shapes until I could discern vast numbers, all dressed alike in uniforms like my father's.

I turned and ran as fast as possible and reached home breathless, gasping out the news to Mama.

'Sshh, child, sshh. Calm down, for goodness' sake. Now, where is the iodine tincture?'

'But Mama, there are so many soldiers and I forgot to get the tincture.'

'Oh Helena, you really are impossible. Do you ever keep your wits about you? Of course there are lots of soldiers about. Now please go immediately and complete the errand.'

'But why are there so many soldiers?'

Mama heaved a long sigh and told me that she had been wrong when she said there was not going to be a war. And I thought of the throngs of soldiers in uniforms the colour of a dark, oily fog that sometimes rolled in from the sea when there was no wind, and the image of our dugout with its gorse and brambles covered in red unripe berries began to spin away from me until it became a dried-up, shrivelled thing, collapsed in on itself in an impenetrable, tangled mass. Seventy years later I would stand in the doorway of a disused prison cell and study the space that was filled with a giant ball of twining brambles by an artist trying to capture the essence of captivity. The brambles had been wound round and round *in situ* until they filled the cell's space from side to side and floor to ceiling, a piece of artwork made from a biodegradable material that would dry out and shrivel in the prison space until all that would survive would be dust.

'Why are they all here?' I asked again.

'They are preparing for embarkation – you know, that is when they leave on the boats.'

'But why are there so many?'

'Because they are needed to protect Europe.'

'Why can't Europe do its own protecting?'

'Well perhaps they do not have enough soldiers and our soldiers have offered to help.'

'William says they are not our soldiers.'

'Helena, don't you ever say that, ever, do you hear? I shall speak to William.'

'Will Papa be going to Europe?'

'Yes, he is going to France with the rest of the soldiers.' Her voice was clear and brusque, the way she spoke to us when she wanted to put an end to an argument, but her shoulders sagged suddenly, so that I thought she was about to lose her balance.

My heart leapt. 'Is he going on one of those boats in the harbour?'

I thought of the regatta in two days' time and the careful plans Benjie had made with me that very morning to take a picnic of food from his mother's kitchen and ginger ale from mine and spend the day watching the race. And I asked Mama if Papa and the soldiers would be sailing to France in the sailing boats for the regatta and felt relief when she said no, they would use the large ships we could see at anchor from our drawing-room window. And she stood very still and straight, looking across the water, her hands hanging by her sides as if she had recently set something aside and was about to reach out to retrieve it. I stood without being noticed, poking my finger into the corner of the tiny hedge-tear on my pinafore, turning down the fabric and watching it spring back up into position again. And I went reluctantly from the room to finish my errand and to find Benjie.

The day of the regatta glowed and heaved with light that bounced back at us from sky and sea and the windowpanes along the seafront houses. The wind was light and brisk, tugging at the flag in front of the Admiralty building and sending the seagulls reeling back from the edges of the waves as if smacked by a large hand. Benjie threw stones at my window very early, long before Mama was awake. I knew that she would not miss me if I did not appear at breakfast, as she was caught in such a flurry of activity outside the house that she had left the routine at home to continue without her. 'It'll be all right in a few days,' Mrs O said at intervals, 'just you see, it'll all settle down.'

The early morning chill made me shudder as I met Benjie outside the back porch and struggled to lace up my boots. He put the bottle of ginger ale into an old fishing tackle bag long discarded by Sean. A faint reek of fish reached my nostrils as I straightened to go and I wondered if the currant cake would taste like the cod liver oil Mama fed us on a spoon as soon as winter arrived.

Benjie had it all figured out – the long journey by train and tram to the regatta in a harbour far to the west of the county. Nothing seemed too difficult for Benjie. I never asked him how he knew that things would turn out all right, mostly I just went along on trust.

We had the train carriage to ourselves and we dozed a little as the morning sun hit the window and made us squint in the glare. The guard on the train knew Sean and asked after him, poking his head into the carriage now and again to keep an eye on us. The tram journey that followed was crowded and I felt sick from the swaying movement and the clamouring noise overhead and the smell of hot wool and strong soaps from the bodies pressed around us. And suddenly we were surging off the tram and down onto the harbour with the noise of clattering ropes on masts and the fluttering flags, the shouting candy-sellers, the organ-grinder and the baked-potato vendors. I remembered the dun ochre pall of the uniformed soldiers in Queenstown and looked at the blue and red and white bunting tugging on lines strung from lampposts along the road to the harbour and wanted to wrap the tiny triangles of colour around them, hide the stultifying muddiness of their uniforms, pin them down in the blue and red so that they could not move, so that the boats would sail without them.

We sat beneath the sea wall on large, round, smooth stones, with great hollows between them which caused them to move and turn over, threatening to trap our feet as we walked across them. We ate our bread and cheese and chunks of ham and cake and drank our ginger ale all at once, forgetting to wipe each other's crumbs from the bottleneck in our thirst and excitement. In front of us, the spectacle of the sailing yawls putting about began. The punt and oar races quickened the pace, drops of water glistening back at us as the oarsmen raised the oars in the air and pleasure boats of all shapes and sizes bobbed on the periphery of the display, their red and white streamers jagged against the blue sky. The band of the fishery school played above the laughter and calling of the crowds and the booming of the loud-hailer as the wind whipped along our cheeks, making them tingle and sting and become hot until we could no longer feel them. In mid-afternoon, when the wind turned chilly, Benjie dug his elbow into my ribs and said we'd miss the train connection if we did not catch the next tram. I turned and took one last look at the boats strung out across the harbour and then along the crowded harbour wall. The dangling legs of young men and the billowing petticoats of young women were rising and falling along the sweeping curve, and it seemed as if the very wall rippled in the wind as I struggled to my feet and followed Benjie to the tram.

I tiptoed into the dining room and squeezed into my chair, without moving it out from the table. Nobody paid me any attention. They were saying grace, heads slightly dipped, eyes down, everyone as usual alert for the sign of an ending. Mama's eyes flickered slightly in my direction but she did not look at me and then it was over. But even though we began to eat it was as if grace was not really over. Papa and Mama were very still, and I wondered if they were still saying prayers, yet they were filling and passing plates among the younger ones. Nobody commented on my windblown appearance. Even though I had tried to tidy myself up, my hair was blown to a frizz and I looked like a hedgehog, William said later. Papa was eating his meal, but more slowly than usual, as if thinking about what was required of him with each forkful he took. Mama was moving her food in tiny darts around her plate and looking at Papa from time to time. Suddenly he put down his knife and fork and dabbed at his moustache with his napkin, then coughed.

'Now, children, could I have your attention for a moment, please.'

'Richard, can't it wait?'

'I'm sorry, Ally, it won't wait.'

'But they need not know.'

'Of course they need to know. Now, children, I'm sorry to have to tell you this, but as of today, a state of war exists between Britain and Germany. We had hoped that it wouldn't come to this but the die is cast. This means that all British forces are called up in preparation for going to France and to help send the Germans back where they belong. As a soldier, I shall go also.'

We sat in silence, watching him speak, his voice deepening with emotion, wishing for him to stop, not wanting to see him tighten his mouth like that or clear his throat the way Mama sometimes did when she was sad. He continued to talk, but there was no more mention of the war. Instead, he told us what he expected of us at home and at school while he was absent. William shot a triumphant glance at me, as if to say that, yet again, he knew more than I or anyone else. And as Papa spoke of the difficult times ahead for us as a family and how we must learn to make sacrifices and look for less for ourselves, I could feel William edging forward on his chair beside me.

'You never mentioned the Volunteers, Papa,' said William.

'Ah, yes, the Volunteers. Well, I suppose we'll need as many as we can get, although they have mixed motives, it has to be said, the same Volunteers. They want to keep Home Rule to the fore at any cost.'

'Richard, it's hardly time for politics.'

'Sean says anyone who volunteers is nothing but a fool. He says they should stay at home and avail of an opportunity when it presents itself, that Britain will be so busy at war it will give the Home-Rulers the opportunity they need. He says things are looking better for them by the minute.'

Papa stared at William for several moments, and as I watched he seemed to have stopped breathing. It went on for so long that I too held my breath to see if I could keep it up as long as he did. Then he rose slowly from the table and walked around to where William sat and asked William very quietly to come with him. Gone was the smirking self-confidence and preening swagger as William meekly followed Papa to the door. And as they reached it I saw Papa's hand move to his belt and then I heard the dull clunk as the buckle swung free and hit the door. Mama went quickly from the room and I heard their muffled voices from the passageway to the kitchen and then Mama returned and began clearing plates, her hands shaking so much that I rushed to carry them for her. But she urged me to sit and she too sat down and we all stayed around the table in stillness until Papa returned. He nodded to Mama, his face pale and taut, his moustache glistening against his skin like coke in the bottom of a milk pail.

Late that night as I crept along the corridor to William's room, I saw Papa and Mama through a chink in their bedroom door. Papa was sitting on the floor beside the bed, his head in Mama's lap, his shoulders heaving soundlessly up and down, up and down, while she ran the tips of her pale fingers very slowly through his hair, her head turned to one side as she looked through the window and the fading light across the harbour.

I was frightened of what I might find when I reached William's room. He was sitting against his pillows in his usual position, but he was different somehow. His poise was still there but the swaggering air was missing.

'Did it hurt, William?' I whispered.

'Did what hurt?' The faint hint of haughtiness in his voice made me think that I had misunderstood Papa's intention.

'I thought . . .'

'Helena, Papa will be going to war in a couple of days' time. Then I'll be the man of the house, in charge, you know.'

He moved to lie back on his pillows in a gesture of closure and a look of pain flashed briefly across his face and he sat forward quickly, looking like the young boy that he was and I felt a great hole opening up before me that grew wider and wider until it seemed to swallow the entire room. And I remembered the carefree legs of the young men at the regatta swaying in and out on the sea wall and the breeze lifting the edges of the girls' petticoats, and then I saw William's boots discarded beneath the bed and they didn't look much bigger than mine.

The remaining days before embarkation were a blur of disjointed movement by dark clad figures who crisscrossed the landscape of our town (although Mama never thought of it as 'our town'). We became strangely enervated by all of this activity, especially as our domestic routine was gradually unpicked, despite Mama's best efforts. But the night before Papa's departure saw this whirl of activity wind itself down. Hundreds of soldiers moved into the largest churches and halls – Christchurch in Rushbrooke and St Mary's in the town. Even so, people were saying that they could not be expected to sleep much on that last night, what with the crowds and the discomfort and the worry of it all.

It seemed strange to us that Papa could not spend his last night at home. Why should he have to go into that large, cold hall with all those other men who had come into the town when he had his own home close by? Even Mama seemed surprised. Mrs O kept saying, 'your poor mother', in a whisper into the air above our heads, a benediction of sorts. She tried her best to impose some sort of routine on our household but even she found it impossible. She settled instead for helping Mama prepare some of the things she wanted Papa to take with him and which he reminded her he did not need.

'Ally, the field-kitchens are well supplied with everything we'll need and I can't possibly carry any extra clothes – you have already packed several changes of underclothes. And you can always send me a parcel, you know. We are not going to be away for long. Just a show of force, that's all that is required and we'll be home in time for Christmas.'

'Christmas, Christmas, Papa will be home by Christmas.' Esmee and Gerald, danced around, clasping hands and chanting their song over and over.

Papa's uniform hung on the outside of the wardrobe door, partly covering the mirror, so that when I passed the door and looked at it quickly it appeared as a headless shape in the fading light. Mama sat at her dressing table, her hands folded in her lap, her hair piled high, the usual wisps curling down onto her white collar, like pale feathers falling to earth. She moved slightly as I peered around the door, as if she was trying to dislodge something, a look of incredible sadness marking her face in shadows. She spotted me and called, pulling the padded footstool towards her. I sat at her feet for what seemed like a very long time, saying nothing, the night lowering a black wing over us.

That night, Benjie and I crept out after bedtime, along the lower road to Rushbrooke. Papa had left home that afternoon in a fluster of kisses and hugs and tears and a pell-mell clamouring into the army transport truck that called for him. As soon as he stepped into the street he became someone I did not know. His voice grew loud and gruff, as he called to the men in the truck. A great energy filled him, so that he visibly expanded. His movements became brusque, sharp, energetic as he lifted his kitbag and swung it upwards into the hands of the waiting soldiers. They laughed and joked about what he had in it, as if they knew him better than we did, as if he belonged to them and we were onlookers. And then he climbed into the truck and gave us a great cheery wave and was gone.

'Wouldn't you like to see the soldiers all together with their guns and helmets and things?' Benjie had whispered to me later as we sat in the kitchen waiting for his mother to finish her work. She took extra care that evening, staying a little later now that she did not need to be gone when Papa arrived. She spent some time in the drawing room with Mama, the door closed, talking in a low voice. I could not hear Mama's voice. I nodded at Benjie, thinking that I would see Papa once more amidst those men with their loud voices and expansive gestures.

'We might even see one of those big guns your father will use in the war.'

'Don't be silly, Benjie, they are too big to carry, they have to be wheeled into place.' Even I knew that much.

Mama said that Papa would spend most of his time motivating his men and seeing that they carried out orders. When she spoke of these things, I saw him sitting at the head of the dinner table, his white napkin stuffed above the first button of his jacket, joking and laughing with us as we tried to avoid his probing questions about our activities. And I wondered was that what Mama meant, would he tell jokes and tease the soldiers and crinkle his eyes and twitch his moustache? For a long time I thought that motives were about jokes and laughter, about openness and generosity. It was only years later, when Mama took to speaking briefly about her childhood, that I understood that there were other sorts of motives, darker, more obscure forces that drove people in directions that even they could not have thought possible.

That night Benjie and I walked down the steep hills, the tall, slender houses shouldering each other into place, 'like a cavalry charge with interlocked knees', my father used to say, 'if one goes, they all go'. I followed Benjie closely, occasionally reaching out, yet never quite touching him, pursuing his darkness in the shadows ahead of me along the long straight road out to Rushbrooke. The shape of Christchurch loomed before us, a fading ochre glow coming from the windows. It was a still, warm night and a side door in the church had been left open. A low murmur reached us like bees preparing to swarm. We remained crouched behind a bush, listening, and now and again a low laugh would break through but it was not Papa's. We crept carefully from the bush and into the porch, the slate beneath our feet damp and slippery despite the warmth of the night. The air had a strange tang to it, musty with a heavy, sweet fragrance that made me feel slightly sick. Benjie said later that he thought that it was incense but it reminded me of the smell that came off the coke in the range or the gas mantles when Papa was lighting them and they were slow to catch. I wondered how the men could sleep with that smell catching in their throats.

We peered around the door into a vast space filled with reclining bodies, some lying flat or on their sides, asleep with heads propped on rolled-up shapes we could only barely discern, some leaning on an elbow, talking in low voices to those beside them, others sitting on the floor, smoking or just staring. I had never seen such a crowd of people. They were so crowded together that whenever there was a movement it appeared as a ripple along the skin of a recumbent reptile stretching, loathe to make a strenuous gesture.

'Can't see any guns,' Benjie said, hoarse with excitement.

'Oh you and your stupid guns, Benjie. Of course there are no guns here. You don't bring a gun to bed with you.'

'You do when you are going to war,' he said, sounding smug.

'Let's go home'. Suddenly I did not want to see Papa. He would be angry with me for coming out after dark, making the journey out to the edge of the town. The feeling I had earlier, that he no longer belonged to us, was stronger there in that dankly sweet smell with the wafting smoke and the gravelly hum of men's voices.

Benjie reluctantly turned away from the door and we crept home the way we had come and all the time our footsteps echoed in my head, 'going to war, going to war, going to war, war, war, war, war'. And when we reached my home, Benjie was too tired to go any further and so he curled up beside the range in the kitchen and fell asleep.

14 August 1914
Midnight

This is the day that Richard departed for France and into
the world of men. Such turmoil. He was so caught up in
the excitement and adventure of it all that he scarcely
noticed the children's tears. Not that they were aware of
them themselves, if the truth be told, laughing one
moment and crying the next. But the men respect him. I
could see that in their eyes.

A matter of weeks, they say, a couple of months at the
most and it will be over. And of course it is what they
have trained for, in a way what they have all been waiting
for, even if they never spoke aloud of it. And now I too
must learn to wait, with the children. The papers are full
of detail about the troops – the expeditionary force, they
call them. I always thought that an expedition was an
adventurous journey full of anticipation and excitement.
Perhaps it is, at least the soldiers seemed to think so. But I
cannot see it in that light. It is really about a show of force
on both sides, and after that, who knows what might
happen? And Richard, in the garrison artillery, the
'muscle of the regiment', as he calls it, is sure to see some
early action and yet I pray to God that he will not.
Already I am losing my nerve. Does this make me
disloyal because I want him first of all to belong to me
and after that to give what is left to King and country?

Shackleton's expedition to the Antarctic is full of the
excitement and anticipation that an expedition requires
and yet he is seen to be honouring King and country by
leaving the war behind. The navy decided that they could
do without him. How relieved his wife must be to know

that his only opponent is nature. How happy he must be.

And how happy Richard looked today as he joined his men. It was a happiness that took a shape unfamiliar to me, one so different to any he has known with me. How I envied them their comradeship, their sense of purpose, of having come into their own time. Richard said that to me once, that I had come into my own time, as he watched me coping with labour pains for my first time, with William. He said he could see the pains visibly carrying me away from him, like a ship heading out to sea, as he is being carried away from me now. Somebody said that war revives the buried honour of men. Is that what they were sensing today, some vague unidentifiable stirring of something lost?

But I must be brave. I have the children to care for, with dear Mrs O's help. There are so many other women doing the same as me. May God give us strength.

And of course there were other women doing the same thing as she was – presenting the brave face to the world. It carried them along for a while until the anger began to show through in tiny chinks and cracks and later in huge personal waves that swept through their homes and dealt blows to their children and sent sparks flying from kitchen ranges. And later still, they would remain loyal to the Crown, while venting their fury on their absent husbands.

But this diary entry was the first one Mama made after Papa's departure. And yet I still cannot infuse an adult's sense of loss into my recollection of the troops gathered in that murky hall in Rushbrooke prior to their departure. A child's recollection, with its lack of depth, that's what I have hung on to all these years. Perhaps as an adult, I took comfort from that lack. It prevented me imagining the horrors awaiting them beyond that place.

'Helena, I cannot understand your consistent lack of curiosity about your past.'

She has been pushing me like this for some time. She sees it as a sort of tidying-up exercise that needs to be concluded before I go, although she never would refer to my death or my significant age. Too sensitive for that, she likes to think. 'Unfinished business', she calls it.

'It has nothing to do with curiosity, Rebecca. I suppose I am comfortable with my version of things at this stage of my life.'

'But the whole box is full of letters and diaries. This is the adult version of things that happened when you were a child. That's all.'

'The adult version. You make it sound so definitive, dear. But I have dipped into the box from time to time. It's not important, really.'

Rebecca has come to visit me today, not one of her regular visiting days, but she is going away for a long weekend with Wolfgang and will not be back until next week. She feels obliged to fit in my full quota of visits even though this places a strain on her and involves complicated reshuffling and rescheduling of her life.

May poked her head around the door a few moments ago and seeing Rebecca here and spotting the box with some of the contents spread across the table, she took herself off abruptly. 'I'll come back later, when you have finished your business,' she said, with a cold glance at Rebecca. She left, muttering 'business is business', or at least that is what it sounded like.

Rebecca is wearing periwinkle blue today, a colour that makes her skin look thin, as if it is stretched too tightly across her cheekbones. She always wears blue somewhere on her person. Someone must have told her it suited her once and she has made it her defining hue. I have come to consider it the 'miserable colour', not that I consider Rebecca miserable. Anxious, constrained, tense, but not miserable. Too busy for that. But blue *is* a miserable colour.

I don't remember the sea at Queenstown ever looking blue. Petrol greens and peacock greens – steely colours, metallic silvers, glassy bottle greens, icy greys, coppery greens, sulphur on the tips of the waves, blackened green in the deepening curl. Mama must have seen all those shades, yet when she spoke of the sea, she only spoke in the colours of ice, Antarctic colours that she could hear rather than see. Sometimes as I listened to her I could hear it too.

'It murmurs, you know, the sea, when it is frozen over. One great mass of silvered ice stretching for miles and miles. And beneath it, the ocean pushes upwards against this icy ceiling, brushing against it constantly, like a silk scarf drawn across a throat.'

I loved it when she talked like this, talking to me as if I were standing a long way off. It made me feel mysterious and grown up, like someone who had travelled far away and returned with interesting stories of my own to tell.

But the sea was green, always green. The ice cold of jade. Subtle shadow of a subterranean flaw. Mama took to wearing jade, a heavy jade bracelet, later, after Papa went to France.

I begin to tell Rebecca this.

'Did you know that all my recollections of childhood seem to revolve around water, the sea mostly? And the strange thing is that it is always green, a sort of jade green.'

'Ummm. Well, I've come to believe that we remember

the nice things exactly as they were and we play around with the rest.'

'She had a jade bracelet, you know – Mama, that is. She wore it for a while after Papa left for France. Mrs O used to say that she wore it because the Chinese associated jade with a long life. It must have been Mama who told her that.'

Rebecca looks down at her own thin wrists, tiny blue veins moving down over her hands.

'Sometimes we don't just play around with our memories, sometimes we bury them, Helena, so that we no longer have to look at them. Perhaps we never could.'

I hold my breath in dread that she will begin once again to tell me about how our lives are one great act of denial, although that is not quite how she puts it. But somehow her view has collapsed for me into a small, brown image, a tiny warped shell we each have built up around us that defies chipping or cracking, so that we live out the lives of diminutive, burrowing insects, moving further and further into the dark.

As she talks I remember a conversation I had with her friend Áine.

'Therapy will change her, you know. You may as well prepare yourself, Helena. It has already started. Have you noticed how she has become more orderly about things? God, maybe she would consider putting some order on mine.'

Not that the sophisticated Áine needs anyone to take charge of her life. She has too firm a grip on it herself. But she was right in a way. There is a sort of heightening of the person Rebecca was in a way I can't quite pinpoint. More transparent, I suppose. It has made her more visible as the young girl who ordered her mother's life, increasingly a hospital life, taking charge of her appointments, slotting in trips to the hairdresser to keep up her spirits, who shopped and cooked and cleaned around Lucinda's haphazard attempts, saying nothing about the oversights as she worked through the chores. I cannot imagine what it is in her childhood that she might possibly have wanted to bury.

'Perhaps that is why men's honour became buried. They couldn't bear to look at what they did in order to earn the honour.'

This is what I do now, dredging obscure items that have lodged unbidden in my memory, ready to spring forth, setting tiny traps for me, leaving me to writhe and wriggle free as best I can.

'What on earth are you talking about, Helena?'

'Oh nothing, just something I read. Anyway, I'm not sure that I believe all that stuff about denial and false memory that you young people talk about these days. The trouble with those therapists is that they see everyone as a casualty, some sort of problem to be tackled. They make the very act of living a problem.'

Walking wounded, the lot of us. That is all she is truly comfortable with. There alone lies authenticity, everything else is lies, shamming, papering over the angst. Rebecca believes that the truth about her life is there for the telling, if only she can be shown how to get at it, scouring away the skin in one great sandblasting, the better to reveal the truth. But we have talked about this so often, played so many word games, that meaning has stretched out beyond us faster than we could speak, until we could no longer understand each other, happy in the knowledge that we each understood what the other could not see.

'I'm sorry you think like that,' Rebecca says. 'I think it is about trying to lead a richer, more aware life. I'm conscious of time passing and there is all this stuff in the diaries and letters. They are all part of it.'

'Part of what?'

'Part of a picture, I suppose – an imprint, my therapist calls it, a sort of legacy we can't escape, like an indelible mark.'

'Wasn't that how original sin was described in the days when we acknowledged such a thing as sin?'

And images of angels tumbling head over heels, falling through clouds, their gleaming white robes in disarray, appear before me, and below them a wonderful orchard, abundant with apples, the ground strewn with perfect wind-falls, gleaming their reds and greens upwards.

'Ah, sin. Well, perhaps, but what I'm talking about has to do with childhood, our experiences of those close to us.' Rebecca sits pulling the pile off her jumper, squeezing the wool into a tiny ball in the palm of her hand.

'Back to mothers again, I suppose? Well, Rebecca, you can't lay that one on me. It sounds like another of those handy excuses for dodging responsibility for our own actions. Always the mother's fault, isn't it?'

I wonder what Lucinda would make of all of this. I can almost hear her laugh, that funny high sound that moved from warm to callous all in one breath. She would have loved to know she held that sort of power, continuing down the years, a sort of edgy shadow dogging us after she had gone.

'I wonder what Lucinda would think of us now,' I say.

'This is not about Lucinda.'

'Isn't it? Well, she was your mother, there's no avoiding that. So if you want to talk imprints, why should you let

Lucinda off the hook?'

Rebecca remains silent and I think about Lucinda, conceived when Papa came home on leave in early 1915, the baby of the family, the one we all spoiled, as people used to say then, petted and fussed over, handing her from one to the other, so that in the end she belonged nowhere.

'Is that it then, Rebecca? Is that what you are really concerned about – Lucinda's legacy to you?'

'Of course not, Helena, she has no bearing on things at all.'

No bearing on things. Rebecca moves around the room, her hands alighting briefly on objects as if intending to lift one, then changing her mind, moves on to the next one. How strange – Mama used to move like this around the rooms in Queenstown. We both know that it is too late to withdraw the reference to Lucinda. She is part of what is there in the diaries, in the spaces and the margins, whether we like it or not.

Beyond the window the spring light glides across the top of the spindly birch and the distant mountains look flat and uniform, slate-blue cutouts pasted onto a grey board. A little like the way Rebecca would have us arranged, really, once she has shaped us to her liking.

'Come on,' she says, 'let's sort these into some sort of chronological order. I can't imagine why it was never done before!'

'Well, Lucinda was never much interested in any of this, was she? "What's the point of keeping all this stuff?" she would say every so often, and each time I had to convince her not to dispose of them. "Dust collectors, that's all they are, nothing more."'

But I'm not about to let the subject of Lucinda drop as

easily as all that, not now. And anyway, I'm anxious, curious too since the day Rebecca began to talk about her grandfather – her *real* grandfather, as she said.

'Who is Mortimer?' she said then.

'Mortimer?'

'Yes, Mortimer. Lucinda took to muttering about someone called Mortimer in those endless days of sleep towards the end.'

Rebecca had always called her mother by her name, since her teens. Something to do with a more adult relationship, she explained to me at the time. But somehow I never got used to it. It had taken me so long and so much effort to deal with Lucinda as an adult that to hear Rebecca calling her name had the effect of hurling me back to my childhood. There we all were, each of the children with a small part in running Lucinda's life, while she proceeded, smiling winsomely and doing exactly as she pleased.

'Are you sure your mother said "Mortimer"?'

'It's difficult to know exactly what she was saying. I thought she was saying Mortimer, or at least part of the word, "Mort" or perhaps "Mor", and then it would run into something else which I could never quite make out. "Mortimer, Mort, Mor", something like that.'

And over the subsequent months, as Rebecca had listened, she pieced together the tiny, barely audible clues, writing them down, juggling them around, piecing incomplete words together in an endless crossword that continued until Lucinda died and continued beyond her going until Rebecca was ready to talk. And she wants me to believe now that Lucinda has no bearing on things.

'I think my real grandfather was Mortimer,' she said to me one day in her sitting room. We had been shopping for some clothes for me, Rebecca having decided I needed sprucing up for the spring. A tray with tea things neatly arranged sat on the coffee table and Rebecca was beginning to place them before us. She always takes care to present things nicely for me on these occasions. She had even managed to find some fragile scillas in the garden and dropped them into a square glass vase, where they all but vanished into the thick corners.

'Your *real* grandfather? Whatever do you mean, Rebecca?'

'It's to do with what I heard from Lucinda, you know, all those things I told you she was saying.'

And I tried to recall what of significance might have started Rebecca on this track. Poor Lucinda – buried beneath a mound of white rugs and sheets, covering a frame that held them above her shrunken body in those last weeks, all her exuberance being sucked in and out through plastic tubes, so that her delirium burbled from her in great panting gasps and nobody among her visitors, with the exception of Rebecca, bothered trying to make sense of what she was saying.

'She was delirious, Rebecca. She was talking nonsense. You read too much into these things.'

'But people reveal things before death that they may never have considered talking about before.'

A little like the loose ends she would like to see me tying up. I am reminded suddenly of the day I disturbed Rebecca in the hospital. It was one of Lucinda's better days, when she was able to sit up, propped carefully against her pillows, her white hospital gown and wheaten skin blending so that she was already a wraith. Rebecca was holding a large hair-brush, the old-fashioned sort covered sparsely with bristles protruding from a curving pink rubber base. I always thought as a child that there was something faintly indecent in the appearance of those brushes on Mama's dressing table. Lucinda's eyes were closed and a tiny smile moved slowly across her face. Rebecca was earnestly brushing her hair, conscientiously slowing whenever she encountered a tangle, the dull sound of the bristles moving through her hair faintly audible. Neither of them saw me. I believe that this is the closest they ever came to each other – Rebecca little more than a child, mothering her mother to the end. And she believes that Lucinda has no bearing on her life now. Perhaps I too am trying to tie up loose ends.

'My father's name was Richard, not Mortimer.' And for some strange reason I started to count the scillas in the vase and consider if she might have arranged them differently, spread them out a little, the better to see them.

'I'm sorry, Helena, of course this is about your father. I'm sorry if I have been insensitive. But who is this Mortimer?'

And Rebecca talked in a distracted, disjointed fashion about love and absence, interwoven with the names of her grandfather and grandmother, whom she had begun recently to call Ally. And all the time I wanted to tell her how false this assuming of her first name sounded, how artificial I found this little device. But I remained silent, listening instead in irritation and exhaustion to her voice as she wove a story of loss and suffering, with the growing central belief that Mortimer was Lucinda's father and not my father, Richard; that Mortimer or Mort or Mor or whatever his name was had somehow saved Ally in her time of great need.

When Rebecca was a child and even into her early teens she had some of Lucinda's spontaneity about her, managing in the tiredness of city streets to make her own fun, searching out the obscure green spaces and neglected squares where childish games could be played uninterrupted out of earshot of echoing calls home in grimy evening light. Her brother William's friends were her friends, leaving home early on summer mornings to cycle to the foothills south of the city and swim in cold mountain streams or fish for pinkeens which slurped from jamjars suspended by string from bicycle handlebars. Her long, thin frame and her frizzy blond hair reminded me for that brief period of Mama.

When her mother became ill and confusion was setting in, Rebecca had already been rejected by her brother's friends. In truth they did not know what to do with this gangly girl in their midst, whose curly hair had straightened, it seemed to them, overnight, so that they mistook it for a loss of spontaneity, a need on her part for something different, something they were not ready to give. They had missed the moment when she had turned towards home, towards Lucinda and the demands of her, as yet undiagnosed, tumour. They stood back and let her move unrestrained into a different place, before her time. And as I listened to her quiet insistent voice, I had a sudden yearning to push her back into that time, back to being that spontaneous child, so that she might have had the chance of shedding her childhood slowly, thoughtlessly, in the way of children. Yes, that was it. Thoughtlessly. I would have liked to see Rebecca live one whole day thoughtlessly. And suddenly my annoyance with her evaporated in a flood of pity.

Her voice had become high and thin, her breathing short and shallow, and I watched the sun touch her shoulder, then wash over her, glancing off the Queenstown bookcase that had found its way to a niche in her sitting room, the dust on the glazed doors in high relief, as if it had only recently come to rest there and was about to fly off again. I noticed for the first time that the timber on one side of the bookcase was much lighter in tone – honeyed almost – than the other end, where the sea light had bleached it. And I remembered Lucinda's love of the salacious, her inability to place herself even momentarily within the sensibilities of others, and recalled the irreverent little games that she played well into adulthood, which spun exotic, dangerous threads around our lives and left us reeling.

'"Dust collectors", is that what she said? Well, Helena, I think we should go carefully through everything, despite what Lucinda thought of these papers.'

Rebecca sits down at the table and begins to examine the tops of the pages closest to her, looking for dates, so that she can arrange them chronologically. She likes doing this sort of thing.

Today she has piled her hair up in a brown plastic, complicated-looking grip, but she has not done it up very well. Some of her hair is escaping in little beige wisps around her neck. It reminds me of Mama, when she tried to manage alone without Mrs O.

'Perhaps she didn't see all this stuff as merely dust collectors. Maybe she just wanted to keep you away from it.' I am feeling mischievous, needing to needle Rebecca a little, knowing what lies at the end of her search.

She remains silent, shuffling the papers, reading quickly then moving on.

'It was mostly journals she kept during the war, you know. There's probably nothing of great interest there. Mama was too caught up in domestic issues to have anything interesting to relate. I'm surprised she even found the time to do any writing at all.'

'It probably helped her, putting all her feelings into the journal at the end of the day. Writing can be therapeutic for those who have no one to talk to.'

And even though I realise that we were all too young to be Mama's confidants, I feel the sting of Rebecca's remark, hearing it as a hidden rebuke for the child that I was. The tone of Mama's voice as she spoke to Mrs O, the rises and falls, the whispered exchanges, the occasional laughter, the closing of a door on certain conversations, the scraping of a chair as they crept closer to each other, all come back to me. And I can see too the heads bent low, the covert glance, the tugging tight of a shoulder shawl – all of this we took inside ourselves without hearing a word and took it for what it was, the slow erection of an invisible shield hauled into place by the two women, a flimsy quivering thing to begin with but one which grew to become a rigid protection between us and the world. It came into being in quietness and subdued light and somehow we children learnt to defer to it, moving around this new space in our lives, in fear that something might happen and blow it away.

But it's not something I can tell Rebecca and even if I did, she would pick at it and pull it apart. A careful, considered inching forward has replaced living for her, where emotions are taken out and shaken like a valuable old rug that is aired on a clothesline once a year and then replaced in its designated spot on a wall, where it is passed unnoticed for the remainder of the time.

She continues to work methodically, this daughter of Lucinda's who no longer resembles her either in looks or in temperament. She is surrounded by a stillness at present that is uncharacteristic as she looks closely through Mama's 'writing as therapy', when I know that she is looking for something specific, some clue, to confirm her belief that Mort or Mor is Lucinda's real father.

Lucinda could have been raving about anything in her last weeks. All that appalling pain, all that morphine. Addictive stuff. God only knows what images were racing through her mind. Rebecca should know better than to pay attention to any of it. And why is there this urgency about it all of a sudden? It would amuse Lucinda greatly if she were here, knowing, as she did, how to survive on a wing and a prayer, or more likely on some light-hearted manipulation and white lies. How harmless it all seems, now that she has gone. But it confused Rebecca, sometimes it seems permanently. It certainly left her and her brothers, Maurice and Anthony, frustrated. And when they reached adulthood they became ultimately dismissive of Lucinda, who remained unchanged.

'Ma,' her eldest son Maurice used to say, 'you're still a child at heart.'

And of course he was right. Her child's view of the world remained subtly destructive, systematically tearing apart the quiet creations of those around her. Once, when Rebecca placed a bowl of tiny quince apples on a table because she had read somewhere that they imparted a subtle scent to a room, Lucinda delighted in pointing at them, laughing loudly in what by then had the hint of her later cackle and announcing each time she caught sight of them that they reminded her of Brussels sprouts. And Rebecca, in quiet defiance, left them in the bowl week after week, and the tiny fruits shrivelled and shrank until they took on the appearance of gnarled green trolls lurking in the shadows of an underground cavern.

It was Maurice who understood Lucinda best and it nearly broke her heart when he joined the British army.

'Don't you think that this family has done more than its share supplying bodies for a war machine?' Rebecca had for once voiced her mother's thoughts. Lucinda had not moved far enough from her family's tradition to voice this sentiment aloud and she remained grateful that Anthony became a doctor, lived in the same town, where he strode around in his off-duty hours with a sense of *noblesse oblige* which made Lucinda proud.

Rebecca must be tired arranging the papers chronologically. She has been skimming fast through them, almost as if she is trying to create a moving image by flicking the pages rapidly. She has stopped and sits, shoulders pushed down harshly, like a posture-improving exercise. She must have felt my gaze upon her because suddenly she swings around.

'It is in here, Helena, I'm not imagining it. Just now, while I was looking through the diaries to see how far they go, I saw several references to him – well, to "M". I've just a few moments ago seen three of them and that's only at a quick glance.'

She continues her frantic flicking of pages, as if she expects an image to leap off the pages, and I notice that the backs of her hands have taken on the beginnings of the mottling of middle age, years ahead of her time.

'M could be anybody, couldn't it? Mary, Marie, Melissa – one of her stepsisters was Melissa, you know. Not that she saw much of her step-siblings. A cold family, with the exception of Bart, that is.'

'Yes, well I'm out of time. Perhaps we can talk about it another day.'

Rebecca stands and straightens her clothes, delivering her usual admonitions to me about all I'm supposed to do while she is away on her long weekend with Wolfgang, the Good European. But now I'm getting piqued, which I suspect is because of reminding myself of Lucinda. Tired. And of course she'll see me soon after her return and she casts a final glance at the letters and diaries before a last wave.

May enters the room quietly behind my back as I shuffle the papers back into the box.

'Finished your business then?' she asks, giving a faint sniff and looking towards the door. She arrived so soon after Rebecca's departure that I suspect she was watching from a neighbouring room and I wonder if James has had his quota of diseases and scenes of lingering death prior to her arrival here.

'Oh yes, nothing very important really.'

'*She* makes it seem very important.' The stiff peaks of pepper-and-salt hair jerk in the direction of the door. 'You would think it was a last will and testament to see the serious face on her.'

I watch small jagged clouds move across the sky and wait for May's disparagements to end, feeling suddenly inexplicably tired, in a way that has taken me by surprise on several occasions recently.

'How is your family, May? I haven't heard about them in a while.'

May turns her head towards the window, looking skywards as if in search of divine inspiration, then shrugs and turns back again. 'God, Helena, my family. Well, if you really want to know, the youngest brother was on the booze again last night, so he probably won't appear out of the bed until late this afternoon, if he even bothers to get up, that is. If he wasn't such a good carpenter, he'd have been given his walking papers from that job of his years ago.'

'I'm sorry to hear that. Has he ever considered looking for help?'

'Patrick, look for help? Not a chance. He doesn't think he has a problem. He's one of the lads, you see, grown-up little boys, in their thirties, single, with all the time in the world, any woman's fancy – you get the picture? They don't see the cut of themselves, the big stomachs and the reek of beer. You'd want to be desperate to look crooked at them.'

May drops into the armchair as if all the oxygen has been suddenly sucked from her body and I sense that there is something that I should be saying, some small solace, but nothing comes to me. I'm too tired. The back of the chair has pushed her hair up in sharp tufts, the light from the window throwing it into spiky relief.

'Drink is a terrible thing, Helena. I can see it all so clearly now with Patrick. His every waking moment is geared around that first drink of the day. He even crosses the river to go to the cattle market to take advantage of the early opening hours of the pubs there – that's how desperate he can be at times.'

It is not clear whether it is the crossing of the river to the north side of the city or the early rising that strikes May as the more desperate gesture and I try to concentrate as she continues.

She shakes her head and says adamantly, 'Men! Who needs them!' This is one of May's frequent closures. She sighs and glances towards the box of letters and diaries, which I haven't put away. 'She's always busy, isn't she,' she says then, turning back to me, 'always got something on the go.'

May is talking about Rebecca again, as if she has only this moment stepped from the room. She has crossed her legs and is watching one foot swinging in the air, one of the leather clogs that she wears for comfort when she is working dangling precariously from her toes. We both remain quiet, as if watching to see if it will fall.

'She is going away for a few days with Wolfgang,' I tell her. 'She's tired. The break will do her good.'

'Yeah, maybe. She looks like someone who could do with a bit of company.'

May draws in her breath as if to say something further but doesn't and I realise that I am startled to hear of Rebecca as someone who might be lonely. She has always seemed to be too busy for that. But she does carry a sort of loneliness around with her. And I've noticed recently that her mouth has become smaller, sort of pinched in, as if she is letting out a silent whistle. But perhaps May was being churlish at the thought of Rebecca and Wolfgang going on a weekend break together. Now she is addressing the red clog, as if she has forgotten that I am here.

'I can't imagine that husband of hers being much fun,' she says at last and I decide in my tiredness that she is being uncharacteristically mean-spirited. Perhaps she is tired too.

'He's a kind man, May, a very kind man. He's just not all that comfortable with people, that's all. He takes a bit of getting to know.'

'Hmm. Well, like I always say, we're better off as we are, without the men.'

She grins at me as she stands up, and without asking,

sweeps the last of the papers off the table and drops them into the box.

I like this place. I have always liked it even though May assured me that it has changed now that it is a museum of modern art. But I'll always think of it as the Royal Hospital, regardless of what it is called. Cleaned up, painted and clinically lit the better to see all these great works, even if some of them don't seem that wonderful to me. But never mind, it is so good to be out of the home for a few hours. The interminable rain over the past week seemed to affect everybody's humour. Nothing to be seen beyond the windows but a heavy mass of grey settling on rooftops as if trying to stifle life.

'It's all modern stuff, Helena, you won't like it,' May said.

Old people are not supposed to like modern things. Perhaps we are not expected to understand them. But this place feels as if it is in my bones. I remember, shortly after we came to the city from Queenstown, standing as a child outside the surrounding wall, outside my grandmother's house, at my mother's side. She had been knocking in vain for several minutes, hoping to see her mother. Not that I understood what was happening then, just feeling a vague unease at her exclusion on a pretext by one of her stepsisters, when she eventually came to the door. The wall towered above us and I pretended I was the child Ally, walking as she had walked in its shadow, along its great length on a trip to see her father at his work in the Royal Hospital. I have to try hard to remember that it is a modern museum.

Rebecca has taken a day off work to take me here. This is

a slack period in personnel, she says, something to do with a break in the recruitment drive that has kept her busy recently. All those hours sitting listening to people, trying to discern their suitability for a job, can't be easy.

'She cheats a little,' Áine told me recently. 'She analyses their handwriting before she meets them.'

Rebecca's friendship with Áine never ceases to surprise me. I have never been able to see any basis in shared interests or anything else on which friendship normally resides. But they work together, there's always that. Sometimes I think that Rebecca is a source of wry amusement for Áine, nothing else. Áine frequently takes little soundings behind Rebecca's back, so that I am not sure what to make of this latest item she has waved in my direction. When I don't respond, she continues, misreading my silence.

'It's all down to whether or not they are ambitious or team players or outgoing – that sort of thing.'

Áine has a lop-sided smile that gives her the appearance of someone who is supremely self-satisfied, even if she is only considering the state of the weather. There I go, judging her again, and I make an effort to listen as she tries to explain how character can be revealed by a series of dots and dashes. But all I can think of is Rebecca and her fascination with any attempt to reveal the truth lying behind things. But I know that she enjoys her work and so I don't mention now the strangeness of her use of handwriting analysis. Sometimes she will talk about some interviewee with an unusual story to tell and it crosses my mind that she is living in the hope that someone will reveal something to her, a tiny clue on how to live. It is something that Lucinda forgot to pass on to her, presuming she ever knew what it involved.

The attendant has directed us to the first floor by elevator and it glides soundlessly upwards, releasing us into a series of long, pale corridors to east and west. The tall windows overlook an expansive courtyard and I regret my lowly position in my wheelchair beneath the sills. We move alongside exhibits of ethnic tapestries of dazzling hues and intricate stitching.

'Wolfgang would like this, Rebecca,' I say, as the mix of nationalities blurs on the catalogue and I give up reading to concentrate on the hangings.

'I think paintings might be more to his liking.'

They are both interested in paintings. Sometimes I think it is the only thing they have in common. They told me they spent time in the galleries on their weekend away – I cannot remember in which town. Wolfgang even tries his hand at painting when he has the time. He is quite good at it as far as I can tell. Impressionistic is how I think his style might be described. Gentle is the word that comes to mind, yes, definitely gentle. He told me once that he would like to live in the country and paint landscapes. That was quite a while ago. Sometimes when they invite me to their home, they tell me about whatever exhibition they have seen recently and show me catalogues and try to explain to me what appealed to them. Once, as they spoke animatedly about something or other, I glimpsed the young people they were when they first met.

All this musing has swept us beyond the tapestries and we are moving in and out of small rooms off the main corridor housing a visiting exhibition. I can tell that these are valuable works, as each room has a very vigilant attendant, and I consider how it might be possible to remove one of the smaller pieces without being noticed. Sometimes I wonder what it might be like to possess something exotic, something I could take from a hiding place from time to time and enjoy, alone. Most of the works here are in sombre colours, unsubtle marks dragging the length of coarsely primed canvases that stand out in stark contrast against all this white light.

'What do you think the artist had in mind when he painted these?' I ask Rebecca in a subdued voice. It seems that all this care and attention to their presentation requires a degree of deference. The careful placing and spacing of the works is the only thing that suggests to me that we are in the presence of great art. The catalogue shows an indistinct photograph of the artist, a gaunt, unshaven man in middle age.

Rebecca doesn't answer.

'Do you suppose that he has ever been to a place like this to see his work in such a nice setting?'

We have paused at the last room of the exhibition.

'Oh, he probably has, he may well have presided over the hanging of this one. What do you think of it?' Rebecca asks.

'Oh, I'm afraid that it is all beyond me, dear. There's too little in them for me. I like something I can keep coming back to but there's none of that here.'

'But don't you find it interesting to see such raw work – like looking at the skeleton of a body or the supports of a building. I like to see that sometimes – where something comes from.'

In this last room we are confronted by a small space cordoned off in the centre of the room. The timber floor is covered with small, acrylic, tear-shaped capsules, the size of a child's hand. They are multicoloured and cover the floor like randomly scattered sweets. There must be several hundred of them. And sealed inside each one of them is a coloured image of a penis. It takes several moments for me to grasp the detail of these images and I begin to laugh, which seems to surprise Rebecca. I suppose it is the unexpectedness of it all, the sheer volume of numbers, the variety – no two, as far as I could judge, were alike – the disembodiment, oh, I don't know, but I am seized with a fit of laughter and I cannot stop. And Rebecca turns my buggy quickly and pushes me out into the corridor.

'You know, Rebecca, we could have taken one of those. Nobody would have noticed.'

The laughter has made me quite giddy and I can sense her irritation rising. And I believe for a moment that, yes, I could have bent down and taken a capsule quite easily and put it in my pocket. And I imagine May's face if I produced such an object on my return.

'Oh don't be silly, Helena, you'll get yourself into trouble. I'm sorry about that, I really had no idea what it was all about.'

She sounds cross and I wonder does she think she made a mistake in bringing me here. I try to stifle the mirth for her sake and notice one of the older attendants grinning at me as we move at speed along the corridor.

I feel quite light-hearted. Lunch next. I love lunch here, great bowls of steaming soup, full of chunky, unexpected pieces and evasive spices. I used to visit galleries a long time ago with Tom. The National Gallery mostly. Soft footsteps on timber, Sunday strollers more interested in talking together than viewing the paintings, glancing briefly towards the walls before leaning in towards each other again. Wet Sundays. That was it, they were always wet Sundays. On dry Sundays we went to the Phoenix Park to walk by the lake, or along by the fence surrounding the zoo, laughing at the zoo sounds of honking and screeching and barking. Sometimes we took the train to the coast and pushed against the wind across dunes and coarse grass, Tom taking my hand when the sand began to slide beneath my feet and I was in danger of falling.

But I liked the galleries then, standing before a painting, contriving stories about the subject. We could make each other laugh. Laughter was safe. Safer than grasping my hand as I slipped slowly backwards in the sand. He liked the *Lady in a Hat*. I think that is what it was called. A strange painting, just a head really, a head with a large hat covered with floppy flowers. The woman is staring vacantly ahead as if she is waiting for something to happen to break the monotony. We used to laugh at it and wonder if she had put on the hat as a joke, and imagine her wearing her nightdress out of sight of the viewer, or perhaps she was wearing no clothes at all, perhaps the artist was wreaking some revenge in painting her faintly ridiculous hat. But secretly I yearned for such a hat and for an occasion when I could have worn it with a flowing dress and elbow-length gloves to the races or to a summer picnic on a clipped lawn. I never told that to Tom. He would never have accompanied me wearing such an outrageous hat. And he only ever held my hand.

The bowls of soup are as I expected, as aromatic and full of surprises as usual.

'I hope you don't mind, Helena, Áine said she might join us for lunch – she said she needs a break from the office.'

'Of course not. I think all you young people work too hard and eat too little.'

We have difficulty talking to each other, Rebecca and I, too many silences, although it suits me. I need to concentrate when I am eating, things spill too easily and it makes her impatient. She has me all tucked up with a napkin under my chin and another on my lap.

Áine arrives wearing strange clothes that look unfinished, the seaming all visible, as if she is wearing her clothes inside out. More of this modern style, showing the bones of the thing, as if we don't have the imagination to figure out how it is all held together. She manages to look dramatic as usual, even if it is in the middle of a working day, all greys and vermilion. I bet she could have worn that floral hat if she wanted to and got away with it.

'Sooo, been viewing the pricks, Helena, have you?'

We have a quiet chortle as Rebecca checks the table nearest to us to see if Áine has been overheard.

Áine and Rebecca chat quietly, drawing me in wherever possible, but less and less, which suits me. The warmth of the place and of the soup is making me drowsy. The murmurs across the table rise and fall – work, colleagues, other people's lives, names occasionally surface and then are quickly dispatched.

'So, have you decided to continue with the sessions?' Áine's voice has risen slightly after the glass of wine she had with the lunch.

Rebecca appears flustered and looks towards me. 'It's the therapy, Helena, you remember I told you about it?'

I make a half-hearted attempt to heave myself up in my buggy and into alertness. I mutter in acquiescence and mumble that she does not need any of it. Áine sips her wine and smiles and I am not sure if she agrees with me or is smiling at something Rebecca said.

'Nothing a good self-help book wouldn't solve, right Rebecca?'

Áine has always disparaged Rebecca's project, her endless delving into books in an attempt to sort out some imagined dilemma, rushing to me enthusiastically with a paragraph to read because she found a vague resonance of her problem lurking there.

'You know who you are really looking for, don't you, Rebecca? You're looking for your father. You've been chasing him your whole life. Admit it.'

Rebecca sits with her mouth slightly open and I think not for the first time that these young people all converse as if they are qualified psychologists. It seems to be a habitual way of talking with them now.

'My father is not relevant – I mean, not to the therapy, anyway.'

Her father, Lucinda's husband. Hard-working, quiet, coming and going on the edge of their lives and then he was gone, suddenly from a heart attack, without any warning. And for the young Rebecca and her two brothers it was almost as if he had never existed.

'He wasn't around long enough to mess up your life, is that what you mean?' Áine has stopped smiling and leans towards her friend. 'I'm only trying to needle you, Rebecca. You make it too easy at times. But admit it, it's worth considering. All this curiosity about who is and who is not your grandfather. What does it matter? You never met this man. You are really hoping that somewhere along the line you will discover your dear, departed father.'

As Áine finishes she manages to look slightly chastened, although it may have something to do with noticing that her wineglass is empty.

'The therapist thinks that I may have to go further back that that.' Rebecca looks towards me, as if fearing Áine.

'This is all beyond me, I'm afraid,' I say.

I cannot concentrate on what is being said, instead my mind is contemplating silken grains slipping down sand dunes, coarse blue grasses tugged almost flat in the wind, skin prickly from sun and the hot smell of sun-baked iron rising from the railway line in a tiny seaside station. And suddenly I have a sense of warmth beginning deep inside me, so deep that I do not know if it is a physical or a spiritual sensation. It is as if I am beginning to melt from within and I start talking rapidly to subdue the sensation.

'There is something that May has said to me recently which has suddenly popped into my head. She says that I never leave the war alone, that I am always picking at it. And you know, she is right in a way. But maybe it is the other way around. Maybe it never left us alone, as a family, I mean. Maybe we are eternally touched by it in ways that we don't really know about, handing whatever it is along from one to another, a vision of horror we heard about or somebody before us heard about, something we never experienced directly for ourselves but gleaned from things overheard. Maybe that is the real imprint you're looking for, Rebecca.'

Rebecca looks at me astonished and again I look for a sign of any of Lucinda's features there, but in vain. And I bluster on, trying to offer her something useful.

'We were left with all those little wounds, tiny little nicks that never healed, just got covered over by a thin skin, so that mostly they are unnoticed.'

Little wounds. Mama would not have looked at her life after Papa departed as a series of little wounds. And yet that is how it was for those of us who were left behind. Everything became diluted somehow, flowing out from those breaches and chinks after he left. And when he was gone into what Mama called the world of men, he truly left the women alone. We have been alone ever since. Mama alone, Lucinda alone, me alone. We never really knew what it was truly like to live among men, there were no blueprints available to us, several generations who lost a footing with men who never really had a toehold in the first place. Perhaps Rebecca knows this. Perhaps this is what she truly fears, this aloneness. I have tried to give her something useful, yet right now she is lost for words.

Across the table, Áine stretches and yawns. 'God, I needed a break from work, Rebecca. You didn't warn me this was a rehearsal for your next therapy session.'

Rebecca apologises and quickly talks about some work problem, while Áine slumps back into her chair, an indulgent expression on her face.

I try to imagine these two friends together on one of those short trips abroad and cannot. A city, a beach, a mountain – it doesn't matter – nothing conjures up a shared energy around them. But I'm an old woman, this is all beyond me, as I said to Rebecca, all this intruding into other people's lives. I'm accustomed to politeness, the grace to know when to advance and withdraw. A little like a dance really. And I'm almost at the point where I won't have a view on anything any more. But right now I don't want to have a view. I'm tired.

Áine unexpectedly reaches forward and touches the back of my hand. 'There, there, Helena, don't pay any attention to all this stuff. It's my bet that Rebecca will surprise us all one of these days. She'll probably open a crèche, full of bright kids appearing to be mini-adults who make meaningful conversation and eat organic lunches – you know the sort, real adult-pleasers.' Her tone is uncharacteristically gentle and we smile at each other.

We drive back to the home, glimpses of old buildings, neglected wedges clinging between recently renovated neighbours that flicker beyond the window and I think of train rides back to the city with Tom, past tenement gables, our feet just barely avoiding contact on the sandy carriage floor. But the warmth that spread through me earlier has gone and only tiredness remains.

10 September 1914

I had another letter from Richard today, a longer one
than last time. He seems to have more time to himself,
now that they have settled into village quarters, at least for
the present. Everything is so new and strange for him and
the men. They seem to have periods of great activity,
followed by long periods of boredom, filled with drilling
exercises and digging. But his form is good and he is
getting plenty of food, although the meat seems to come
mostly from tins. He says they got some leave to visit the
local town, where they visited an hotel and ate a decent
meal of chicken and fresh vegetables and had some drinks
later. It sounded so warm and comfortable. It's an elegant
town with water-gardens, he says, a place where the
slow sliding of punts on water stands in such contrast to
the crowded disorder they must experience when
on duty. But I can only try to imagine this, as
Richard tells me so little of his life among the soldiers.
They have recently moved further into the
countryside and they don't expect to have any leave
for a while.

    The papers are saying that reports of figures of large
numbers of wounded are false and have been put about by
enemy agents. It is very worrying but Richard has said
nothing of this. He talks of the excellent morale of the
men and of their determination to send the German
soldiers back where they came from within a matter of
weeks. And yet the papers are full of notices urging
farmers to till their land and grow wheat for next year, as
the country has only three weeks' supply of the crop left.
What on earth will we do for bread when that runs out?

But as soon as all this commotion is over in France, I expect that the Government will be able to import wheat from Europe. It is all so disruptive, even if it is only for a short time.

Mrs Coakley is taking measurements in Clonakilty for her cloaks. Richard promised to get me one for Christmas but I expect that will have to be postponed now. Perhaps I should give her my measurements anyway. I would so dearly love to shrug one of her cloaks around me in midwinter and snuggle beneath the hood, with its intricate gathering of pleats at the back. Mrs O laughs at the notion when I tell her, saying she prefers the comfort of her old plaid shawl. Perhaps I could surprise Richard when he returns home by wearing it to meet him. He would like that. I can imagine him smiling at the sight of it. It would be useful too for wearing to the army wives' afternoons as the days get colder. It would certainly set them talking!

I must remember to go along and meet them all next Thursday. I quite forgot to go these last few weeks. But there was so much to do then. And now things are so very changed – the talk will be all about the war effort and preparing bandages and food parcels and the difficulty of obtaining woollen socks and of course it will be in truth about the men and how much they are missed, although we will refrain from saying that. Their absence is something we are skirting around already, as if somehow it will be prolonged, become permanent, if we allude to it.

I shall ask Mrs O if she can stay a little later on Thursday. She is such a great friend, especially now. And she has her own troubles, yet she never bows to them but remains always cheerful. When the fishing is poor or the weather bad, I know that life is particularly hard for her and her family but it is still difficult for me to broach the subject with her. Helena, bless her, helps me get around that at times by bringing little gifts with her when she visits. And always on her return there is something for me – a brown speckled egg, a beaker full of honey. 'We leave the jam-making to you Protestants,' Mrs O likes to joke, 'but we have the best honey!' She likes to give the occasional nod at our differences, when Richard is not here, and now it is happening with greater frequency, almost becoming a continuous joke.

'I see Home-Rule has been postponed once again, Mrs Galvin,' she said this morning. 'My Sean won't like that one bit.'

And there it is, lying snugly between us, as if the difference belongs to others, to her Sean and to my Richard, as if it has nothing to do with us. Sometimes I think she likes to gesture towards a separateness that the two of us occupy together here, an aloneness that we need to preserve. And yet she shelters me from aloneness and absence, with her bustling efficiency and her gruff dismissals of my gratitude.

'Let duty be your watchword,' she said, reminding me that these were the King's words to the embarking soldiers. 'Sometimes I think that duty is really about the giver, not the receiver at all,' she said, noisily riddling the range, 'salving our own consciences, so that we can manage to live with ourselves a little better, that's all.' And then she stopped abruptly, as if she had already said too much and she lifted the ashes and clinker from the ash pan and carried them out into the yard.

And yet my duty is to keep on doing what Richard said I do best – taking care of the children and overseeing the home. And perhaps Mrs O is right. Perhaps it is salving my conscience.

I remember Mrs O's plaid shawl – every last scratchy encounter with it. I sheltered beneath it, bumping at each step of her angular hip, as Benjie and I, one on each side of her, ran up the ochre clay street in the rain to her house. I lay on the floor playing with baby Róisín, my cheek rubbing against a worn patch of the shawl, avoiding the baby's drool, a shimmering strand of silver across the woven wool. I huddled beneath it as Benjie told me ghost stories and we postponed throwing the shawl away from us for fear of what we might see. And once, when I had fever, Mrs O wrapped me in it and placed me close to the range to 'sweat the fever out of the poor lamb', as she told Mama.

The fabric was different from Mama's Clonakilty cloak, which was softer, a looser weave. Mama said that the wind blew through hers, that it was not as warm as she would have liked. Maybe that's why she drew it so tightly around her, as if she was protecting something or hiding something beneath it, as she bent over slightly, hurrying out the door on her way to one of the army wives' afternoons.

But she did not always have the cloak. It was something she had talked about having for some time and then, when she finally made the decision to obtain one, she became impatient when she discovered that it would take a while to have it made. She was determined to have it ready in time for Papa's homecoming and as the weeks passed and Christmas drew near, Papa wrote to say that it was unlikely that he would be home.

I think that was the time when Mama stopped speaking to us directly about Papa and the important work that he and his men were doing safeguarding the people of Belgium and France. She began instead to speak obliquely to us about the war, dwelling on tiny gestures of self-sacrifice we might make, of helping the war effort in a vague way that we could not understand. She put us to work on little projects, teaching Esmee and me something she considered useful, as she deemed it, such as turning the heel on a knitted sock, and the boys were shown how to tear muslin into long narrow strips. But somehow, she forgot to tell us exactly what use they might serve. Instead, she concentrated on the refinements of the task, her head bent low, two fine lines appearing between her eyebrows as she talked in a distracted way about how important it was for each of us to be involved, about how these tasks of ours were a real sign of a commitment to helping the forces in France. Somehow we knew not to question but to leave intact the fine gauze that held these endeavours in place for fear of what lay beyond. And the idea of involvement and commitment lodged in our children's psyches, so that in different ways each of us would either seek or shirk these measures of perceived worth throughout our lives.

We huddled in the kitchen while working on these projects, sustaining ourselves in the heat of the range. But even that seemed reduced, as Mama put less coke into it each time it needed replenishing and we understood that this too was part of the great, vague sacrifice. It became identified for us with a slowing down of everything, a waiting, as we stood alongside Mama and watched as she showed us how to perform each new task, how to arrange the coals in the range so that they burned more efficiently, so that the smaller pieces would not fall through the gaps in the firebox. Everything contracted for us. We had entered a different time, where the days drifted past like a mist settling over a pond and we existed in the tiny ripples beneath. Even the light in the house changed during that period of low-burning coals and dimmed gas mantles. We moved quietly around the house, as if we were afraid we might bump into something in this subdued light. And we played along with this, thinking it was only temporary, never wondering why Mama never taught us how to turn the sock's toe or how to roll the long strips of muslin into tight little sausage shapes for taking to the Admiralty building, where the local war effort was co-ordinated. We were only too happy to leave all this aside and sidle out the door unnoticed as she left us to stand at the window and look across the harbour to the island at the time when Papa would have normally returned home for the evening.

I cannot recall any of her outings to the wives' Thursday afternoons when she was not wrapped in her Clonakilty cloak. She cannot have worn it in warm weather, yet, try as I might, it is always there before me when I think back to those occasions, encapsulating a demeanour, a stealth that crept into her movements over that first winter. But perhaps I'm telescoping time, collapsing all those winters into one. Three winters spent living in hope must have been interminable for her.

'Mind how you go now, Mrs Galvin', was the constant reminder called out to Mama by Mrs O as she moved into the low afternoon light on her way to meet the other wives.

'There's a lot of practical work to be done, Helena,' Mrs O would explain each time Mama departed, and I found myself wondering on those occasions why Mrs O did all of Mama's practical work, while Mama dressed up to do her practical work somewhere else. 'Now, like a good girl, take these onions and peel and slice them for me and we'll put them quickly into the stew. And mind your fingers. Nobody likes to find fingers in their food!'

And on those days I sat and prepared onions with the tears streaming down my face because I had once again forgotten to bypass the root end with its sprouting creamy root-hairs. And I imagined Mama passing along the streets, struggling along Westbourne Place as the wind whipped at her cloak, one hand clutching the front edges together, the other holding the hood over her hair as she turned into the square and trudged up the steep hill to Barrack Street, where the houses stood leaning into each other, propping each other up like a deck of cards, as the locals liked to say.

'Look after Esmee', was her usual farewell to me, which really meant 'Don't ask Esmee to do anything too taxing'. And Esmee willingly took these opportunities to rest in the afternoons, her face wan, made frailer by the fact of her delicacy, a condition constantly placed before her by Mama.

'Nothing that a good dose of fresh air wouldn't cure', was Mrs O's dismissal as Esmee smiled, her eyelids lowered in a way that indicated that she had already entered that enveloping cocoon of half-sleep where she lay suspended hour after hour, replenishing her strength.

'She thinks she is living in a fairytale,' William observed to me once as he shovelled coke into the range, his angry scooping sending rasping noises across the kitchen and down the hallway.

'Mama says she is delicate, William.'

'There's nothing delicate about Esmee. She wants to avoid chores, that's all.'

William was always angry on Thursdays. He hated having to remain home, helping to look after the younger children, instead of wandering around the town with his friends. And he resented the frequent reminders from Mama that he was the man of the house while Papa was away. 'He's not away,' he would utter furiously to me after Mama had gone, 'he's at war. Why can't Mama say it, why does she talk as if he is only visiting France, as if the war has nothing to do with him? He has gone to war, that's where he is, gone to war.'

William's neediness tumbled out on these occasions, a mixed-up froth of alignment with the manly world of the soldiers and a covert pride in Papa which had not yet freed itself from the influence of Sean. This sort of angry talk from William shocked us children and Mrs O would try to placate him and ask him not to upset the little ones.

'They've gone to war, the lot of them, answering the call of the King and yet the Home Rule Bill for Ireland has been postponed again. Does that sound fair, Mrs O?' William's voice was deepening by then and I could not tell if it was deliberate, an exaggeration, to make him sound more like a young man, more like Sean.

'Where did you hear that, William? Have you been talking to my Sean?'

Mrs O would become slightly breathless on these occasions as she tried to answer William's posturing and contain her own opinions at the same time. Her own thoughts on politics and religion were never a matter for conversation in our house, at least not in front of us children and certainly not when she was in charge in Mama's absence. She was adept at filtering everything through Mama's eyes, setting aside what would upset Mama, realigning events with meticulous care so that the gap was filled in, a brief aberration banished to some other adult place. Sometimes this took more than one attempt, especially with William.

'Yes,' he said, 'I spoke with Sean. He says if the men were stupid enough to march off to war for a foreign king and a foreign country, then where's the honour in that? And furthermore, if some of them went because they thought they would get Home Rule for Ireland as a reward, then they were more stupid than he thought in the first place.' William paled as he spoke, a look of fierce concentration on his face, as if he was trying to repeat verbatim what he had heard from Sean.

'Young man, don't you ever let me hear the likes of that from you ever again. And your poor father off in France! You'll upset your mother no end if she hears you speak like that. Home Rule will only bring another set of troubles around our ears. You mark my words. It's not as simple as you think, William, not as simple at all.'

And of course she was right. William's grasp of things could not take him any further with Mrs O. And I could tell from his rapid blinking when he was finding himself out of his depth. Sparks flew up out of the range as the coke hit the clinker and I watched Mrs O to see if she would check him for overloading it and running the risk of smothering the embers. And though she watched him closely and tightened her lips, she waited patiently as he dropped the round cover into place and opened the damper with harsh tugging movements.

'That Sean will be the death of me yet,' she said, in what had become a frequent signing off she used to these episodes. 'Him and his Home Rule. It might be all right for those Irish representatives sitting in parliament in Britain and who want an Irish parliament of their own, but what about the rest of us? It won't help to put food on the table, will it?' And she looked quickly at me and swept the flour to one side of the marble slab with the side of her large, freckled hand. 'Come here, Helena, and we'll have some nice scones ready for your Mama when she comes home.'

Mrs O and I had become accustomed to working quietly side by side in those early days. It was just the two of us on Mama's afternoons, with Esmee resting and the boys doing boys' things in the garden, and William – well, increasingly we didn't know where he was or what he might be doing, until he could contain it no longer and a few nights after an escapade he would divulge it all to me.

To stand near Mrs O was a little like standing on the platform of the Queenstown railway station as the steam engine arrived, coming to a slow, laboured halt. It was something to do with a surfeit of energy that was only barely contained by the confines of the space in which she worked. Sometimes I would listen carefully to her breathing, expecting to detect something unusual there, an inner secret mechanism at work that wound her up and set her going in a way that stood in stark contrast to the slow, dreamy movements that carried Mama through her day. I expected Mrs O to make snapping, creaking sounds generated by her brusque movements but try as I might I never heard anything. She was so enormous, appeared to have such great girth to us children, yet she did not carry any discernible excess fat, was just a solid mass that ducked and weaved efficiently in whatever space she happened to find herself. Sometimes I tried to imagine her when she was young, seeing a tiny child that held her exact proportions in miniature, like a clumpy clay figurine newly prised out of a mould and placed carefully on a beach among sand and shells, looking so top-heavy that I expected her to topple in the first gust of wind.

'Now, Helena, stop dreaming and pat a little milk on top of each scone with the back of your hand and we'll put them in the oven. They'll be just perfect for when your Mama arrives home.'

And in the beginning that was how it was – Mama coming in with her cheeks uncharacteristically pink from the walk down the hill, the hair around her forehead blown into a creamy froth by the salt air. She was full of talk in the early days, of the wives who were at the afternoon and how they looked well or were sickening for something. She loved to describe their clothes, how one of them looked beautiful in violet and another wore a lovely garnet brooch placed high on the neck of a silk blouse, and another had dark lustrous hair and she wondered how she maintained its lustre in the damp blustery weather. And overall, there was a vividness to these homecoming stories that is still with me, as she set the rich dark colours in place for us, laying them across the scene she described like bolts of silk scattered on an ottoman.

As she talked then, Mama and I drank tea and ate Mrs O's scones beside the range and the sea-green Clonakilty cloak lay draped over a chair, while around us the evening drew in earlier each week, yet I never remember anybody standing to turn up the lamps as we sat and let the glow of the range spread its orange-red hue across our faces. Mrs O would join us at Mama's invitation, sitting on a straight-backed chair with a woven seat which Mama said had been in the house when we arrived and which Mrs O called 'the súgán'. It was really too narrow for her and when she sat down, the chair vanished completely from view, so that she appeared to float and I watched fascinated, believing that only the centre third of her body could be accommodated on such a narrow chair, with two thirds of her body held in suspension on either side. As the days passed and became colder and we drew closer to the range, she moved to a wide, low, slackly sprung armchair to one side of the hearth, which seemed to have been moulded around her shape. This was a chair Papa used to occupy on the infrequent occasions when he sat in the kitchen.

But by the time Mrs O took over the armchair, Mama had taken to making her extended walks along the seafront, walks that took her out of sight and beyond our knowing for hour after hour, as she began a period of scanning the sea for sight of what the newspapers were calling the 'commerce raiders'. Mrs O reluctantly told us this when we queried the length of Mama's absences. 'It's something to do with protecting the merchant ships that are bringing food and fuel across the Atlantic. I was reading about it in the paper yesterday.' Mrs O imbued the reading of the local newspaper with such a reverence that I always pictured her sitting upright as if in a church pew, her plaid shawl covering her head as she slowly turned pages. Papa once told me that all the local people called the *Cork Examiner* The Paper. 'They think that paper has some divine access to the truth of every situation it reports, that there is no other version of events possible,' he had said in exasperation one day, as he disputed something which William had read. But he had never had occasion to dispute the paper's standing with Mrs O.

Her large floury hands flew in a blur as she threw fruit into the soda-bread mixture, turning it over, digging in with her thickening knuckles between each turn. Benjie and I had come in from school together and had finished our bowls of thick onion soup when she began to explain why Mama had not yet returned from her walk.

'Some German boats are attacking the supply ships to deprive the soldiers of food and ammunition.' She continued to turn the dough over, slapping it continuously into shape, as if she had forgotten what she was doing. 'Anyway, your Mama is interested in these things. She says she must be vigilant, that the King said to the troops that duty must be their watchword and so she believes that it must be hers too.' She spoke in a low voice, urgently, as if she wanted to finish what she had to say before someone might interrupt.

'Is that why she walks along by the sea?'

'Well, child dear, I'm not too sure. She likes to walk, sure enough, but she also wants to do her duty, as she likes to say. But the Lord knows that there's duty and there's duty.'

Mrs O's cryptic musing beneath her breath lodged between us and I knew not to ask her what she meant by the set of her mouth. She gave a last dull thump to the dough, turned it over and slammed it down again. 'As long as they don't stop the sugar and tay from coming in, we'll be all right, girleen.'

I loved it when Mrs O called me girleen, loved when she let her speech slip into the strange place where syllables slithered about to emerge sounding like one thing yet meaning something else altogether. When Mama was there, it happened less often, as Mrs O made an effort to be comprehensible to her, so that Mama did not have to ask her to repeat something as sometimes happened to both their embarrassment. And Benjie shot a look across at me and I knew that our days would be filled with lurking behind beach boulders for hours, our fingers sticking to the icy rime of rocks, Benjie telling me our white breaths in the cold air would give us away to the commerce raiders.

But while she walked and watched, Mama's thoughts, unknown to us, must have already begun sliding across the metallic sea to another sea of mud, churned up by thousands and thousands of boots, mud that clung to their soles and sucked their energy, seeped into their clothes and chafed their bodies until she could think of it no more. Then she must have covered it over with one gesture in mist and frost and ice and snow, freezing the quagmire by an act of supreme will until it shimmered and sparkled back at her, solidified and became opaque, so that she could no longer see the bodies and the faces beneath. It must have been in some glide across ice like this that her mind took her to Shackleton.

'We are approaching our coldest time of year here, but in the Antarctic it is approaching the warmest time of year,' she said one day, throwing her cloak over the back of the súgán chair. 'Yes,' she said into the silence, 'Shackleton's expedition really did set off at the right time.'

'Avoided the war, you mean, ma'am?' Mrs O peered closely at Mama as she continued to speak about the expedition and its slow movement south in a white haze of ice and gales and snow, oblivious to the sound of Mrs O's voice as the tiny, imperceptible slip of her mind, already begun, continued, although we didn't know it at the time. Later Mrs O would refer to Mama's crabwise drift in conversation as an 'accommodation', and I came to think of it as a little room she slipped quietly into for shelter on occasions. 'It's just one of her little accommodations,' she would say, when one of the younger children would query what Mama was talking about, usually after she had left the room. 'She can't bear to think about more difficult things, you see, and so she talks about other things that are not so difficult but that rest alongside the difficult things in her mind.'

And somehow we accustomed ourselves not to ask about the more difficult things which I pictured lying there in her mind, side by side like skeins of unbleached wool in a dyer's chest.

It was about that time that Mama began to talk about the spy who was arrested on the coast to the west of the town. Doubtless this was one of her accommodations, one of those less difficult things with which she could preoccupy herself and which was heightened in significance by the speculation in the newspaper and in the town. He was a stranger in the area, arrested in the hills behind Timoleague village with a view of the lengthy bay of Courtmacsherry fanning out beneath. The *Cork Examiner* was expansive in its accounts of the shadowing activities of the police as the stranger moved around the area, and of how he was taken into custody and held overnight and was mistakenly released by a local magistrate, whereupon he retraced his steps to Courtmacsherry, where he was recaptured on the beach in possession of extensive sketches of the area. He was handed over to the general commanding the military forces in the region to be dealt with under military law.

We heard this account in fits and snatches over a period of days, mostly overheard as Mama and Mrs O talked quietly together. And when we questioned them about it, and especially about what might happen to him next, they answered vaguely and made it all sound routine and ordinary, a blunder of sorts, but it was not clear whose blunder it was. William seemed to be in a heightened state of tension as he listened, saying nothing. One night he called me into his room and told me that he was concerned that the spy might be Sean, whom he had not seen for several days. The fact that Mrs O did not seem at all concerned, he swept aside in his absorption with the event. He picked it over night after night with me, believing that Sean's subversion could extend to providing intelligence to the Germans. The possibility grew in his mind that Sean was indeed intent on using this opportunity for his own purposes. And while Mama talked to Mrs O about the possible dangers of these spying activities to the soldiers in France, their heads almost touching as they huddled, William moved in his parallel world, where native spies plotted subversion at home. As for me, I could not decide which world offered the greater excitement.

And so Mama's list of accommodations was slowly extended from the commerce raiders to local spies and any person or event that might thwart the war effort. And behind it all, her fascination with the Shackleton expedition continued as it forced its way into the blue ice of the southern hemisphere, seeking to honour an Empire which Papa and his men also served.

7 December 1914
Approaching dawn

I have had such exciting news today. Bart has written to
say he is coming to visit after Christmas. It seems like such
a long time since last we met. It must have been that time
before William's birth when Richard and I went to
Dublin for Melissa's wedding. Such a strained affair it was
– Mother trying to be cheerful and seeking to keep us all
included and Stepfather strutting around, fiddling with his
watch-chain and avoiding Richard at all costs. But it was
lovely to see Bart then, the same wicked humour and
pretence of seriousness. It will be nice to sit and laugh
with him again. He can have the large front bedroom –
Helena won't mind moving in with Esmee, even if her
coughing disturbs her for a while. He will enjoy the view
across to the island. It's very different to what he has been
accustomed to at home, looking across at those massive
walls around the Royal Hospital. But sometimes even I
miss them. They seem less dreary in my imaginings than
when I looked at them from my old bedroom window
and thought that the walls had been smeared with soot.
What a long time ago it all seems, when I was the only
child for so long in a house that was later filled with so
many children. And a new father. Such a long time ago. I
must remember to ask Mrs O to help me prepare the
room. That nice lavender rug will look bright on the bed
and will keep him warm when the winds swing into the
northeast in January. And I can bring up that bunch of
heather that Helena has been drying in the kitchen and
hang it from the mantelpiece with a piece of purple velvet
ribbon.

Today was full of activity. We had one of our afternoons, full of talk and laughter and of course the inevitable tears. And we all seem to have had hopeful letters for a change and there was no great worry from any of the men, not like the time when Amelia's husband was seriously wounded. But at least he is out of the war now, in a hospital in England. But Marcie wasn't so lucky, with her young husband missing, presumed dead. It happened so early for her, right at the beginning, before we thought things were serious, before we understood anything at all about the war. She is suffering so badly right now that she is not able to come to our afternoons. I must call to her tomorrow and see if there is anything I can do.

Richard is gone almost four months now, yet it seems like four years. Memories of his homecomings in the evenings from the island are blurring already, so that I have to go to the wardrobe and smell his clothes to remind me of his closeness. Sometimes I stand inside his wardrobe and close the door and feel in that blackness that I am in some other place, where he has just left the room and will return at any moment and light will slice through the darkness once more. But this silliness is not what he would want to hear and so I tell him all the cheerful things about the children and school and Mrs O and the clamour in the town as the war effort moves along and the complaints of the merchants whose horses have been commandeered. And I told him about the endless notes in the newspaper about pigs and their feeding problems and the proposal to let them feed on open ground 'as nature intended'. He laughed at that – he said so in his last letter.

But he is hiding the horror of it all from me, the way Mrs O hides the newspaper when the news is especially grim. And this sets my mind racing and my imagination begins to work on what I do know, and then my nights are frequently filled with dreams of water-filled trenches and endless darkness lit by sudden, blinding flashes from the armaments and the sighing and moaning of death in the wind, until I awaken from the sheer terror of it all and wait for my breathing to quieten down and the pain in my heart to subside. And lying there, listening lest I have disturbed the children, I think of the sea beyond the window and imagine it icing over as winter progresses and the ice spreading and thickening in one great sheet of palest, duck-egg blue, stretching in a shimmering line across the North Atlantic and on to the southern oceans where Shackleton's ship must encounter it on his journey to South Georgia. It is said that there is a sighing and moaning to be heard there also, rising from the straining timbers and the soughing of the wind in the ropes, the shifting, hissing sound of ice as water rushes and pushes beneath it, making the ice creak and groan in an endless resistance. And I let the brightness of it all spread out and out, until it fills my room and I can look at it no more, for there is nothing left to see but this endless blankness.

Blankness is what I slip into with ease now, a quiet, floaty place that our Thursday afternoons have begun to offer, a place to slip into with M, to rest awhile in that comfortable space, unassailable, held fast in a grip as if frozen in ice, only this grip is warm, soothing, a place where I can stay, unquestioned, if only briefly. 'Harmless,' Amelia says. 'M will comfort you in your hour of need,' Kate says, as if she is talking about praying to her favourite saint, as if for once we share religious aspirations. And perhaps in a way we do, at least in that place. But she always says this with a sly look, a certain native knowingness that tells me she will not say anything about this sharing we have, yet leaves me feeling tainted by a beholdedness that I cannot name.

The weather has grown colder and the wind is moving into the east. How much colder it will be for the men with no way to dry their heavy uniforms and socks, which stiffen from the freezing mud. Last night I tried to sleep on the floor to see what it might be like to lie on something other than a feather mattress. My body became rigid, stiff and cold, until I could not tell where it ended and the floorboards began. I felt as if I were part of the floor, the earth, the same earth Richard stretches out on at night or in quiet moments in the day and I thought that my body was continuous with the earth and with his body, hard, round, rigid, like an acorn in the ground.

My memories are filtered endlessly through the eyes of a child and yet I am an old woman. It must be possible to look back from this great vantage point with the experience and, dare I say it, the wisdom of the intervening years and have something sensible to say, shed a little light before all is lost to view. Yet, try as I will, it is my child's view that seeps through relentlessly and my ragbag of experiences is to no avail here. Surely I can shed some light on Mama's life? She appears almost as a child from this vantage point. I am already three times the age she was when Papa left for France. And yet I feel no closer to understanding what was happening to her than she was.

The weaving of the Shackleton story that Mama had begun for us a few weeks earlier continued above my head as I sat on the floor with Esmee. We watched as she divested herself of her green cloak and sank into a chair, stretching her small feet towards the fire, having shed her narrow leather boots, her mouth very slightly open as she breathed in the warm air and the kitchen smells. It was clear, even to a child, that she occupied a different place to the rest of us then, of this I am sure, a place she had entered into on her walks, a place full of sensations that crept in on the sea wind, filling her senses with tiny particles of ice, so that her re-entry into our world was arrested and she became like a grain of pollen trapped in amber. And yet I suspected that she remained isolated from us by an act of will, postponing her return indefinitely from that place where cold and wind raked her emotions.

'It is so cold out there,' she said, 'that I think the wind must be sweeping up to us directly from the Antarctic.' Mama spoke softly, as if to herself, and Mrs O's stolid body leaned towards her to catch the sound.

'Well, I don't know about that, ma'am,' she said. 'My Sean and the fishermen he works with always talk about the southwesterlies and how they bring all this soft weather with them, so they must be blowing from somewhere a little warmer than the Antarctic.'

Watching them, it was difficult to detect a gesture, a hint from Mama that might indicate that she had heard any of this.

'They are moving continuously south, you see — Shackleton and his men — so it must be getting steadily colder.' Mama leaned slightly towards the range as she spoke.

But of course by then Shackleton was already out of contact, moving steadily into the vast whiteness that was beginning to envelop her.

'And the snow is very different to what passes for snow here, on the odd occasion when it falls. It's drier, you see, it falls away from your clothes like hawthorn blossom.'

'Mostly slush, ma'am. You could hardly call what falls here snow, the way it gets churned up with the march of feet, turning it that dirty grey.'

But Mama did not want to contemplate marching feet, had winced as Mrs O spoke. And they fell into a silence while Esmee and I slithered the ivory fish from Papa's parlour game across each other in their dark timber box with the tips of our fingers. And it was the start of a new pattern between Mrs O and Mama, a game of point and counterpoint, where Mrs O tried to insert little nuggets of fact and common sense into Mama's speculations.

We became accustomed to Mama's delayed settling back into the kitchen space, happy to let Mrs O continue with whatever it was she was doing. Almost overnight, or so it seemed to me then, Mama had slipped out of the formality of the domestic routine that had structured our lives prior to Papa's departure for France. She seemed to be slotted into our lives in a new, ill-defined series of ways that left her wafting free like a loosely anchored piece of bunting. We were never sure any more when we might encounter her next, whether she would be home in time for the evening meal or arrive late and breathless, smoothing her hair and offering some vague excuse about encounters along the way and the endless whispers of injuries and losses (they were always losses or missing in action, never deaths) that rustled along the walls of the town, an unwanted missive that passed surreptitiously from hand to hand.

'He says the rain has churned up the soil into a sea of mud,' she said one day to Mrs O, after having received a letter from Papa, and I wondered how far I could take the island ferry in such a muddy sea, and its familiar bobbing

shape became an oozy amorphous thing in my mind,
sinking into a sea the colour of wet peat.

'The men are suffering from blisters and trench foot,' she
said almost to herself another time as she turned the page of
the letter and fell silent again and I considered asking her
about trench foot and decided against it, knowing she
would not hear me.

Mrs O had taken to clicking her tongue on these occasions
in a mixture of sympathy with Mama's having to read about
such horrors and disgust at what she was saying. And
somewhere in there too I thought there was annoyance at
Papa for telling her about these horrors in the first place.
She watched Mama closely, with a gentle sidewise look,
the same glance I would see her giving a stew pot to make
sure it did not boil over while she was occupied with her
baby, Róisín. One day, when Mama thought that none of
the children was within earshot, she read part of a letter from
Papa to Mrs O.

To fight hand to hand, you have to be crazy. It requires
the craziness of my boyhood, Ally, the sort of fisticuffs
we lads indulged in along the Dodder banks over
matters I cannot now recall but which seemed worthy
of all the violent aggression we could summon up with
no thought for the consequences. Even now I can recall
my mother's admonition to us then, to use only the
amount of force that was required to defend ourselves
and no more. But I have since set that advice well to
one side, it is a mere echo now, which gets dimmer
with each passing day.

'What does he mean, Mrs O? There is nothing in the
papers about hand-to-hand combat. The reports are full of

stories about success and battles won, of vast numbers of prisoners and guns captured. Why does he talk about the need to be crazy? People who are crazy end up in asylums for the insane.'

'Now don't you go upsetting yourself, ma'am. He was probably tired when he wrote that letter, getting things a bit mixed. You have to look on the bright side of things. It's just a lot of talk about some other soldiers, that's all, just a load of talk.'

But playing out of Mama's view in the corner, even I could not imagine the soldiers sitting around talking. It made no sense at all. All the bustle that went on each day around the Admiralty in the centre of the town, all the comings and goings of people helping with supplies, whom Mama spoke about as doing their duty, how could all this activity go on at home if the soldiers had nothing to do but sit around exchanging stories in France? Yet the two women remained silent on the subject in front of us children, and anything I knew at the time was overheard by me or by William. And in the town the horses were rounded up for sending to France, while the merchants complained endlessly to anyone who would listen and wondered what they could do to make their deliveries with their horses gone, and the price of wheat drifted slowly upwards. Listening to Mrs O's long list of anxieties had me imagining horses and sacks of wheat, honey-coloured tea chests and brown paper bags of sugar all spiralling upwards in a gigantic funnel that sucked them up and twisted them across the sea to vanish in a tiny point somewhere over France.

I suppose some of the muslin strips of bandages the boys cut up were wrapped into tight little sausage shapes and delivered along with the completed knitted socks — completed by someone other than by me or Esmee — to Admiralty House. But Mama made frequent trips into the town and told us of the goings-on at the British Legion's supply centre.

This is what I came to consider in later years as the visible aspect of Mama's Protestantism. It was something she stepped into from time to time, like donning a sensible winter petticoat and pulling the strings firmly tight. It became apparent after Papa left for France and with it came a subtle change in demeanour, like a shadow passing across her which seemed to alter her posture and the way she moved, so that everything appeared purposeful. Even her speech changed from something speculative to a more precise, carefully enunciated tone, as if she hoped that it might be taken for an assuredness by those who did not know better. It was as if she wanted to convey the image of someone who could deal with recalcitrant kitchen maids — of which she had none — and organise extensive sock-knitting and bandage-rolling groups, while at the same time devoting herself to her young family. It was apparent too in the occasional encounters we had with visitors to our home, when these subtle changes were evident in her dealings, when she became so much more this visibly coping person.

But it all vanished when she went for her long distracted walks and then returned. It vanished with the removal of her cloak, in one great vapoury rush of air as it swung across our heads to lie in deep folds on the chair. Sometimes I thought I could detect it twitching as it lay there. And when she would ask me in a little while to take it out to the hallstand and hang it up, I appproached it cautiously and kept my eyes riveted on the stuffed red squirrel that rested on the stand as I aimed the cloak at the highest hook that I could reach. Standing there, I could lose myself in the brown opacity of the squirrel's eye that sent the hallway glinting back at me in a swirling, enveloping movement that, if I looked long enough, would make me dizzy. Beyond the kitchen door the low murmuring voices continued until Mama's fell quiet and I knew Mrs O was snuggling back into the low armchair and talking about life in the ochre street in an attempt to seduce her away from the bleached-out whiteness of her increasing mental instability.

There was something faintly exotic about Mrs O's version of her life on that edge-of-town street. It took its rhythm from the rising and setting of the sun, from the tides and the seasons, from the cats with their litters and the children tumbling in doorways. But what added to the sense of the exotic was an overriding absence of men. They spent their days on fishing boats or in the fields beyond the town, engaged in sporadic farm labouring. Sometimes they could be seen waiting around the shipping agents' offices, helping passengers with their luggage as they boarded the huge ships for America or lounging around the centre of the town in the hope of work heaving sacks of produce for the merchants.

Mrs O's husband was a small, thin man, with large pale eyes that gave him an appearance of being in a permanent state of surprise. Sometimes in a fit of exasperation Mrs O would tell Mama about some escapade of her husband's, and finish it with a deep shrug and sigh, 'Ah well, sure he's harmless', as if she were waving aside some tiny insect. When they walked together, which was seldom, he scurried to keep up with her, while she strode along as if trying to shed an irksome presence. Once, when Papa thought that he and Mama were alone, he laughed aloud at the sight of them both passing the drawing-room window and said that Mr O'Sullivan should hold on to the hem of her skirt if he wished to keep pace with his wife. He was seldom at home when I visited Benjie and on the odd occasion when we met there, he moved in and out of doors, always carrying things of one sort or another – a few small sods of turf for the range, some onions from the store shed, a basket of potatoes, some unidentifiable tool which he carried vaguely before him, uncertain what to do with it. He reminded me a little of a bedraggled bird, unable to find a perch on which to alight.

These were the twin poles around which Mrs O's life revolved. It was as if all her movement forwards in her life had been towards the care of these two families. Invisible lines extended out from her, keeping us all aloft like kites on a wind. As Mama's preoccupations grew and as she moved away from us, she too became one of these kites, for a time a lighter, more erratic one that blew higher than the rest of us and took up more and more of Mrs O's attention in order to keep her from drifting away altogether.

Not that we children had a sense of Mama's mind altering, although we sensed a difference, a relaxation of her routine, a little more freedom for us once we came home from school, where meal times were filled with chattering and uninvited reaching across the table beneath the level of her gaze, which seemed to be permanently fixed half an inch above our heads. Sometimes she snapped out of her reverie in a vain attempt to discuss our activities with us and even occasionally tried to indicate to us something of her day. But we were not interested in her day nor she in ours and so we all settled quickly into our new routine. Once she began to tell us about her afternoon with the army wives and names passed in the air around us – Marcie and Kate and Amelia and Marjorie – and we giggled at the names and pulled faces at each other as she talked on, failing to notice our mischievous wriggling and giggling.

But unknown to us, her Thursdays had evolved into something unique for her that she came to guard closely. And Mrs O sensed something too which caused her to ease back from Mama and wait quietly to one side of the hall and watch her adjust her clothes in the narrow mirror. In the early days all her preparations for the walk up through the town were finalised in the hall with Mrs O waiting to bid her farewell while we children rushed in and out of doorways. But after a while Mama took to donning her outdoor clothes in her bedroom, coming carefully down the stairs, one hand holding the cloak wrapped tightly across in front of her, as if she were already encountering the first blast of wind from the sea. Mrs O stood more erect then, as if responding in some way to Mama's determined exit.

'Don't let the talk get you down, ma'am,' Mrs O would sometimes say if Mama had been particularly downcast after her previous afternoon with the wives and she would draw her cloak even tighter around her and look towards Mrs O, her pale, thick eyelashes lowering briefly over her eyes and then she would raise her head as if hearing a sound and leave quickly without a word.

It is the quiet, solitary station that Mrs O occupied at the end of the hall on Thursday afternoons that I recall now, the sheer, solid immobility of her bulky figure there in the shadows and then a quick heaving movement that sent a ripple of air down the hall as she started into her more familiar rhythm as soon as the door closed on Mama. The swooping draught of wind with its salty bite dropped towards the floor to rasp at our ankles and chill the warmth beyond the kitchen door.

Benjie and I decided to follow Mama one Thursday afternoon. It wasn't because we wanted to spy on her, despite Benjie's preoccupation with the intrigues surrounding that particular activity since the war began. It was simply boredom. Benjie and I saw her turn the corner and begin her ascent of the steep hill that led up to the house where the army wives' afternoons took place. When I asked her once why they never came to our house for their afternoons, she said it was because Marcie's house was in the centre of town and easier for people to reach.

She moved along the edge of the square, staying in close to the buildings for shelter, moving carefully around the fruit and vegetable stall that the greengrocer had set out on the pavement, the hem of her cloak wrapping itself briefly around the legs of the trestle. We held our breaths, thinking that she might pull the whole stand along the pavement with her, but it snaked away at the last moment and she moved on unknowing. Benjie and I continued to dodge in and out of doorways, not needing to watch where she was going yet pretending she was leading us. Up through the town we climbed, along the steep street, the narrow limestone houses glinting back at us. Once we reached this street there was no longer anywhere for us to hide and so we remained crouching at the end of the row of houses, bent low beside the steep steps leading to the front door. When she had been admitted, we still remained in our crouching position, the mid-winter light fading fast, our limbs stiffening in the cold. When eventually we thought the half-light offered sufficient concealment, we crept along the street until we reached the house where the wives had gathered. Because of the steep incline, the window was above eye level for us and we tried to see in through it by standing on the topmost step and leaning sidewise across the handrail and towards the window. This was a position we could adopt only one at a time and which gave us a partial glimpse into the drawing room or into that part of it that was visible beyond an imaginary diagonal which I had drawn across the room as I waited for my turn to take a peep.

Many of the wives lived on this street. It was what Papa called 'the officers' patch' and when we asked him why he did not live in the officers' patch, he said it was because we had more children than anybody else and needed more space.

By the time Mama arrived to join them, most of the wives were sitting around, talking. A parlour maid was waiting to take her cloak when a small woman with dark hair reached over and took it, placing it quickly around her shoulders and twirling and swinging it in great swirling gestures while the women all laughed and Mama stood smiling quietly as she fixed her hair into place where the wind had whipped it from her combs. Around her, some of the group sat on an array of chairs, reclining back comfortably in easy postures that Benjie and I were unaccustomed to seeing. Languid, I suppose, is the word that best describes these few women, definitely languid, their bodies leaning back into soft upholstery, while the rest of the group looked on enthralled from the margins. They watched closely the behaviour enfolding before them – a slowly dangling shoe hanging in a half-grip from a silvery stockinged foot, the folds of a skirt draped between knees placed apart in a way that Mama would never permit Esmee and me to sit, two pale hands clasped loosely between. The women were reticent yet mesmerised by the scene. We saw disembodied legs and feet, the backs of heads with twisted chignons and braids of hair carefully pinned in place, pale necks and pleated blouse collars. Now and again when someone leaned forward we saw the full upper half of the owner of feet or hands and sometimes when they arose we saw the entire person. The mirror over the mantelpiece gave us a view of a sort, a tilted cameo, people caught up in a skewed world.

We made this trip several times over the course of that first winter and watched undetected from our perilous leaning position on the top step in the fading light. There were times when we caught a glimpse of a covered face in the mirror, hands covering the face entirely, mimicking the start of a game of hide-and-seek, until someone crossed the room rapidly to clutch the shoulders and rock the owner wordlessly in a desolate dance. Then another figure would cross the room and pull the window-blind, glancing distantly across the sloping street as if in an effort to see beyond the greyness of the limestone, beyond the ragged edges of the town into the countryside to the west and beyond to the broad viridian reaches of the Atlantic. But I'm putting an old woman's view on it all now. All Benjie and I saw then was a face that came briefly close to us and then was gone, into the dark velvety opulence of the wives' afternoon.

Rebecca is bustling around in her huge kitchen, cooking and tidying and handing out drinks to Wolfgang and me. It is truly a wonderful kitchen, full of quiet creams and greens, natural timbers and gleaming tiles. Everything has been carefully lighted so that we are enveloped in a soft glow, like gaslight. Wolfgang looks quite healthy in this light, his customary pallor washed over with colour. Rebecca, however, has managed somehow to retain her usual strained look despite the softness of the light and the harmony of the rustic colours. She carries this air of intensity about her always now, regardless of the task in hand. She appears to be tackling each job to be done as if it is a matter of great delicacy and importance, demanding her utmost concentration. At the moment she is opening a tin of green olives, pulling with little strength at the metal tab.

'I couldn't get any fresh olives, Helena, the delicatessen closed early today. You'll have to make do with the tinned variety.' She continues to pull on the metal tab, her knuckles raised under the strain, looking too large for her thin hand, as if she pulls at her finger joints to make them pop.

'Oh they're every bit as nice, Rebecca, and probably more hygienic. I sometimes wonder about all those open barrels of olives outsides shops. They look inviting but they can't possibly be the safest way of displaying food.'

'I think the oil and brine keep them safe enough.' She waves the tin to and fro in the air in the direction of Wolfgang, who pulls at the tab and effortlessly removes the lid.

'May told me today the delicatessen is closing for good – something to do with complications in the marital lives of the owners. One of her sisters lives in the area and she had all the details.'

Rebecca upends the tin into a flecked pottery bowl, then flings the lid into the empty tin with a clatter. 'May really takes an unhealthy interest in other people's lives,' she says, rearranging items on the table as she speaks.

'Oh, I don't agree, she is interested in people. The people in the nursing home love her.'

Rebecca carries a large dish to the table.

'That looks nice, what is it?' I ask.

She stands crookedly, in mid-turn, looking at me over her shoulder, which gives her an uncharacteristically provocative look, before relaxing. 'It's nothing too exciting, just a vegetarian quiche,' she replies. 'We're almost ready. The salads are made. Wolfie, would you take the wine from the fridge, it must be well chilled by now.'

'You look pensive, Helena,' Wolfgang says as he pours the wine, a careful half glass, the better to appreciate the bouquet, as he reminds us.

'Just savouring the moment, Wolfgang, that's all.'

Wolfgang moves about in his poised style, talking quietly about his latest conference. Something to do with welfare subsidies and how to use them more efficiently. He moves between the table and the far end of the kitchen where Rebecca is working. But he constantly stops short of where she is standing and Rebecca continues to work without entering into the conversation. As he speaks, using the jargon of bureaucracy, I cease to listen and nod and smile. Once again I hear how he rolls his words around his tongue as if he is trying to hold something in place behind his teeth, something only he knows about and wishes to conceal from us, like a child with a sweet. He does not smile as he speaks and makes no sound as he crosses the dark tiles, his face almost immobile, so that I have to watch carefully to detect movement.

I knew a family a long time ago who never smiled in photographs, who seemed to be honouring the solemnity of some occasion known only to them. They looked like images of families who stood outside famine hovels a century and a half earlier, having been evicted by a land agent. It was only years later that I learnt that the reason the family never smiled was because the father told them not to. He thought it would be amusing to reproduce those tragic, gaunt famine faces with their deep-set eyes and sunken jaws. Wolfgang reminds me of that cynical father, except that he is not cynical. Neither is he a father. And of course that is really none of my business. Who knows, perhaps they may not have any choice in the matter, which is none of my business either. Oh dear. These young people believe so ardently in the idea that they have a choice in everything they do. They don't differentiate in any way, everything seems to be of the same order of things. All is choice and negotiation. To do with equality, I suppose.

'Helena, you are very quiet. Are you tired?'

'Oh no, not really. I think that taking that glass of wine before eating was not such a good idea. It has made me a little drowsy.'

'Well let's serve. I'm starving,' says Wolfgang as he continues one more round of the kitchen before sitting down and topping up our glasses, despite my protests. 'One glass of wine is surely not enough to make you sleepy, Helena. You'll be fine once you eat something and it will definitely be an improvement on what they feed you at the nursing home. It always looks a little overcooked to me.'

I wonder how he could have noticed, as he seldom visits and when he does, he never remains for long, shifting around uneasily as if he has interrupted me in the middle of some act of intimacy or has spotted a large pair of bloomers drying on a radiator.

'The problem these days is more to do with what happens to the food before we buy it rather than afterwards. We don't know what we are eating half of the time.'

Rebecca speaks softly as she and Wolfgang continue to talk about additives and preservatives and goodness knows what else. I try to intervene to say that my poor jaded taste buds are incapable of telling the difference, but think instead of the bumpy, irregular shapes of childhood apples lying beneath a crooked apple tree at the end of the garden in Queenstown and Mrs O gathering them in her apron, the corners gathered in her hand to contain the windfalls, and what we children called the Hallowe'en smell, the russety, woodland smell of apples that reached us as she cut them in halves and spread them around the perimeter of a white enamel plate for us to help ourselves.

'A penny for your thoughts, Helena?'

'I doubt if they are even worth a penny, Wolfgang. I'm just musing about how we think that some things will remain in our memory forever and then one day the memory has become fuzzy and imprecise, diminished.'

'Maybe it has to do with the wisdom we acquire as we age. It allows us to change our view of things, which cannot be a bad thing.'

Wolfgang sounds tired. But I don't want to talk about this. I don't want to hear myself say that sometimes we have to act as though change has not occurred, until we cannot talk about the things that have changed, about the person we loved who was dead. How could they understand about swearing children to secrecy, so that they had to pretend that nothing had changed in their lives, at least not to the world beyond the home? That doesn't allow people to move on, it locks them in the past, pins them to a memory until it becomes some shadowy thing, until they cease to remember what it is that holds them back.

Wolfgang is piling food onto my plate – he calls this 'high food' and says it is a popular way of presenting food in restaurants these days. Oil is glistening in beads around the edge of the plate, tiny signals of light to let me know this food involved a great deal of effort to prepare. And to honour this effort I begin to pick over the salad, murmuring as I go, while Wolfgang apologises for the absence of pine kernels and tells me of all the places he tried to get them and failed. I smile at him and wonder why he cannot recall how I always leave them on the edge of my plate.

'Wisdom – was that what you said we acquire with age, Wolfgang? I'm not sure about that. It's memories that fill my head now since I began reading Mama's letters and diaries. I really didn't expect them to hold such a fascination for me and yet there is this strange apprehension at the same time.'

I try telling them about these parts of Mama's private life that we never knew existed as children, which were carefully hidden from us and which she never expected us to see. And in a way she tried to protect us from it – the awful war news, details of prisoners taken, numbers killed and injured – she kept it all from us as far as possible. And for us the war was always exciting, a great adventure happening to Papa, whom we always thought was far away from the fighting. And even though I have become familiar down the years with the awfulness of war, it is still that childish sense of an adventure that surges to the surface first whenever I think of that period. But maybe I am regressing to my childhood. When I mentioned to May this morning that I am finally making progress with the diaries and letters, she told me to leave 'those damn things' aside, saying it's best not to rake over cold ashes, as it raises nothing but dust. Perhaps she's right.

'Oh, May and her rules of thumb. I'm not sure if it is wise to speak to May about things that are so personal, Helena. She's got those wild brothers – heaven only knows what sort of political allegiances they represent.'

'Rebecca, it's really quite funny to hear you talk like this. Isn't it time this family came out from behind the parapet? It really is all right to tell people these things now, you know.'

Something young and rebellious stirs in me and then is gone, leaving a whisper of a family rule, the forbidden fruit of communication that was politics and religion.

Wolfgang leans forward suddenly and gently pats the back of my hand. 'It's OK, you know, it really is. Sometimes we learn the lesson of concealment too well.'

The unexpectedness of the gesture shocks me and I feel suddenly that I am going to cry. Wolfgang raises his eyebrows as if he is about to query something, but instead he leaps to his feet and joins in with the clearing of dishes. We make small talk while the dessert is being carried to the table. At the same time the doorbell rings.

'Oh, I completely forgot – Senan and Áine said they'd drop by.'

'Well, they certainly got their timing right.' Wolfgang's mouth tightens at the corners and he hastily tidies the remains of the dishes onto a tray and we move into the sitting room.

I find the sudden transition from kitchen table to squashy sofa difficult, especially as I am required to deal with a frothy dessert without a table to lean on. The voices around me rush to and fro, the pace seeming to speed up since the arrival of the friends. Áine and Senan always strike me as the high priest and priestess of bureaucracy, both wedded to their jobs in a way that is usual for young people but is totally foreign to me. Rebecca is slightly in awe of them and I suddenly want to shield her pale figure from the sleek blackness of Áine's hair and the creaminess of her skin. Áine pushes the dessert – the name eludes me – around her plate in complete indifference. The voices speed up further, so that I am unaware of changes of topics until they are well into each one. Even the language they use is largely unfamiliar to me, full of unfinished sentences, oblique references. And every so often they seek good-humoured endorsements from me that make me feel as if I am being stroked, an unconscious connection by each of them in turn with a feeling, an emotion they wish to preserve. It all serves to remind me that I am an old woman and for an instant I feel as if I have stepped outside of my own skin and see my shrunken self, sunk down in the over-upholstered sofa, leaning slightly forward, like a parrot crouched on a perch.

Áine's hair fascinates me. It looks as if a sleekly feathered crow has descended onto her head and carefully laid its wings on either side of her face so that the ragged edges lie flat beneath her high cheekbones. Even her forehead has a dainty point of black hair, slightly off-centre, which has me carefully searching for a sign of a beak in the arrangement. She has dark smudges beneath her eyes. I've always liked that in people, especially in men. It makes me think they have other lives. But on Áine's creamy skin it looks as if she has rubbed her eyes with dirty hands.

Once when I was a child in Queenstown, I saw a wedding party moving sedately in a horse-drawn open carriage along Westbourne Place towards the Queen's Hotel. The wedding guests in this carriage were all elderly, dressed in muted greys, as I recall, sitting straight-backed, staring ahead, moving through a ritual they had performed many times before. And what I recall over seventy years later is the strength of the yearning I felt as a young child to ride with them in that carriage, not as a child but as an adult. And the yearning was so strong and so vivid that I remember exactly how I wished to appear. Aloof, that was the most important thing, aloof, sitting slightly apart from the elderly guests, in their dove and silver-greys. I too would sit like them, erect, but I was not elderly like them but young, slim and attired in a dazzling emerald taffeta dress, tight-fitting through the bodice then billowing out behind me, a flat hat to match and a flowing ultramarine veil wafting out from beneath it, with a myriad of tiny jet beads glistening on it in the sun. And as I made the slightest movement the folds of the dress melted into lapis and midnight blues and all the time I sat serenely erect, smiling in a world of my own.

Áine's dress is black and no matter which way she turns, it remains just that, a matt, flat black. Not that Áine is flat, far from it. She oozes from the dress, over the top, from beneath the short skirt, around the tightly fitted shoulders. The light has given the skin beneath her arm a yellow, scraggy look, a bit like a lightly smoked fishtail. She turns to me. 'Don't you agree, Helena?'

'Oh, I'm sorry, I'm afraid my mind wandered.'

'You are amusing, Helena. I was just remarking that Rebecca is looking pale and in need of a break of some sort.'

'Well, yes, you do look a little pale, Rebecca, dear. Perhaps that would be a good idea.'

Wolfgang brings the dessert bowl and offers second helpings, then places it on the coffee table as he speaks. 'It seems like no time since you and Senan were off on a holiday.'

Senan rolls his eyes to heaven and says nothing. He is a short, rotund man, his prematurely grey hair set atop a perfectly round head, and angelic features set in a permanent, complacent smile.

'Now, Wolfie, don't be jealous. We girls work very hard *and* manage to put up with you and Senan as well. You can't begrudge us a little fun away from you now and again, now can you? After all, we don't have the excuse of foreign conferences to break up our working year, do we Rebecca?'

'Well, we never did get more than a cursory account of

your last long weekend away in – where was it? – oh yes, Prague,' Senan says to Áine.

As they speak I try to recall where Rebecca went recently with Wolfgang or if they went anywhere at all. But of course they did. They decided to go to the West, to some little village overlooking the Atlantic whose name I have forgotten. There was incessant wind and rain, they said, but the hotel was quirky and comfortable and they looked rested when they came back. Strange how I had almost forgotten it. And now Rebecca is off again. She looks slightly perplexed now, watching Áine as she stretches her long, creamy arms, raising them slowly towards the back of her head, a languid cat waiting to have its stomach scratched. I try not to look at her armpits and think again of the marriage group in the open carriage and listen for the straining of leather and the creaking of carriage springs. Instead, I hear the chill clatter of Rebecca's shoulder strap as it drops onto her luggage on the floor on her return from Prague and her gleaming face floats back to me as the appearance of someone renewed in some new, mysterious way. But there is no sign of that renewal in the pale face spreading out on either side of the candle flame that shudders between us in a tall, slim candlestick.

'But that was months ago. We did all the usual tourist things, Senan, you know, all the things that bore people when they hear them delivered in lists at dinner parties. "A sophisticates' Disneyworld", I think you called Prague, if I remember correctly, wasn't that it? Too Central European for your taste, you said.'

Rebecca looks at Wolfgang and then drinks quickly from her glass, stiffening suddenly in her chair as if someone has tightened a grip on her.

'I think it's time we left, folks,' Áine says, 'I've got a presentation to make tomorrow. Well, thanks for the lovely dessert, and don't forget, Rebecca, we'll arrange the date for that weekend break. Oh do stop pouting, Wolfie, your face is too gaunt to get away with it. It makes you look like a sick giraffe. Bye, Helena, great to see you again.'

Senan moves in Áine's wake, pulling a quizzical face in Wolfgang's direction and shrugging his shoulders. He looks briefly at Rebecca before hurrying after Áine, waving his hand above his head, as if attempting to discard something but which we take for a farewell.

A pink tray, that's what I see now, a pink tray. Product of a craft class all those years ago. 'Brothel pink' Gerald called it once when he came home unexpectedly. I don't remember asking him how he knew such a colour. Home to recuperate after the operation on his leg. Not that the surgery helped. His limp seemed more pronounced afterwards. But nevertheless he was pleased, he smiled in a quiet way each time he stood and steadied himself before beginning to walk, always locating things in his life as having happened before or after his operation. 'That was before my operation,' he would nod, retreating briefly into his thoughts before resuming with a gentle reiteration, 'yes, that was before my operation', and I was always left wondering if he had expected something to change, if he thought that his life might have been turned around after the surgery and that it marked a time when he knew that hope would never be realised.

The tray was a dull, flat pink, functional in its shape and proportion. It was larger than any ordinary tray I had seen, as if the craft class instruction was to use up all of the pink formica on offer to us. It was edged with plaited cane strips which were unwieldy to use and had resisted bending and stretching, so that the oval shape of the tray was irregular and graceless where the cane had buckled and bent awkwardly. It sat on top of a sideboard for a quarter of a century, rocking gently on one edge, the base against the wall, so that all might see the brothel pink. And then it vanished and I didn't miss it for years. And a vivid picture of it came to me recently in a dream, one which has recurred. The tray appears without warning, unadorned, floating free, no obvious support, nothing but the plain brothel-pink tray.

Perhaps I should see how much of my life I could cram onto the surface of the tray – office accounts books and end-of-year reports, pens, pencils, office clothes and scarves, shoes and stockings and all those craft tools gathered and discarded over the years, parts of my ancient Raleigh bicycle, spectacles and false teeth, make-up and hair-grips, photos and books and letters. Such an ordinary life. What a small mound it makes on the tray. Oh, I nearly forgot, the diaries would be there too. My life as a pink tray. And in there lies a tiny shard, a diminutive projectile waiting to emerge as – what is it I'm trying to discern here? Dread. That's it, dread.

It's been eluding me all week. Low-slung heaviness in the pit of my stomach, like a pack animal whose saddlebags have slipped and are about to strangle me. Inelegant picture. Old age *is* inelegant, full of sloppiness and messiness, faltering movements and sudden clumsiness. And today is definitely showing all the signs of incorporating each of these unwanteds. Drifting off at Rebecca's lunch is more of it. The tumour will make all of this worse in time, a sidewise list, a rambling collection of unrelated words and all the accompanying smiles and cocking of the head and nodding in the belief that everyone knows what I'm trying to say. Is that next? Hard to imagine that something the size of an innocuous pea will eventually wreak such havoc and destruction.

I can see it quite clearly, this tiny green cannonball, rattling out of control down a labyrinth of nerves and veins and arteries, sometimes sliding down smooth, white chutes, entering thick, red, viscous channels and effervescent, magenta streams, all the while its tiny green curves retaining their colour, yet some hidden energy straining beneath the surface, and I see a sudden ripple, as if a tiny animal is striving to hatch free of the green capsule. And yet the doctor says this tiny pea-thing is static, is inoperable, which, I suppose, means that he would have to remove too much of what little grey matter is left to me, so that I would go instantly gaga or worse. But of course I don't say that to him, just nod sagely the way any old woman of my age is expected to. (I prefer to consider myself an old woman than an old lady. It is so much more substantial; 'woman' captures the essence, leaves niceties and pretensions aside, although May refers to the female inhabitants of this place as ladies, sniffing that some of them don't deserve to be called that.) But I have attained this period of wisdom as is required, haven't I? And yes, of acceptance, or is it resignation?

It is something I feel I owe to Dr Brady. He relies on this attainment of sagacity in the belief that ahead lies this possibility for him too. It's all a bit Chinese, really, this sudden acknowledgement of great age. It's not the way we are generally treated – brushed aside, tidied away, is the best we can hope for. And yet he has this almost mystical expectation, as if, like Confucius, he too has been to the mountain to watch his father dispose of his ageing grandfather so that he also might know what to do when it came to his father's turn. As if he might discover a better way. But there is nobody here, just he and I. I wonder does Rebecca know about Confucius on the mountain? Unlikely. She thinks my tremor is due to a touch of Parkinson's. I suppose I shall have to tell her the truth soon. People don't die of tremors, as far as I know.

Those therapists Rebecca consults have been staring the death of the self in the face for so long now that they think that it is the only death there is. And of course they think they can prevent it. Mortality is something they don't consider much, seeing it as an unexpected bonus, the endless phases of bereavement it produces, unfolding in wave after wave, each with its own neat label of guilt, rage, resentment and goodness knows what else, on and on, waves crashing in spent eddies and pools around their feet where they paddle about, trying to make patterns from the detritus that came in on the last emotional tide. I wonder what Rebecca would make of the detritus of my life.

God, I wish things didn't always come back to Rebecca. Sometimes I think I hate all the endless attempts to make sense of things. There really is no sense to it all, no matter how momentous we believe something to be, we just muddle along, some better than others. And if we manage to find a usable crutch *en route*, then so much the better. I don't seem to have been so successful there, at least not as successful as some of my colleagues here, with their daily trips to the little chapel on the ground floor. Soothing quietness and fractured stained-glass light is the most that registers with me these days, try as I might to concentrate on what is going on. And there's the morbid interest in those around me to further distract me. James shuffles in wearing his slippers – something he never does when he is going to the dining room, always wearing well-polished shoes. Perhaps he considers that going to the chapel is merely slipping into the next room for a quiet chat and he need not bother to change. Fr Morgan would like that idea and would probably use it in his next sermon, if he ever noticed James's feet, that is. Even Elvira is only faintly distracting now, with her morose, bossy demeanour and her large bosom drifting down towards her stomach. May tells me she serviced the entirety of the British forces serving in the Falkland Islands, although it is difficult to try and see beneath the jaded veneer a more sensual self that made a play for others a long time ago.

I have also ceased to watch the tiny wizened woman, named after a film star whose name escapes me, who looks twenty years older than her age from a lifetime of chain-smoking and whose continued existence has to be worthy of scientific study. She likes to whisper to those alongside her as they wait for the priest to appear out of the sacristy door that she is expecting visitors later in the day, that today's visitors are dropping some business of great importance in order to be with her. And she smacks her lips as if to emphasise this enhancement of her stature, so that her unhealthy pallor is marred by a narrow gash where her mouth is, and she pushes her glasses up the bridge of her nose, smudging a lens with her short nicotine-stained finger.

And even as my interest in these people tugs my attention away from the Mass and the genuflections and benedictions of the priest, whom I glimpse out of the corner of my eye, I know that my belief in whatever it was that had held me in its thrall throughout my life has been leached out of me without my noticing. The ritual has taken me along beyond the point where I might have questioned my unbelief. And now I'm like James in his slippers, wearing the ritual like tired footwear. Skeleton of belief, that's all that remains to me now. And perhaps that is fitting.

Rebecca is in Barcelona with Áine for a long weekend, looking at the architecture. She showed me photos of some of the buildings – extraordinary edifices, large cakelike structures with every sort of man-made adornment clinging to them, as if the buildings themselves were growing, some looking as if the concrete had been too wet and had dripped down the buildings' façades, like sugar icing. But it will be fun for them both, even if they seem to take in way too much in such a short space of time. It makes me dizzy to contemplate it.

It is so different from my last trip to Paris, the one I made alone a few years after Tom's death. Leisurely, that's how it was, leisurely. All that aimless sauntering through streets whose names I cannot recall, yet whose pavements remain vivid, the slabs appearing subtly exotic in their texture and shape, only because they were different in an inconsequential detail from the limestone slabs of home.

Rebecca put me under orders to move faster through Mama's papers on her last visit to me. She has become utterly focused on the reference to M in the diary. She moves so readily into Mama's world that at times she might be living in another time. She admits to spending lengthy periods musing about her life, although she doesn't voice an opinion on it. Recently she mentioned the absence of a husband for Mama over the greater part of her life and quickly began to talk about Lucinda and her equally early widowhood. And there it was again, this great gaping hole, this lurking absence lying behind the women in this family. I could almost discern her laying out the structure of a dissertation that would take her neatly up to her chosen device, this imprint she talks about, a psychological legacy of sorts about which we are never warned. I have believed for some time now that aloneness is all she has come to expect.

I think that May, more than anyone, would be capable of understanding aloneness. In the midst of that boisterous group of brothers, whose every need she answers, although she would be the last to admit it, she is truly alone.

'Fried cabbage on Sunday evenings, that's what I look forward to,' she said recently. 'After they are all fed and the dishes washed and put away and the floor swept, I put my feet up with the Sunday papers and have a good read. Not that there is anything new there – just a rehash of the week's news. And sometimes I have a doze. And then around five o'clock, when the brothers have gone to see the football on the telly in the pub, I take whatever remains of the cabbage from lunch – I always make sure to keep enough leftovers – and I fry it up quickly in a big nut of butter and plenty of salt and pepper. It's like my own private party, sitting there in the kitchen, eating the fried cabbage. And sometimes I even turn on the television and listen to *Songs of Praise*, may God forgive me. But I always think that the Protestants have the best hymns. And one day I'll give in to the temptation to eat the cabbage straight off the pan. At least it would save on the washing-up.'

When May isn't close by, the image I conjure up is of her sitting in her tiny kitchen, with a heavy cast iron pan on the table and a mound of cabbage on her plate, munching happily alone. I wonder on these occasions does she carry images of any of us here in this place? Does she entertain her family with stories of our eccentricities – James constantly mislaying his false teeth, Nora forgetting she has been to the loo and demanding an escort every few minutes, me and my placing and re-placing of Mama's papers on different surfaces around the room in an endless procrastination. What was it in our earlier lives that produced this particular set of fixations in old age? I wonder. Tiny pieces of a mosaic whose picture we may never comprehend – that's all we are left picking over now, forever turning them around and around, the better to arrive at a perfect fit.

But some of the pieces are too large, or we are too close to see them properly. Hellebores. Now as flowers go, they are not too big. Delicate, drooping heads, greeny creams, flashed with delicate pinks and mauves and burgundies in tiny veined presences, strappy leaves raised like Queen Anne collars behind them. *Helleborus orientalis*. I thought that Mama liked oriental things then. I thought that she liked them because of her black lacquered boxes, with their Chinese sampans painted on the lids. Mama liked to place hellebores in a crystal decanter, which she kept especially for them and which magnified the blood-red specks on the stems as if they had blood poisoning. The decanter was always placed in exactly the same position on a small mahogany table to one side of the bay window in the drawing-room. It was placed so that the crystal caught the light, yet the flowers never stood between her and the view of the sea beyond.

After Papa was gone some time and she became more distracted and confused, she would lie on the chaise longue beneath the window, her head raised on a rolled cushion and spend hours staring out to sea with the light fading slowly around her. Many years later I remember seeing a drawing of a Chinese opium den frequented by European merchants and their mistresses. One of the women reclined on a narrow sofa, her head supported by a rolled cushion identical in shape to the one Mama used, the heavy tassel dangling from the end. In the drawing the cushion had been placed beneath the woman's neck, so that her head lolled backwards in a gesture of indolence, while the stem of the water-cooled pipe rested in her hand, which trailed languidly towards the ground. The entire scene was wraithed in smoke and the air seemed stained.

My memory of Mama lying in the drawing room has a different light to it, not stained, definitely not stained, but suffused by an underwater eeriness. Everything in the room appeared to swim in an ethereal green that emanated from the dark leather upholstery on which she lay, its aged patina giving the impression that it floated several inches above the floor. And as the light faded, her gaze would move slowly across the window until it came to rest on the hellebores, where it remained until somebody, usually Mrs O, would come in and light the lamps.

Once, when Mrs O sent me into the room to see if Mama required anything, I heard her murmuring to herself, something about drooping heads looking like giant icebergs, 'Shackleton's bergs' she called them, and catching sight of me she said, 'Don't you think so, Helena, don't you think that they look just like icebergs plucked from the sea by a giant silver ice-tongs and deposited here on our table?' And she turned briefly towards me and I caught for an instant the wistful look on her face and I knew that she wasn't really seeing me. 'If only we could pluck all the icebergs from the South Atlantic, it would clear the way for Mr Shackleton to reach the South Pole. And then we could drop them on all the German soldiers in France and freeze them where they crouch in their trenches. Just think of it, Helena, lines and lines in their hundreds and thousands in ice-filled trenches, their bodies frozen, only vaguely visible from above, among the clouds, so that down below it would be possible to stand and walk and slide and skate along the white icy stretches all the way to the coast. Can't you imagine it? Thousands of miles of narrow, glistening white ribbons of ice, all leading to the coast and home. And all the horrible muck and filth and stench of death would be buried beneath the ribbons of ice forever.' And the mesmeric murmuring stopped abruptly and she released one heart-rending sob and put her hands over her entire face, so that all I could see were the creamy blobs of her hands blending in the half-light into the creamy-greens of the hellebores. And the door opened and Mrs O ushered me out, telling me not to upset Mama, and I was too stunned to say that it was none of my doing.

But of course it took some time before she became more consistently 'confused', as Mrs O said. That was after the period when she referred to Mama's early strange behaviour as her accommodations. And in the way of children, we didn't question her accommodations or her confusions, making our own accommodations by ceasing to notice her vague presence. And Mrs O moved imperceptibly into the gap left by her quiet and steady withdrawal. Once, when Mrs O was heating the large tin bath on top of the range for washing the bed linen, I told her I hated hellebores.

'Ah, what's got into you child? Sure why would you hate flowers? They wouldn't do you any harm, girleen.'

'I just do. They're sort of sad flowers, the way their heads hang down, so that you only see the back of their necks. Well maybe they are not sad, more like sly, I suppose. It's as if they are peering out from beneath those droopy heads at us and trying not to be seen.'

She tightened her lips and I thought she might be angry with me. But suddenly she burst out laughing. 'Look, Helena, come with me.'

She took my hand and brought me through the back porch and into the garden. It was dark and gloomy, everything laden down by moisture, clumps of leaves whipped into decaying peaks in the corners, great brown papery heads on the hydrangeas like mummified skulls. Bending down beneath a shrub, she pointed at slim, coiled twists of creamy green poised above the soggy black soil. 'Now what's sly about those harmless little buds, Helena?' She placed one stubby forefinger beneath a pale bud, the edges suffused with palest pink, her finger crisscrossed with tiny cracks in the skin like ice after rain, and raised the tiny bud towards me. 'Your Mama always does everything so nicely,' she said almost in a whisper. And I knew from her voice that these flowers had the power to make Mrs O sad too.

'Mama sometimes brings these flowers to church, Mrs O. She puts them on a side table, where the hymn books are stacked.'

I wanted to keep talking, afraid that Mrs O would start to cry.

'I didn't think they went in much for flowers or candles in your Mama's church – something to do with flowers and things being frivolous. But I don't really know much about it, just what your Mama tells me.'

And my head whirled with notions of Mama who loved flowers going to a church where nobody liked flowers and I thought that Mrs O also was becoming confused.

Mrs O took my hand tightly in hers. 'But look how you have me talking too much with all your questions. Your Mama would be very annoyed with me if she heard me filling your head with all these anxieties. Hush now, Helena, and let's go inside and leave these ... these flowers ... what did you call them?'

'Hellebores.'

'I'll never remember that name. They look like green poppies to me. I always think of them as pale, green poppies.'

I wanted to tell her that I couldn't imagine a church without candles – the stagnant, languorous smell of the tottering candles on either side of the altar in what I thought of as Papa's church or the tiny flickering votive candles that clustered at the feet of the statue of Mary, whose flames lurched sidewise each time the church door opened and where we placed a halfpenny, reaching up to place another flame alongside the rest, each one no higher

than a finger, offering its tiny gift of light in the dimness of
the church. But I said nothing, knowing I would only be
told what she considered to be harmless.

We went quickly back into the kitchen where the
steaming bath of water on the range spread a fine mist
across the kitchen, which settled on window frames and
delft on the dresser. I thought of Mrs O's own garden with
its onion rows and drills of potatoes and lines of vegetables
and her quick gestures as she tugged a head of cabbage from
the ground and sliced through the stalk, separating the head
from the root, hurling the discarded stalk in an arc before her
onto a heap of garden refuse that lay steaming beside the
fence. What a grand gesture that was, it seemed to me,
encompassing in the arc of her arm her garden, her home,
her family, all that she did for them, and somewhere in
there too she encircled me and my family and the bath of
hot water steaming on the range.

The picture that comes to me now is of two giant
bubbles, one full of heat and movement and laughter
enveloping the kitchen and somehow containing all the
comings and goings of the children and Mrs O, so that the
bubble appears to pulsate at the edges, to move about and
bounce slightly, as if tethered against a buffeting wind. And
the other bubble is blurred, as if someone has breathed on its
surface, so that the internal image is indistinct, aqueous,
shimmering through hues of pale green, getting lighter and
lighter towards the edges, which vanish into an icy white
glare. I know instinctively that this bubble encapsulates
Mama's opaque world, where she reclined in a half-light
for hours on end. And try as I might now, I cannot put
these two enclosures together, cannot bounce them off each
other to make them merge. If anything, Mama's bubble has

become more indistinct with time, the life of the occupant within more opaque. But perhaps it is my memory playing tricks on me, like a ball of wool that has been knitted and ripped and knitted again over and over until it retains so many kinks from multiple unpickings that it can no longer be unravelled.

That was the time when William became distant from us. I was the one most affected by it, as he had not been in the habit of confiding in the younger ones. If I tried to creep into his room at night as in the past, he did not always want to talk to me. Sometimes I would find him writing in a small, black-covered notebook – lists, with one or two words written on each line. But he always snapped it shut when I came in and put it quickly under his pillow. Neither of us ever mentioned the notebook. Once, I thought I saw him showing it to Sean, but I couldn't be sure.

I have always thought of this period in William's life as the period when he began to darken. It was his brow that first caught my attention. He looked darker suddenly, as if he were standing beneath a tree. His eyebrows had thickened, not gradually, it seemed, but overnight, into one almost continuous line, as if someone had laid a crooked stick of willow charcoal above his eyes. His face had grown shadowy, sallow with hollows where previously his cheeks were slightly plump. And his voice had changed suddenly, so that he began to sound more like Papa. Once, when I was sitting with Mama doing some sewing, he called to Esmee from the hall, beyond the drawing-room door. Mama turned her head so sharply that I dropped the petticoat I was repairing. And when William stopped speaking, she held her hand to her throat and remained frozen for a long time.

'Perhaps you could go walking with Mama in the afternoons,' he suggested to me one evening, in his new, deep voice, so that I thought he was play-acting. 'She looks pale and spends too much time lying on that sofa.'

'She's tired, that's why she lies down.' I didn't like William telling me what to do. 'And anyway, she walks on Thursdays, up the hill to the wives' afternoons.'

'Oh yes?' He turned towards me and even his look had a hint of the imperious as he raised his chin, perhaps in an effort to gain more height.

'You know she does, I've seen you watching her as she walks along the seafront. You wait until she turns the corner and then I have seen you run out of the house and down to the Queen's Hotel. What do you do there?'

'You nosy parker, Helena. I was doing nothing, only meeting a friend, that's all.' His posture collapsed instantly and he assumed his dark-browed belligerence.

'What friend?'

'It's none of your business.'

'Well, Mama says that I must keep an eye on everyone when she is away.'

'Does that include her?'

'What do you mean, William?'

'Well, I've seen you and Benjie sneaking up the hill after her on several occasions. What's all that about?'

'It's none of your business.'

His eyes flickered sidewise and rested on his boots before he spoke. 'All right then. I'll tell you what I was doing in the hotel, if you tell me what you were doing following Mama.'

And I told him about the Thursday ritual with Benjie, how we stood beneath the window and how we watched

the figures beyond the glass moving like marionettes, to and
fro, bending gracefully towards each other momentarily
then turning away quickly, heads thrown back in laughter,
pale throats and pale hands and the glow from the fire
spreading outwards, suffusing the room with its light until
someone stood and lit the lamps and pulled the curtains.

'Can you hear what they say?' His whisper was hoarse.

'No, of course not, we can't let them see us.'

'But you must hear something. They might be discussing
important things. You might hear something about the war,
about Papa.'

'Well, sometimes they cry and sometimes they talk and
then fall silent or cry again. And sometimes someone reads
a letter aloud and that makes them cry too. But mostly they
are merry, as if they were having a party. Don't you think
that is strange? They giggle a lot, although there never seems
to be anything funny happening that we can see, just the
group of them giggling into their hands whenever
somebody says something. I've never seen Mama behave
like that before.'

William's face grew darker as I spoke, appearing to close
down, draw inward, as if it were shrinking and all the
hollows were accentuated. He jutted his head forward,
staring at me so intently that I became nervous. And I
waited for him to tell me what he had been doing at the
Queen's Hotel. But he never said anything, just stared at
me as if willing me to say some more. I sat holding my
breath, afraid that this new William, with his new, hoarse
voice, would act in some uncharacteristic manner, and
while I tried to vanish into stillness, he quietly left the house
and I thought how glad I was that I had not told him about
the Chinese box.

Suddenly, without warning, the image of the Chinese box is before me, Mama's lacquered box, the largest one of the set. It was Benjie who saw it first, nudging me in the ribs and pointing towards the window as we watched from the twilight. One of the wives was walking towards the centre of the room, while, around her, the women were sitting passively, almost listlessly, as she placed the black box on a small supper table as if she were making an offering and then one of the wives nearest the window stood and drew the curtains.

'Perhaps they keep their letters in the box,' Benjie whispered.

'That's Mama's Chinese box. Why would they all put their letters in her box?'

'Well, perhaps it's because they like to read them aloud and pass them around, so maybe they keep them there for safety.'

'Safe from what?'

But Benjie had already moved away from the window and was stamping along ahead of me down the hill. Our footsteps echoed back at us from the flagged pavement, while the deathly quiet rose in a pall and I knew from the silence that this was merely a pause, that the tide was about to turn, bringing with it the wind once more. And then Benjie began to hurl questions at me as we reached the seafront. What did I think it was really like to be in the war, really in it, in the fighting? Did I think the Home-Rulers would take advantage and organise a rising while the British were occupied in France? Should we try to take the Chinese box and see what was in it and see if the letters from the soldiers to their wives should be given to the Home-Rulers, who might find some useful information in them?

I had not been paying much attention to him, as my thoughts were too wrapped up with Mama and her strange laughing, languid behaviour, in contrast to her distracted absence at home. But Benjie persisted with his questions until I stopped as I finally heard what he was saying. Benjie too was changing in a way that was not unlike the close questioning stance that William had taken with me. What could be wrong with them that they needed to keep up this questioning? Benjie was forcing me to step outside the safety of our make-believe world, beyond the window on the hilly street, and steal into the wives' world to retrieve Mama's box. And the strange sensation returned to me, the one I experienced the previous summer when we went into the foothills behind Rosscarbery with Sean. An image of the tall man called Mick, with the cow's lick of hair, flashed into my mind and for a brief moment he carried Mama's Chinese box before him, clutched tightly, high against his chest. And I vowed then and there to retrieve the box and its contents and hide it from Benjie, from William, and from the wives. I vowed even to hide it from Mama. But of course I never did manage to secure it.

But this is still the child Helena's story, one of derring-do or at least the endless hope of it. But I can still recall how, even as I planned such a daring exploit, I sensed my childhood slipping away from me on that walk downhill. I also realised that, try as I might, I could no longer see Mama's fixations with icebergs and snow and ice and sea or her drifting on the edge of reality as her little accommodations any more. They were only some of the things in a life that was becoming more and more confusing. And Benjie, who was sounding so like Sean and William, was no longer the one in whom I could confide this.

8 January 1915

This journal is slowly taking the place of Richard. I talk to it the way I used to talk to him on his return from the island, burying myself in it the way I used to bury my nose in his coat. He used to say that, from the ferry, Queenstown looked like a series of children's wooden building blocks, slipping down the hills towards the sea. He said that he liked to look at the houses, made tiny by distance, to see if he could detect a slippage as they clung there, defying gravity. That's how I feel – defying gravity here, nothing between me and the sea but this billowing piece of lace at the window. I have been thinking of removing it. It has begun to remind me of gauze bandages the children roll for sending to France. Oh God, how many of the men known to Richard have had need of them already? In this failing light I can see their shapes moving beyond the lace, a blurred procession, faceless, floating above the island.

Not that I tell Richard any of this. Tales of the children's doings, happy events, that's all I tell him – Esmee's latest drawing of Mrs O's hen and her new chickens, the precarious, rickety tree house built by Gerald and Peter, where they spend endless hours – but at least I know where they are, William and his endless wanderings abroad. I seldom know where he is – and of course I don't tell Richard that. But Helena is close to Mrs O, which is a great comfort. The war was so far from their world it seemed as if it would be possible for the children to continue doing as they have always done, creating their make-believe games, into which they could slide effortlessly, like snails into shells. At least it still seems

possible for the younger ones. And Richard enjoys these
titbits about their world and their occasional little notes
slipped into the envelope with my letter.

He too keeps to happy events, if one can consider
anything from France a happy event at present. He told
me of the occasional few hours of leave spent in a sparsely
provisioned café in a little village on the banks of a river
whose name I cannot recall – an unimportant tributary, he
said. I try to place myself there, in a place where he found
respite and a brief peace, a place where he said that
painters met and ate and drank and talked, before the war
began. But now the soldiers are lucky to find this café
equipped with rough red wine and coarse bread. How
difficult it must be for the owners to make a living.
Richard liked to say that he would take me to Paris some
day, where we would sit in a café and watch the barges
on the river. He planned the visit in meticulous detail, so
that I knew exactly what we would be doing at each hour
of the day and night – the barge trip downriver past the
riverports and the islands, letting the river set the pace
until we would reach the sea. He liked to talk about it
when the children were in bed and the lamps were low,
before the fire began to sink in on its embers.

Now, when I read the papers and the reports of troop
movements, casualties and prisoners taken, I try to picture
all the tiny villages and towns of which I have never
heard before and I cannot do it. All I have is a picture in
my mind of the great sweeps and loops of the meandering
river of Richard's plans, with its lush islands and small
flat-bottomed boats lurking in the reeds and the slap–slap
sound of water on timber and the laughter from strolling
couples on the river-path. I believe that if I can hold that

picture steady, transfix it before me, then Richard will
remain transfixed in that little café he found, that he will
never have to go back to the troops, that the war will end
and he will return safely by the time that I can no longer
hold the picture in my mind and it begins to shudder and
disintegrate. Oh God help me.

M helps me transfix this scene. When I feel that
everything is about to rush away from me, M is there to
support me, that cosy, comforting support that I need
more and more. I haven't felt like this since my
childhood. My 'inside–outside' feeling, was what I called it
then. Bart knows what that means. Not, of course, that he
knows about M. I think he was the one who described
our life then as an inside–outside life, one day when
Mother refused to let us run down the lane to play with
the mill children, because she feared Stepfather's anger if
he found us playing with Catholics. This was the first
time anybody had offered an explanation to me for
Stepfather's anger, for his seething presence, his silence, his
dark looks towards Mother, which always caused her to
stop mid-stride. And though I had never before
understood his anger, that day I understood that I had an
inside–outside life, where my life in the home was careful
and considered, and I learnt the importance of presenting
myself in a particular, acceptable way, while my 'outside'
life was conducted down the mill lane, with the Catholic
children despised by Stepfather, where exuberance was a
taken-for-granted thing, where all my flaws and foibles
were as essential to me as the hair on my head, not
something to be hidden, but there by the grace of God, as
Richard might say.

Not that Richard really understands any of this, for

how could he possibly imagine the all-pervading routine
and discipline that had settled over my mind, or the
constant harping presence of Stepfather reminding me
hourly about the importance of work – house-work,
school-work, garden-work, sewing repairs, church-work –
whether studying Scripture or the Psalms or covering
hymnals. And yet Stepfather's work had always remained
vague – I was quite old when I discovered that he
managed a printing firm – and this vagueness had created
in my mind a continuum so that I thought that what he
did by day and what he did at home were one and the
same thing, where he doggedly forced people to do his
will and work. And throughout all of this, he seemed to
single me out for special attention, always finding
something additional to the allocated tasks for me. And
here too it was Bart who eventually supplied the clue. 'I
suppose it is because you are his stepdaughter,' he
whispered to me. 'It's not so much that he is harder on
you as that he is easier on the rest of us because we are his
children.' But even then I knew that Bart, at that young
age, was trying to be kind.

But why am I thinking about this now? Absence, is
that it – my natural father's and Richard's? Or is it
memories of my inside-outside life with Richard? For he
too was part of that hidden life. And at this distance it is
like a great glass dome that arched over my childhood
home outside the walls of the Royal Hospital, arched over
the hospital itself, spreading outwards to include the
garrison church of St James's in Thomas Street on one
extremity and the garrison magazine fort in the Phoenix
Park at the other. And in between lay the green picnic
swards, dotted with crisp squares of linen and cotton to

carry food and drink, discarded parasols caught by the wind and drifting slowly towards the river, banks of brambles that we guarded as our secret blackberry store in autumn along the Camac river, the occasional ceremonial guard whom we watched in awe moving between the hospital and the garrison church.

And in the centre of the glass dome is my 'real' father, for whom I don't have a name – did I call him Papa or Father? I don't remember. He stands in front of my mother's dressing table, brushing up his whiskers, before stepping out the hall door, taking my hand and walking slowly down the road, beneath the towering hospital wall, to enter the back gate and the solid square building of the Adjutant-General's office, where he picks me up and gives me a resounding kiss and tells me to turn around and walk straight home. 'And remember,' he says, 'a good soldier never looks behind.'

And somehow I knew that my real father knew about my inside-outside life, that as soon as I left him, I would run down the lane to play with the mill children, and I came to believe that he knew and let me go there to that safe place because he realised that he would not return alive from India, that he knew that he would succumb to disease and burial at sea. And I believed that he secretly approved of my outside life. And I knew too, that he would have approved of Richard.

And Richard, you were so much a part of both 'inside' and 'outside'. As a military man, you were part of that acceptable, disciplined life, but as a Catholic, you could only, ever, be part of that outside life that I was forced into more and more, the one that came to define everything about me in Stepfather's eyes, the part that made both you and me finally unacceptable. Ah Richard, all that harshness and condemnation, all that exclusion and heartbreak. And poor Mother, lacking the courage to stand up to Stepfather, caught up in trying to protect my stepsisters and Bart from the rages and anger. At least I had you, but she had to remain. I could step outside forever, outside the glass dome, outside the fixedness of the relations that existed between the mill children and me, outside my subservient position in my stepfamily, outside the newness of mother's distancing from me and Stepfather's brooding moods. I thought that once I stepped outside the glass dome, I could return on my own terms, but I was wrong.

I never expected to find myself cast out because I loved you, Richard, and find myself on the outside forever. I thought that everybody could understand love. And now that I am on my own there is nothing but confusion to mask my days. Perhaps I should find a different church to attend, a starker church, one with a pared-down service, where the candles and flowers are unknown, then perhaps God would accept this as a gesture and keep you safe. But you have always loved candles and flowers. 'You like to be adorned, Ally,' you said to me once, 'you like your pearls, your gold pin, your rings – tokens of love,' you said they were. So why then is it not all right to adorn the house of God with tokens of love and veneration? I don't know if what I believe is right any more. I don't know what to believe in any more, except to believe in you, Richard. And I must write this now, here, because I cannot let you know that I am lost, not now when you need to know that I can be strong.

Shackleton is lost too in the wasteland somewhere on

the way to South Georgia. He has failed to contact
anyone since December 5th. There are no flowers where
he is.

Cafés, Richard, you spoke of cafés by the river in your
last letter. Small cafés with lots of people singing and
eating and drinking and laughing. So much gaiety. You
said you will take me there but your letter seemed
somehow too flimsy to contain all that gaiety. Did you
imagine it, or were you really there once, as you said? Or
did you perhaps see all those people sitting at the water's
edge in wide hats and straw boaters in a painting
somewhere? Such gaiety seems too loud, too irreverent in
a way, for these times. The images have become muddled
in my mind, have become enmeshed in images of snow
and ice, so that the gaiety slows down, like a music box
whose tune is winding down, the tiny drum pushing
fruitlessly against mounting drifts of blinding white snow.
I feel so tired, the bone-weary tiredness of endlessly
pushing against something. Snow-tiredness.

Bart will be here in a few weeks. It will be wonderful
to talk to him after so long a break. This place is so far
from Dublin – another world really. And Bart is still in
that other world, still there in Stepfather's house, in his
narrow, bigoted world. I have never been able to use that
word 'bigoted' aloud, was always afraid that saying it
would give it a reality far greater than it had in
Stepfather's household, that it might seep out and ooze
down the mill lane, washing the mill children before it
and sweeping away my outside world at the same
time. It was enough that it had flooded Mother's life
and mine.

Bart used to tell me not to go against Stepfather so

much, as it only drew his attention to me. He tried hard to comfort and help me after Stepfather's rages had engulfed me and left me with hours of extra chores. I tried to explain to Bart that all this trouble had nothing to do with me, that it was really my father he did not like. I told him then how my father was gentle and kind and loved the mill children because they made me happy. But Stepfather hated them, he said they were lazy and careless and ignorant. He would not listen when I told him how they knew so much more than we did. And when Bart looked doubtful, I told him how much they knew about fishing for pinkeens in the river, where to find the juiciest blackberries, where the hop cart slowed down on its way to the brewery so that we could jump on without the carter seeing us. Bart listened and tried to defend his father as best he could. And in a way it was easy for him – the only son amongst four sisters, he was singled out for special treatment that had taken him into the adults' world at an early age. Perhaps it was this forcing of maturity that placed him in a vantage point that was to serve me so well down the years.

It is strange to see what I have written about my life, my secret life, my buried self, doubly an outsider in my home once I announced that I was marrying Richard. His military background would outweigh the religious difference, we thought, but we did not fully appreciate the weight of Stepfather's intolerance. To think back to my home from this great distance, lodged there between the Royal Hospital and the Camac river, is to stand outside the glass dome and look inwards on Mother and my step-family sealed beyond my reach. And yet even here in Queenstown, I remain separate, with Richard's military standing at once raising us up and casting us out from the local community.

It is only with M that I can forget all the loneliness and hurt. And I firmly believe that Richard would understand what has drawn me to seek this solace that takes me briefly from this torment of anxiety that occupies my every moment. It is only with M that all this fades and vanishes, if only for a short while, so that I am made briefly whole again. I believe that Richard would understand. I believe that Bart would too. But, God help me, I can never tell them.

Well, there it is then, out in the open, Mama's involvement with M. Rebecca will be pleased with this acknowledgement, believing that this is something I need to know. But I'm not sure that I want to tell her, not yet anyway. I don't want to hear any more about how this will cast a different light on my life and on hers. I like my memories exactly the way they are. This is the city where Mama, Lucinda and I finally came to rest, three lives secured to each other like marker buoys. I like that image of the three of us – all cheerfully bobbing about without rhythm or pattern, just the occasional appearance, a now-you-see-it-now-you-don't movement.

'What was it like, Helena?' May asked me yet again, yesterday. 'You know, your father being in the British army?'

May had idly turned on the television, something I never do during the day, and was flicking her duster across the top of it, as pictures of the latest Belfast riots flickered across the screen. She frequently comes back to this subject of my father. It intrigues her in a way that I don't fully understand, surfacing as it often does on the heels of a fracas with one of her brothers. It is as if it allows her to snuggle up to some dangerous place without any danger to herself, so that she can sniff and turn away in a manner that she wants her brothers to follow, as if she might sample and then understand whatever it is that they derive from their peculiar brand of pub politics.

And I try to tell her about this hidden life of a military family, that unspoken way we had of going about things, of quietly conforming on the surface until that conformity had seeped into the densest part of our bones, reappearing as an understated style, a pared-down aesthetic, a quietness in everything we said and did, a minimalism of taste before its time.

'My mother always said that she'd know a Protestant at forty feet,' May said once.

And here I was, breaking my family's first rule – never to speak of religion or politics outside the home. But I didn't tell her that even at home there were lines we did not cross, that there was no neat category into which my family fitted, with my Irish Catholic father in the British army – an 'army of occupation', as I suspect May's brothers would call it now – and a Protestant mother. And as she presses me further, I tell her how we went to the school in the town, where we were unquestioningly Catholics, bringing cowslips for the May altar and performing the endless visits to churches on All Souls' Day to rescue a soul from purgatory; while on Sundays we attended Sunday school with the military children and church service with Mama and brought sheaves of corn at harvest thanksgiving.

'I suppose our life then was a little like a hidden valley, when I look back now,' I tell her.

May looks blankly at me and I wonder if she heard me, if perhaps I did not speak, and turns up the volume on the television, turning her back to me, the better to see the rioting. She is trying to sniff danger again.

'From more than forty feet, she used to say. It was the skin, she said.' May spoke without taking her eyes from the television. 'Soft, more than soft, very fine, the sort that you would think you could see through, the sort that wrinkles early and lets you see through to the tiny veins beneath.' May leans forward and turns the volume down completely, leaving the rushing, stone-throwing groups heaving to and fro as if in carefully choreographed movement. 'She said that you could tell from their eyes, too. Catholic eyes are deep-set, too deep-set, I think myself, but Protestant eyes are clear and wide open, innocent-like, do you know what I mean?'

Innocent. Was that it, was that what set us apart – innocence? Bewilderment, more likely, at least for Mama and the five of us. We seemed to fit in nowhere, always gazing about, as if trying to second-guess what the rest of the people were about.

'Do you mind if I push your chariot closer to the window, Helena? I need to pull the furniture out. Matron is cranky these past few days, so I'd better not leave any slut's wool in here for her to find.' May pushes my wheelchair at speed, then stoops and picks up a clump of dusty fluff and waves it aloft. 'Now wouldn't she just love to discover that.'

She drops it into the wastepaper basket and tells me about

the latest trouble between her brothers. The more of these incidents she recounts, the more she appears to be stepping back from her family, shrugging at their eruptions, shrugging them off, these four middle-aged brothers, eternal bachelors, even the married one. Not that I have met any of them but I feel I know them well. Their gruffness, their great bulk, viewing themselves as young, laddish, believing their lives stretch endlessly ahead of them. They have developed the habit over the years of telling their life stories, in all their quotidian detail, to each other, and to anyone else who cares to listen, so that it has become one story, so that they take it in turns to pick it up, passing it over mid-sentence to the next brother to continue it, like a sampler frame with a series of dangling threads, passing from hand to hand. To listen to May recounting what they say is to hear the same story told over and over, embellished with each telling, so that each mundane act appears in high relief. Once I had a dream about them in which they appeared as a gigantic four-headed monster with long sinuous necks that twisted and turned endlessly, yet remained locked into a single body. The heads had features that were larger than life, huge mouths, each with a grey tongue, constantly licking and preening one side of the body. The endless preening went on and I knew that it was the verbal preening of their real lives and I kept trying to intervene, to tell them to stop, to point them towards the other side of their body which was in shadow and which they seemed to view with disdain. And it is this preened and polished identity I see when I think of them, this unassailable identity they have created and which everyone around them accepts. Except, that is, for May.

'My brothers would like to think that they would have

ambushed your father and his like if they had been around at that time,' she said. She turned the television off and continued to speak. 'But you know something? They wouldn't have had the guts. All talk. I think if somebody ever showed them their lives for what they are, they would fall apart. It's all talk, that's what it is, talk.' May whisks my wheelchair away from the window without warning and I have to use the brake to prevent it slamming into the wall. 'A nation of cattle dealers, that's what you'd find if you scratched us – wheelers and dealers, every last one. Good at putting a gloss on things, that's us.'

May is standing in the place where my wheelchair had rested, looking across the canal to the distant mountains. She has recently speeded up the analysis of her brothers, although analysis is not an activity she would own up to doing. But she is unpicking them, a slow, resigned unravelling, as if expecting intractable knots and tangles, yet determined to continue. She works from the general to the particular, wriggling in and out through lengthy soliloquys on the state of the nation, usually triggered by a news item glimpsed over my shoulder in the newspaper. She will slowly negotiate her way downwards through lengthy tangential detours to one tiny piece of the mosaic waiting to be placed, one tiny identifiable piece that has one of her brother's names etched on it.

'Have you ever noticed, Helena, how men don't really listen to each other when they are talking? They're just waiting for the other fella to pause for breath so that they can have their say. And then it's always about besting the other fella. That's what really matters, besting the other fella. It's not what's said that matters. That's never important at all.' She stops at the window while the tiny green catkins flick about on the birch tree, as if anticipating her naming of the brother who is to be unpicked today. 'Tommy thinks we should breed labradors.'

I try to remember which brother is Tommy. They have all appeared briefly and infrequently at the nursing home, a blur in large checked shirts and enveloping anoraks as they stamped their feet and moved restlessly in the courtyard below, waiting for May. Tommy, I decide, is the short, squat one, with thick hair like a badly thatched roof.

'It's not that he cares about dogs, you know. It's all about money, you see. He says people are prepared to pay big money to own a pedigree dog. He says it's to do with image. In the countryside they count a man's fields and his cattle to get a feel for his wealth. In the city, it's down to image. And that, he says, includes pedigree dogs.'

'Well that sounds like a nice pastime, May.'

'Pastime? It's not a pastime he is considering. This is big-time breeding. He wants to make a lot of money. And you can guess who will be left with the cleaning up after the pups – yours truly.'

'But surely your brothers would all lend a helping hand?'

May shrugs, a clumsy gesture that makes her shoulders appear too big for her frame. 'Oh, sure they will, they're full of it at the moment. But I know them too well.' She turns from the window and sees the box in the corner at the same time as I do and gives a quick nod in its direction. 'So how are those stories coming along? Find any skeletons yet?'

I tell May some bits and pieces to indicate I am making progress through the diaries, that I am serious in my intent. But her thoughts are elsewhere, ensnared in untangling skeins, wondering perhaps where her own story has gone.

She doesn't hear most of what I say.

'Great big, slobbering mastiffs, that's what they are planning on breeding,' she muses as she pushes the hoover towards the door with her foot.

And somehow the faces of the mastiffs she described appear before me with the faces of her brothers, soft, moist lips slack below squared teeth, heads hunched down into their shoulders as if preparing to spring.

May sinks down onto the edge of the bed, suddenly tired, her round face sagging. 'Tell you what, Helena, when I'm finished at midday, I'll take you down to the garden for a quick trip before lunch. You can stroke a rock, how's that?'

She straightens, defying the exhaustion. She hasn't mentioned Rebecca's return tomorrow but her invitation to get close to nature is not lost on either of us.

Rebecca is sitting across the table from me, wearing black. We have come to this pub on the canal bank because it is wheelchair friendly and because Rebecca feels it has not been redecorated in the new, brash, pub-decor style that wipes out the small-scale cosiness of old pubs. The black makes her look like a mafia widow, May said, when she peered down into the courtyard this morning as we waited for her to arrive. But of course that is not how she appears at all. Her colour is all wrong for a start. The black enhances her pale colouring slightly, making her appear fragile, yet assured, the high fake fur collar framing her face and recently shortened hair like a tulip newly opened. She has two fresh spots of colour on her cheeks and I cannot tell if these are natural or a cleverly applied artifice. Overhead, a large glass dome in the roof-space – the single gesture to the modern here – magnifies a cumulus cloud against a blue sky, casting shadows downwards that manage to lodge below Rebecca's pale eyes. It makes her look lit from within, a neon strip mistakenly left on by day.

We order open salmon sandwiches and a glass of wine each. It is easier for me to go along with whatever Rebecca is ordering, as food is now something that is of little interest to me.

It is several weeks since Rebecca's return from her trip to Barcelona with Áine. She has talked in a stilted manner about the holiday on several occasions – brief anecdotes, vague descriptions of buildings and museums, released in a slow drip-feed, almost reluctantly, so that I expect her to plead, like a child who offers to share a bar of chocolate, saying 'now only a little piece'. Even the language she uses is unusual for her, full of harshness and clipped references to things which remain outside the conversation and which I cannot understand.

'There are several Irish pubs in Barcelona now,' she says 'not a sniff of Spanish culture gets inside the door. Áine says it took several generations of hard drinkers to get us where we are now in the drinking stakes and we can't afford to dilute the tradition.'

She doesn't smile as she speaks, as if she is delivering a vital statistic rather than one of Áine's glib ironies. The light shows up some tiny broken veins on either side of her nose which I have not noticed before. May said once that such broken veins are the sign of a secret drinker. Rebecca continues to eat, leaving her wine untouched.

'That holiday really gave you a well-deserved rest, Rebecca. You look well and I think that you have put on some weight.'

She colours suddenly, a strange, pale hue that seems to creep in from her ears, as if they were slowly releasing a fine spray that sprinkled her face in uneven blotches, like an underripe raspberry.

'I suppose it was the holiday . . .'

'Sorry, Rebecca, I realise that you young people don't like to be told you're putting on weight. But in my day, people liked to hear it, they heard it as an affirmation of good health, when many around them were fading away with TB. But that is a long time ago.'

'Your sister Esmee died of TB, didn't she?'

'Poor Esmee. Barely twenty-one.'

Rebecca is sitting very still, so still that I cannot detect her breathing, and I wonder if she has been listening. I consider telling her that all of Esmee's life seemed to be a preparation for her dying, full of fragile half-gestures at living, timorous little stabs that were sucked down beneath the blankets that wrapped her winter after winter, while the windows rattled in the teeth of the southwesterlies sweeping across the harbour. But I decide against telling her, trying to avoid the narrowing spiral that is my family and which sweeps us time after time, when we are together, into its strengthening vortex. But of course once again we are creeping towards it, the slow pick-pick-picking of Rebecca's scrutiny awakening again as she says something which I don't hear.

'But we were fortunate, I suppose. She was the only one of the family who contracted it.' Suddenly I want to make it difficult for Rebecca, I want to sit back and watch her pick her way back into this personal project of hers.

It seems so long ago now. Almost seventy years. And what I remember most vividly is trailing Lucinda by the hand onto the train to the mountains south of the city.

Later I tried to restrain her and keep her at a distance from Esmee and her coughing, standing around the foot of the bed, clasping the cold, black, iron bedstead. Esmee cheerfully quizzed us for news, while we tried not to look at the dark hollows in her cheeks or the flushed blotches above them, looking instead into her eyes as if all hope lay there, believing that if we stared long enough, the unnatural sparkle would seep outwards and light up her face, her body, burn away whatever it was that was sapping her energy. Sometimes I would dream about her and then waken, only able to recall her eyes. I can still see them, all these years later. It is all I can recall.

Across from us some new arrivals are settling themselves into a corner, three generations on a family outing, long, colourful clothes drifting to the floor, dark, honeyed complexions and jet-black hair held in place with glowing hair ornaments, carrying the timelessness of immigrants before them, a defiance, a triumphal banner. One of the women is flamboyantly pregnant, lowering herself gingerly into a seat while her family jest.

'How is Wolfgang?'

Rebecca starts and I realise that she too has been watching the arrivals.

'Fine. He's fine.'

I follow her gaze across to the family. Wolfgang should be here. This is his territory, the bureaucratic terrain of reception centres and integration programmes, retraining and placements, empowering skills and on and on, in an endless flat bleakness. The newcomers voices rise and fall in cadences and rhythms we have never encountered before and that leave us with nothing to say.

'Helena, I'm pregnant.' Rebecca says this in a rush, not

looking at me but looking at the pregnant woman across from us, as if she is trying to understand the essence of the condition, as if it might be concealed in the vivid oranges and yellows and reds of her long skirt or the white and gold of her teeth or the blue-black gleam of her hair or the beeswax glow of her skin. For a moment I think that this is a pretence, that what she said is something arising out of a longing. And now she is speaking again, telling me that Wolfgang doesn't know yet, that she wants things to settle down first before she tells him. 'I expect I shall tell him this evening,' she says.

'I'm sure he'll be delighted, dear.'

Rebecca doesn't appear to hear me.

A tiny child detaches from the group and wanders across to stand to one side of Rebecca and gaze with huge, sad eyes at her before turning and wandering back to the family.

Bart came to visit us after a prolonged Christmas of half-empty churches and sermons spoken in solemn, newly subdued tones, with visits to houses where plates of rich cake were passed around and left largely untouched, while guests sipped velvety port and pulled heavy drapes against a darkening world. We children moved surreptitiously to and fro out of the view of the adults, organising games that brought us beyond earshot. Benjie took to visiting us less and less, something to do with being 'out and about', Mrs O said. I wanted to know where that 'out and about' was exactly and why he wasn't bringing me along with him. And Mrs O would give me a sympathetic smile and pat me on the head and say, 'Hush, child, sure it'll all work itself out, you'll see.'

Bart came to a house that seemed shrunken in size, or perhaps it was the semi-darkness that prevailed in each room that caused it to appear smaller so that at night I dreamt that perhaps it would eventually vanish. Mama had taken to leaving the curtains half-pulled across the windows and the blinds half-down. Once, when Mrs O went to pull them back, Mama placed her forearm across her eyes and winced, and Mrs O withdrew, apologising, muttering in the hallway that Mama looked far too pale for her own good, that she was in need of some sunlight on her skin.

But with Bart's arrival, she came alive again. Her cheeks glowed and her halo of fine blond hair became almost translucent around her face. As I watched her head nod and turn towards Bart's conversation, I would sit and study the light moving through her hair and think about threads of golden toffee trailing from Mrs O's wooden spoon as she dropped the boiling sugar mixture onto a saucer of water to see if it would set.

He arrived in the second week of January, late in the afternoon as the light was fading. He stood in the open doorway, in a long, dark travel coat, the wind crashing the door, while he and Mama remained locked together in a silent embrace. I remember being startled to see when he removed his hat the same blond unruly curls that she had, though they were prematurely beginning to thin even then in his late twenties. Mrs O had explained patiently to us all what stepbrother meant and how Bart was Mama's stepbrother and I tried to piece it together in my mind and understand why he too had blond curls. The two pale heads together at the end of the hallway appeared disembodied in the wintry light and I thought of the pale faces and whispered voices looming out of the darkness in the church the night before Papa embarked for France. It never occurred to any of us to call Bart 'uncle', we never managed to fit him into our frame of things.

His presence seemed to set the house a-shimmer. He opened the curtains fully and rolled up the blinds so that the metallic light off the harbour seeped into the house in furtive darts. He pushed back chairs and tables as he moved about, smiling at each of us in turn, a strange, absent-minded drifting from room to room, as if looking for something he had mislaid. This was another thing he had in common with Mama. It was as if he was studying the detail of her life, getting to know it, wishing to absorb it through familiarity with the surface of things. And all the while, she stood in doorways twirling a curl at her neck, watching him with a half-smile.

Mrs O herded us into the kitchen for the first few days, insisting on giving us our meals separately, while Mama and Bart ate quietly in the dining room, a low murmuring of voices reaching us each time she opened the door to bring in food or remove dishes. And even though it was several days before we began to drift back into their presence again, we sensed that something new had entered our house, was floating beyond our reach and moving around us, loosening the stays on our lives, pushing us along in a way that we vaguely liked but which we did not comprehend.

Slowly a whole new set of relationships and words to describe them filtered into the kitchen and with them a torrent of questions from the younger children for Mrs O, for they were hearing this for the first time. William and I, feeling superior with our prior knowledge, speculated in whispers.

The younger ones were mesmerised, a real, live, wicked stepfather and in Mama's family, and they plagued Mrs O with questions. She was reticent to begin with but eventually she relented and her innate compassion for Mama's situation surged within her as she began a rant against our step-grandfather that continued sporadically for days. It seeped outwards into dire mutterings about 'that narrow freemason and all his kind', and we were left with pictures of a man who wore a blue apron whenever he met his friends, whose five children were cosseted and spoilt while his only stepchild was shunned by her siblings, and whose wife – Mama's mother – remained a shadowy figure in the background, 'hiding behind the mason's apron', as Mrs O said. And when she calmed down, she tried to retract some of this, saying that, of course, now that he was an adult, Bart was completely different from his father, that he was a good brother and friend to Mama, even if it was behind his father's back, for she could never go so far as to grant him a full dispensation for his father's behaviour.

''Tis why your Mama is spending so much time talking, you see. She has this great thirst for news of her family. Well, at least she wants news of her mother. That's it, news of her mother.'

Mrs O was at pains to explain away all of this talking behind closed doors. She was accustomed to being Mama's only confidante since Papa went to France. Even as a nine-year-old, I sensed that her position had been usurped by Bart, even if only for a couple of weeks. She filled the void by attempting to piece together the words and phrases that floated out to her as she came and went past the drawing room, finishing the interrupted sentences, creating a context from all that had gone before, between herself and Mama, unwittingly making us children privy to a family history that was never intended for us.

But after a few days of incarceration, waiting for Mama

and Bart to emerge, we became impatient. We wanted to
dine with her, to hear her voice again, to hear Bart and
some of what he had to say. Also, we were becoming
bored with Mrs O's account of things, we wanted to hear it
for ourselves, all of this business about Mama's stepfamily.
All of it. And why she had not told us herself. Especially
that.

'Your Mama doesn't want to talk to you about
unhappiness,' Mrs O said, 'only happiness. She wants to
make your lives happy.'

And this made sense to us. Stepfamilies and unhappiness
were part of our story-life, and Mama's stepfather could
only signal unhappiness for his wife's daughter. We knew
that much. This was the stuff of our nightly story fare. But
we wanted to creep closer, now that it had entered the fabric
of our lives, we wanted to experience terror first hand, to
feel a stepfather's presence, even if at a remove, through
Bart. We wanted to sense him around every corner, to feel
his breath in the air, his smell on the coat-stand in the hall, see
his cane leaning against the wall.

After a few days, the talk from the drawing room had
become lighter, the tenor of their voices gay and lilting, as
if they were trying to float their voices out through the
tops of the open windows, to mingle them with the high
harbour winds. It was then that they began to take walks
along the seafront, along by the bandstand with its funny
pineapple-shaped ornaments, past the Queen's Hotel, out
towards Rushbrooke where Papa had spent his last night. I
never saw them walk up through the town or along the
route Mama took to her wives' afternoons. Perhaps she
wanted to keep that to herself, a sort of secret place. I used
to watch them from an upstairs window, their two blond

heads bent against the wind, blending into one golden orb as they moved into the distance, leaning in towards each other.

Bart seemed to turn towards us reluctantly, as he and Mama emerged into the life of our home again. I could see his eyes flickering across our heads, as if he were counting to see if we were all present. He was slightly bemused by us, the way Esmee had appeared once when she was looking at chickens hatching their way unexpectedly out of their shells. There was a strange little dance that occurred between himself and Mrs O on these occasions. He would stand back, hands clasped loosely together behind his back, a quizzical smile on his face, watching Mrs O marshal us to the table to eat or to our rooms to study. And when her marshalling was complete, he would bow briefly in her direction and she would blush and scurry from the room, dismissed, her task finished for the moment at least. I don't remember them ever exchanging a word.

And yet Bart was curious about Mrs O. When we all found ourselves eating together again in the dining room, Bart would gently question us about her family, slowly leading us along until we began to talk freely about her. And all the while, Mama ate quietly, nodding now and again as we talked about her house and her ducks, about Benjie and the baby. Somehow, we never mentioned Sean. He was too difficult for us to pin down, too shadowy. We associated him, his friends and acquaintances with silent places without names in the hills behind the town, with men who, we understood from Benjie, were always dressed in winter clothing regardless of the time of year, as if permanently ready for a long journey.

'He's not accustomed to country people,' Mama

attempted an explanantion of Bart's curiousity once, 'he doesn't meet many of them in the city, you see.'

Suddenly the city of Dublin became illuminated for us as a place where people always wore formal dress, like Bart, who never appeared without a freshly starched collar with tiny studs holding it in place, where people visited by invitation and where servants stayed in the kitchen and scullery to emerge only at preordained times.

Once, Mama and Bart took their walk along the seafront in the opposite direction, Bart self-consciously carrying a basket filled with grapes and oranges which had recently arrived unexpectedly in the town, nobody knew from where. The oranges were small and underripe, but he assured Mama that they would ripen with time. Benjie told me a while after their visit to his home that Sean had removed the oranges when his mother was absent, saying that no mason's gifts had a place in his father's house. I never told Mama.

I felt then that she was missing her Thursday afternoons and all the merriment with the wives. She seemed edgy as that day approached and I saw her a couple of times in her room, her head bent low, her back towards the door. In the dressing-table mirror I could see her holding her Chinese box open on her knee, idly turning something over and over in her hand. I thought then that she must have been looking at a sheaf of letters that she was perhaps considering bringing to read to the wives. I noticed how thin her hands had become and how they quivered slightly, as if the remains of a tiny shiver running down her arm was spending itself there. With a sound like a slap, the lid dropped and she hastily moved towards the wardrobe and out of my view. Later at dinner I again noticed the quiver in her hand as she passed the sauceboat to Bart and I saw him noticing it too. But next day I could not see any sign of it and she was light-hearted and jolly. Bart watched her as if from a long way off, not wanting to intrude, yet anxious not to miss anything that passed in her day.

She was slowly growing into whatever it was that Bart was noticing in her, like a tiny flower reaching for light. If Bart admired the way she arranged her hair, then for the rest of that day she carried her head at a slight tilt, and I thought she did this to allow him a better view, continuing like that for hours until the compliment was overtaken by another one. Perhaps it might be an admiring remark about a pearl pin she wore high on a blouse, at her throat, causing her to appear for dinner with a pearl necklace wound tightly above the pearl pin, fingering it from time to time as she spoke to him, the tilt now gone from her head, her chin raised in a gesture that made her look at once defiant and vulnerable. The effect on us children was one of dazzlement, caught at the edge of some strange light that bathed us, threatening to drown us as it seeped out into the shadows that surrounded us. Sometimes we sat through a meal in this way, a hazy murmur of voices moving to and fro above our heads, yet I could never recall later anything that was said, with the exception, that is, of the Shackleton mill.

It entered the conversation surreptitiously, and suddenly Mama was recounting a visit she had made long ago, before we children were born, before she was even married to Papa. Somehow I had missed the important details and I had to struggle to piece together what it was they were talking about.

'Such a beautiful place it was, such a peaceful place, with the sound of the millrace constantly in the background. It was a lovely, cooling sound on that hot day. It seems such a long time ago.'

Bart sat there quietly responding, but she was almost talking to herself, slowly building up a picture of the Shackleton-owned mill, bought by a relation of the explorer. We sat quite still, listening, lest she might remember we were there and for some reason stop talking. She reminded Bart of the journey from the Shelbourne Hotel in the centre of Dublin by jaunting car along the north bank of the Liffey, with gently wooded hills and rolling fields spreading into the distance. We could almost hear the creaking of the cart's springs as it bounced along country roads until it reached the gate-lodge to the mill and the passengers disembarked to saunter along the river banks and speculate on the twelfth-century origins of the building, once known as the devil's own mill. And that, of course, was what we children clung to, the terror at the possibility of a diabolic apparition. Yet for her, it was a place of utter peace.

She spoke gently of three tiny islands in the centre of the fast-flowing river and when we asked her if she had visited them, her glance flickered briefly at Bart before she began to speak rapidly of the features of the house adjoining the mill and the sparkling jewel-colours in the fanlight above the imposing door. And as she spoke of the light from the river refracting from the glass, we became entranced and forgot to press further about a trip to the islands on the river, but remained instead silent, listening.

'He's out of contact,' she said suddenly and Bart's head whipped upwards, so that for a brief moment we thought that she was talking about him. 'Nobody has heard from him since sometime in October.'

'Oh, I'm sure Shackleton is all right. These explorer chaps

know what they are about. You'll see, he'll turn up like a bad penny.'

Bart, who seemed uncomfortable on the subject of the trip to the mill, began to talk about his new printing business – he had followed in his father's footsteps – and the difficulty the war was presenting in trying to source good quality inks now that he could no longer import them from Germany. He spoke about different types of printing presses, of monotypes and linotypes and letterpress and lithography and lithos and photogravure, and we could smell and hear the giant printing presses and feel the speed and the urgency of the tasks. To this day the stale-biscuit smell of a newspaper reminds me of Bart.

Around that time Mrs O prevailed on Benjie to accompany her to our house. He had not been to see us since before Christmas and Mrs O had stopped offering excuses on his behalf and I in turn had stopped enquiring after him. The short winter days had always meant that we had less time to spend together, what with school and homework and too little daylight in which to visit and wander abroad. And I tried to convince myself that as soon as spring returned, Benjie would arrive back at the kitchen door, enquiring after me. Mrs O was spending more and more time with us, helping Mama with meals during Bart's stay, and she was anxious that Benjie should not be left alone for lengthy periods. And so he began to appear, reluctant and with a brooding sullenness, a demeanour that was new, reminding me of his brother Sean, who had, he told us, recently left home. William had smirked to me one day that Sean must have changed his mind and decided to go to war after all, that he had not got the courage of his convictions. And Benjie had fixed William with such a look of silent disgust that William never mentioned it again. But Mrs O would not be drawn on Sean's whereabouts.

Benjie spent most of his time in the kitchen playing with the younger children, pulling drawers out of the dresser and watching as they took the contents out, one by one, disentangling them from old skeins of wool and loose spools of thread, helping them sort the discarded playing cards, count the crushed and battered metal thimbles and fence with the knitting needles until Mrs O confiscated them in horror, chastising Benjie for his lack of common sense. Sometimes he would steal from the kitchen and be absent for an hour or two, then return, sitting once more idly by the range, waiting to accompany his mother home.

Once, he forgot his solitary vigil in the kitchen, forgot his new, aloof demeanour and crept upstairs to find me at my homework, laboriously copying out line after line of handwriting exercises. This was the occasion when he told me that he had followed Mama and Bart, out of habit, I suppose, because, as he explained, he was bored. He watched me out of the corner of his eye as he spoke, and when I said nothing, he continued.

'They didn't go up the hill,' he said, 'they went along the seafront.'

I heaved a sigh. But of course they did. That was where they always walked. Still I said nothing.

'They went all the way to Rushbrooke, you know, out where we went that night your Papa was leaving with the troops.'

And still I remained silent. He was trying to move back into the place he had vacated, the warm place of confidences we used to occupy together. He wanted to be back in that time a few months earlier when we exchanged this sort of information as a matter of routine, to step back into that place as if he had never left it. I remained watching him, stonily waiting, to see what he would say next. He looked at his feet.

'They kissed,' he said, without looking up, 'not a goodbye kiss, but, you know, a sort of a slow kiss.'

He remained sitting at the end of my bed, fiddling with the fringe on the bedspread as I sat in silence, then he rose and slowly walked from the room.

Bart left at the end of two weeks, on a day of drizzle, petering out on the edges of the harbour into an indeterminate mist. I didn't come down stairs to wave him off. I told Mama later that there were enough children crowding around in the hall and that I had waved from the window. Anyway, I knew by now that Papa had been granted home leave from France and I wanted to turn my thoughts exclusively to him. I wanted to blank out everything that had intervened between his departure in August last and his arrival. It was something that I would have to work hard at, now that I was on my own, without Benjie, without William's confidences and without the attention to our lives that Mama had finally and absolutely abandoned.

'Heroic peaks.' That was Bart's phrase many years later. Heroic peaks. And what was he talking about? I can't really remember, something to do with family matters, as always, yet I can locate it back in that time when Papa returned briefly from France, in early 1915. But it is an image that I have retained through the years, can never see a picture in a magazine of some soaring pinnacle without considering yet again the epithet 'heroic'. But that, of course, was in the safety of afterwards, that wisdom-filled post-hoc nest from which we view and reshape our lives and try to re-create them as heroic.

We were so sure that Papa would be home by Christmas and when he did not come, he became lost from sight, subsiding into that flatness that still represents for me the dull, lowly lit days of January. And then Bart arrived and stirred Mama's spirit for two weeks and then was gone, and in the coming and going, I expect that she forgot to tell us children exactly when Papa would be home on leave.

One grey, wet Saturday morning towards the end of January, about two weeks after Bart's departure, Papa appeared. We were in the kitchen, listlessly teasing each other and waiting for the rain to stop so that we could go outdoors. The air was clammy from the vapour rising off damp clothes hanging on the clothesline above the range. This was one of the things that Mama hated about this time of year. She said that she felt hemmed in. She spoke frequently about this feeling of being hemmed in that winter and for once, on that morning, I thought I knew what she meant. Esmee sat near the range, idly tossing a ball at the clothes overhead, the thump of the ball on the wet clothes sounding like the echoless thud of snow falling from a roof. The swollen sound of the back kitchen door opening, dragging along the flagstones, reached us and then all was silence. Mama's voice carried to us faintly, sounding unusually high and thin, followed by a deeper voice that uttered a few words, then silence. Esmee had stopped throwing the ball and had discovered a piece of wool trailing from the bottom of a smock. In her boredom she began to pull on it, so that it slowly unravelled, a crinkled line of dark blue that she wound around her hand as if preparing to knit. The boys had upended a box of cards on the floor and were squabbling over who would replace them in the box. I was drawing squiggly lines in the condensation on the side of a glass fruit-bowl on the table when the door opened. I heard a tiny hiss of air from Esmee, as if she had been squeezed too tightly, and turned to look at her. She was looking upwards from her place on the floor, her face white, and it was only then that I looked towards the door.

Papa seemed to fill the entire space of the doorway,

standing with his arms slightly bent at his sides, as if he had just dropped a heavy load. His eyes moved around the room in a slow movement, reluctant to move on from each face, smiling in a tired way. And of course, as the realisation sank in, we jumped and leaped around him, swinging from his arms, wrapping ourselves around his legs, elbowing each other out of the way. Through it all he stood there, his head bent towards us, smiling that tired smile which we had not seen before and which did not make his moustache twitch in the old way.

And suddenly I am that child again. Or am I? Surely it is no longer possible to see things with a child's eyes, to set aside my grown-up self, with its raggle-taggle experiences. A child's eyes hide too much. It is true that Papa's eyes were tired, yes. And I think of him momentarily as Richard. Even at this distance I can detect anew the sense of something unknown slipping in between us, something that even my nine-year-old self knew he had brought back with him from France. Richard. Papa. But there was more. His mouth was lined on either side, which was something new, as was the lean look to his face, even though he was not yet gaunt. That would come later. But that was something I learnt after the event from war photos, posthumously issued. A handful of printouts, all the same, as if by multiplying his image they might deny the scattering of his body, make it whole again. The bureaucratic tidying of a war graves commission. There were no photos of war then available to us, not a single dead or mutilated body stretched in the clamouring mud. It would take years before we were confronted by the crushing pictorial engagement with our own inhumanity. But my child's eyes then saw only the tiredness, the nobility of uniform, the sheer rightness of a father protecting others as he protected us. Not for a child's eyes or a child's mind the failure of language to dredge up the horrors that he had left only days before. Not even for him was there the facility to represent the baseness of it all, or even to accept that it had been real, when at home everything was as it had been, unchanging, in the face of another place he had left recently, where everything had changed utterly.

In thinking back to that homecoming, my parents seemed sundered, so that they appear to me now no longer as a single unit of Mama and Papa but as two people who circled each other tenuously, fearful of doing damage. Ally and Richard. Richard and Ally. But the thought disintegrates in an instant as I remember how we finally began to settle down, Mama coaxing us away from Papa, and William retrieving his kitbag from the floor, scrutinising it, trying to see through the rough canvas. Mama carefully took his coat, as if afraid of what it might reveal, and his leaner frame became more obvious. His face as he sat in towards the fire was hollowed out by leaping shadows. She said nothing but of course she noticed his thinness and feared it as everyone feared weight loss then, a spectral consumption waiting its opportunity. He coughed and quickly smiled at her, letting her know it was not what she feared, that it was the remains of a chill that he had caught in the trenches. Later William, taking on his old role, told me about trenches.

Papa carelessly opened his kitbag at some point during that first evening. Worn socks, a change of underclothes, mouldy cheese, a few letters, a photograph of Mama, some scraps of paper, a few salary chits and an oblong cardboard box covered in waxed paper. Slowly and deliberately he drew the box out of his bag, all the while keeping his eyes moving across us as he detected our curiosity. Somehow on his journey home he had bought a box of turkish delight – Haji Bey's turkish delight, made, very strangely it still seems to me, in Cork. He had protected it in a woollen ribbed scarf so that it would not become crushed. On the lid was a vague desert scene, the type that I have seen over the years on boxes of dates, with what Papa told us was a desert schooner – a camel – trudging hopefully towards a cluster of date palms. Esmee immediately told him about another schooner, Shackleton's ship *Endurance*, which she said she saw in the drawing on Mama's dressing table. And I recall Papa saying to Mama that such a boat would never withstand the southern ocean, or if it did, the ice would surely crush it, break it up like fire tinder. He tightened his fist as he spoke as if to emphasise its fate and she winced and said nothing. The next day as I passed their bedroom I saw that the drawing was missing from the dressing table and I thought that perhaps she had placed it in the Chinese box. But she may not have put it there at all, merely tidied it carelessly into a drawer somewhere. It may have been destroyed by Lucinda years later along with all those photos. Whatever happened, I never saw it again.

The irregular chunks of turkish delight were adrift in the box on squares of white paper laid carefully in a crisscross pattern, with icing sugar sprinkled liberally and the honey and rose-coloured pieces laid side by side. Papa was the last one to take a square, and as he ate, his moustache moved up and down, up and down, as if in preparation for his old teasing way, when the twitching moustache signalled the commencement of the fun. That was the only time on his brief home leave when I saw his moustache twitching.

He never mentioned the war, at least not in front of us children. And yet something of the war seeped through to us during that slow ten days, as he did his best to elicit tales of school and playmates from us and talked quietly out of our sight with Mama. I think of it now as an exercise in breath-holding, a suspension of life almost, as we each strained to hear something of what was being said. Of course we could have asked him to tell us what the war was like – William certainly wanted to know – but nobody dared. And as usual, it was William who was the most successful in gleaning information and in making sense of what little the rest of us gathered.

'Ducks,' he explained to Esmee, 'is only part of the word. It wasn't ducks he was talking about, but duckboards. They are long planks of wood erected along the trenches to allow the soldiers to run along them without having to step into the mud all the time. But they have to be careful and keep their heads down below the level of the top of the trench or else they will be shot.'

Fortunately the younger children did not pay much attention to this, happy that the occurrence of ducks in the French countryside made sense. But sometimes at night the ducks and the turkish delight became dream-tangled and I saw Papa trudging along trenches bogged down in wet, sticky turkish delight covered in duck feathers that clung to his boots, so that in the way of dreams, he moved slower and slower, sinking deeper and deeper into the sticky mess, while overhead, the three timber masts of the *Endurance*, with their broken crossbeams, tilted crazily on the edge of the trench, trapped and crushed by a rising bank of white feathers.

Mama stood in the centre of the kitchen wearing a burgundy woollen skirt and a cream blouse. Mrs O was preparing pastry for the evening meal, carefully rolling it on the slab of marble she kept especially for this purpose. They had been talking quietly together for some time, Mama taking dishes from the dresser and slowly placing them beside the range to heat. Papa had gone to the Admiralty Office about some business he had not discussed with Mama.

'I suppose it is something to do with the separation allowance,' she said shortly after he left.

She had continued to discuss her personal preoccupations with Mrs O, all the tiny details of survival that had previously only been discussed with Papa. Mrs O didn't always reply to these statements because she was sometimes unsure if they were being addressed to her at all or if Mama was merely thinking aloud. She was aware that this also had something to do with Mama's general air of distraction.

'It is as well that there is less to spend on these days. At least it will let the money go a bit further. The children are growing so fast they seem to grow out of their boots all at the same time.'

''Tis a pity the summer is a long way off, ma'am. Doing without anything on their feet is so much better for them.'

'Summer? I can hardly remember last summer — just a bustle and crowds everywhere. Bustle, noise and then silence.'

I remained sitting very still, my hand hovering over the slices of apple on a plate, remembering the last summer with Benjie, when our games were our reality.

'Well, we don't hear the clatter of horses' hooves much any more, that's for sure, what with the merchants having to give them to the military, whether they liked it or not. Poor Mr McAuliffe finds it very difficult having to do his bread deliveries with his sons on those bikes of theirs. Can you imagine trying to push them up these hills? I'm sure the military could have spared one horse,' Mrs O said.

'It would be difficult to make an exception. Soon everyone would want the same. But I have heard talk in town, people are certainly finding things difficult. Mrs O, be sure and put on some extra vegetables for Richard — I don't think he has eaten any greens since he left home.' Somehow, without my noticing, Mama had taken to using the affectionate name we children had for our housekeeper, as if the old formalities belonged to another, vanished life.

Beneath my hand, the edges of the apple turned the colour of dried fern and I wondered if Papa had eaten any apples since he left home, if he passed any orchards in the fields of France.

'But surely they get a bit of cabbage and potatoes from the field-kitchen — is that what you call it?'

'I don't know much about that. The wives were telling me one Thursday that it is mostly some sort of tinned meat they eat and beans. Can you imagine eating that food day after day? It must be horrible.'

Mrs O and Mama had stopped their movements around the kitchen and turned towards each other as if they might better convey the horrors of their talk by facing each other, each seeking for a tiny gesture from the other that might reveal a denial, a negation of what they described.

'What does the Officer say about the food, ma'am?'

'Not much. I mean, he doesn't talk about it at all. He doesn't want to talk about his life in France at all.'

And they talked in low voices, forgetting I was there,

about the scraps of information that Mama had managed to coax from Papa about the rain and the way it churned up the ground so that it was difficult to walk. About how they sometimes had to walk for miles to a place, only to turn around and walk back to where they came from, with Papa beginning to get angry at the recollection, saying something about inaccurate maps, but stopping and changing the subject, talking instead about the men's feet.

'What about the men's feet?' Mrs O allowed her gaze to drop momentarily to Mama's feet before she spoke, then she watched closely as Mama replied.

'Well, it seems they get badly blistered from walking for hours on end in the hard leather boots, which get harder as they dry out after all the rain. And then they begin to crack, which adds to the discomfort, and their socks are permanently wet too. They get foot infections and something called trench foot.'

As Mama related the mundane details, she sounded like a child, proudly presenting information as a gift to a parent, evidence of a task completed, awaiting commendation. Suddenly she sat heavily into a chair, as if the waiting had taken its toll and she looked hopelessly towards Mrs O. 'But you know, all the time he was talking about their feet I felt he was trying to bite back a huge anger, even when he had stopped talking about France and was asking about things here. But maybe anger is too strong a word. Impatience may describe it better. He seemed to be impatient with our lives here, each time I told him something about how we try to keep doing all the usual things, and I felt that I had to be careful, sift out accounts of difficulties. I stopped myself from telling him about William always wandering off and not telling me where he is going.

It is difficult to explain, but it is as if none of this matters to him any more, as if he thinks life is suddenly too easy here for us, somehow.'

I wanted to get up and leave the kitchen and run into the garden or the street, away from the kitchen and Mama's talk. I wanted to run among the rocks and the scratchy limpets, drag my feet across their surface, feel the jagged edges make incisions on my skin. But I could not move from the room.

'Well, you try your best, ma'am. But it must be strange for him to sit in a comfortable chair in a nice warm room after what he has been through. I hear some of the women in the town talking in the shops and they say the same as you – that the men won't talk when they come home on leave.'

But Mrs O didn't tell Mama that Papa had also spoken to her about his anxieties. She avoided looking at me, knowing that I was in the kitchen, unnoticed by my father in his rush to question her. And this too was something new, this seeking her out when she was alone, enquiring ostensibly about her family until he felt comfortable to talk about his wife.

'I think she has got thin this past few months, Mrs O. I hope she is eating well.'

'Oh yes, sir, she eats well enough, considering. It's just the worry that does it, that's all.'

'I see. There seems to be a slight tremor in her hands, something that is only noticeable in the evenings, when she is passing the plates. And then there is that pallor, sometimes even a film of moisture on her forehead – do you think it comes from stress? Perhaps she should see a doctor.'

And Mrs O steadily reassured him that, no, Mama did not need to see a doctor, that she was merely a little tired by evening, that she was not taking medication and that perhaps Papa should speak to her himself.

'I wanted to talk to you in case it was all my imagination. I don't want to add to her worries.'

'Well, there is no need to worry, sir, honest to God there isn't.'

Papa left the kitchen abruptly and Mrs O stood looking into the garden for what seemed like a long time. Half-heartedly she began the dinner preparations, silently placing some carrots on the table for me to slice until she heard Mama coming along the hall. She visibly hauled herself upright and after the usual chat about the dinner arrangements she seemed to lose energy and sat down. Sensing that she had something to say, Mama sat down too.

'You know, ma'am, the Officer is worried that you might be taking medication, he thinks you are too pale, you see. It's your health, is what I mean to say – he is worried about it.'

'But why would he worry? And how do you know this, Mrs O?'

And I noticed how Mama's voice had become quieter with each fresh response, and I thought that if they continued to talk, Mrs O would soon be unable to hear her at all.

'Well, I'm sorry, ma'am, but he enquired yesterday. He didn't want to trouble you. He thought you took medication when you were upstairs because you seemed to be more cheerful in yourself when you returned. He was concerned, that's all, ma'am.'

'Well, I'm sorry that he didn't come to me himself. I shall talk to him.'

'Oh, ma'am, I didn't mean to cause trouble. I just thought

you might like to know that he does worry, even though he doesn't talk much now.'

Mama left the kitchen and entered the dining room, her tall thin shape bending and stretching, her movements breaking up the reflection in the mirror above the sideboard, pushing her image back further into the room, distancing her from the intimacy of her surroundings.

'There has been so much rain this winter, it is as if the sea has reared up and relocated itself right down on top of us.'

'Oh, Ally, my dear, you are so melodramatic sometimes.'

'It's true, Richard. The wind is so loud at times that I fear the windows will come crashing in on top of us. The sound gets inside my head so that I cannot tell where the noise is coming from any more.'

'Well, let's not think about the weather for now. Look at this wonderful fire, it is so good to be in here, snug and warm. So good to feel dry, not having to think about the damp all the time, hoarding the last pair of dry socks because we don't know how long the rain will last.'

I was sitting in the hall with Esmee and Peter, having been told to supervise them as they finished a jigsaw puzzle and ensure that they did not argue. The tray holding the incomplete image had been placed on the floor at their request, close to the half-open door into the drawing room where Richard and Ally were talking. The young ones were keen to keep their father in their sight immediately after his homecoming. I was tired and the task suited me, as I sat with my back to the wall, watching the shadows from the fire, which was out of view, shuddering on the wall beyond the door.

Papa and Mama sat in the room, the gas mantles turned low, the firelight flickering between them. They talked in low voices as they reached back to the time before Papa's departure, when the domestic rhythms of Queenstown, the comings and goings of the island ferry bringing him to and fro, the bustling exits of Mrs O just prior to his arrival home each evening all imposed a careless order on the days. The apparent thoughtlessness of the arrangement must have created a huge yearning in them both as they sat together.

'We hear so little about what it is like in France,' Mama said. 'The newspapers are so optimistic and full of talk of the numbers of German prisoners taken in some encounter or other. But it is so difficult to make sense of any of it, especially as these little towns are not mentioned in our atlas or else are impossible to find.'

'I'm afraid, Ally, you can forget about atlases and maps. It's just a quagmire. Even we don't know where we are half the time. Direction makes little sense there – there is nowhere to go, direction doesn't matter, it's all just names on signposts all pointing to the same horror.'

I could hear Mama pressing him to tell her more but he resisted, always concluding by saying the same thing. 'There really is nothing to tell. We are doing what we are trained to do. That's all.'

'But it is a very honourable thing that you are doing, Richard. That is surely no small thing. And you are doing it for us all.'

Mama's frantic searching for a solace for Papa, for some hitherto unacknowledged vindication of his life in France, always came around to this, that he was doing it all for his family. This was the sticking point for me as a child, that he was caught up in violence on behalf of his family. Whenever

I heard Mama's plaintive response, I sensed that their conversation was about to end, not open up.

My attention moved between flickering shadows and my parents, responding to the rise and fall of each voice.

'Have you noticed it, Ally? Have you noticed it, this vague sense of shame slithering around us here? Shame and, yes, anger too. Definitely anger. And I can't understand either of them. Well, anger – perhaps I can understand anger. But not the shame, definitely not that. Shame has to do with something hidden. But we have never hidden, Ally. We have worked and lived openly here as soldiers, so why should we suffer shame now because we are continuing to pursue our chosen loyalty?'

Mama said something which I could not hear and Papa began to speak again, his voice rising, his breathing changed.

'And in another way it is as if I have never been away, as if the war is not really happening. Life here seems so unchanging. That makes me angry too.'

Mama's mounting desperation broke through then, a breathy, gasping plunge backwards into her fortified domesticity. 'Well of course it is unchanging, Richard. What would you wish us to change? We have been trying to keep things as they were, it seemed the best thing to do, to keep to our routines here, keep the children at their studies, with Mrs O continuing to help me as in the past. What else would you have us do? The children have rolled bandages and knitted and packed socks and gloves for months now. What else could we do, Richard? What could we possibly change?'

I heard the gas escape in a startling hiss from a burning log. By then, of course, he had seen too many explosions too many jagged flames tearing across the blackness, leaving behind screams and melting flesh in the charred earth. What use would our gauze bandages and woollen socks have been to the mangled bodies and bloodied stumps? But I knew nothing of such things then, nothing of the endless peering into the darkness, waiting while his men crawled on their elbows towards enemy trenches, wire-cutters at the ready, preparing for an attack at dawn that might never happen.

'No, of course change is impossible right now. You're perfectly correct to continue on as you have been doing before. It is the wisest course. The wisest. And of course you must keep on helping with the emergency supplies and keep the children involved. It is all required. It is all important. For King and country, isn't that what we say? We must not forget that, whatever else we forget.' His voice had settled into a low monotone so that he sounded as if he was beating out a rhythm in his head in time to some distant drum that only he could hear.

'Richard, I know that it is very difficult for you in France, but you must not let it make you bitter and angry like this.'

'Angry, is it? No, Ally, I'm not angry.'

'Then what is it?'

'It's not knowing why we are really there. I know why we are supposed to be there, but nobody seems to know how we should conduct ourselves there, where we should be at any one time or even, God help us, how we might get there. It is hard to believe that anybody is really in charge. I'm sorry, Ally, I shouldn't be saying any of this. Perhaps it is not as out of control as it appears, perhaps someone knows what is really going on.'

'But of course someone is in charge. And you are too,

aren't you? I mean you are in charge of the men who report to you, aren't you?'

'Yes. And responsible for them in ways I could never have imagined.'

'But you can't be responsible for them all of the time.'

'Oh, Ally, if only I could remove myself from that, from the decisions that determine if they live or die. In a way, although it is hard to believe, that is the worst part of it all. Motivating the men, building up their spirits in a huge act of falsity, in the hope that they believe all the hollow praise and false promises only to send them moments later to their death. Blown away to kingdom come, to misquote the prayer. And what use is a prayer? We seldom have time for prayers. No, there is no time for that any more.'

'But I pray for you all the time – for your safety, for the safety of your men, that the war will end soon – I pray for all that. Don't you find a few moments in the day for prayer? Surely there is a quiet time in the day?'

'Well, the nights are fairly quiet.'

They remained quiet there before the fire, replicating the quietness he spoke of, willing it to last.

'And do you pray then?'

'Pray, Ally? No, I don't pray. But isn't this war really one great prayer, the ultimate gesture on behalf of those of us who honour our country and King?'

'Stop it, Richard, this cynicism is corrosive. Don't you believe that what you are doing is good and honourable?'

'I don't know what I believe in any more. I don't know that in sending men out to crawl through the French mud, to be hailed on by bullets, that I am doing it for the right reasons.'

The hall had become chilly, and I could tell from the

slowly flickering shadows that the fire needed replenishing. But neither of my parents moved to deal with it.

'Perhaps you should pray for strength, Richard. Perhaps we should both pray.'

'I can't, Ally, not even for the men for whose deaths I am responsible. I cannot pray even for them.'

'But you are not responsible. You were only doing your duty.'

I saw Papa's shadow bend then towards the fire, as if seeking the essence of his unquestioning sense of duty in the flames. Duty must have seemed to him like one great net in which he and his colleagues were enmeshed, fish caught by the gills, lifted out of their own lives, unable to breathe in this new place. He must have wondered how many other men were having similar conversations in their homes to the one he was having with Mama tonight.

'And who holds in any regard what we are doing over there? Isn't the only talk to be heard here about wringing Home Rule out of Britain when all this is over? Aren't the likes of Sean O'Sullivan only waiting in the wings for an opportunity? And what would he know about the nobility of serving a cause or fighting alongside the best?'

'Richard, please, there is nothing to be served by getting angry.'

'Angry? No, it's not anger, Ally, it's confusion.'

Sitting in the hall, my child's mind could not have contemplated the vista of horror with which he was confronted, of fighting, so he thought, for the highest principles, in the midst of a descent into the greatest levels of inhumanity he could ever have imagined. Nor could I have understood Mama's silence as she sat waiting to hear what he had to say, to hear something, anything, that would reveal to her where the man she married lay hidden now in the midst of all this anger.

'How can we cope with the so-called nobility and the baseness of war all at once? That's what I want to know. Oh, God, Ally, I never wanted to speak to you of this. I'm sorry. Please forgive me.'

'I'm not sure I understand you when you speak of baseness. We hear so little here.'

'Let's stop talking about this. I'm very tired.'

'Please Richard, I'd really like to know.'

'Don't you see, Ally? I can't talk about it any more. I have a little game I play, where by not talking about it I can convince myself, if only briefly, that it is all a bad dream.'

And Mama would have truly understood the game he played with himself in the coming months.

Mama and Papa retired early. The night had become uncharacteristically still, so that for once the sash window did not rattle and occasionally I could hear the splash of a wave against the sea wall. Earlier I had watched their two figures moving slowly along the corridor in, what seems to me now, an exhaustion of duty and love and desperation. Perhaps they came together that night in an attempt to grapple each other back from the darkness that was enveloping them.

I suppose what surprises me most about Rebecca's pregnancy is that it has happened at all. The truth is that I always thought she preferred women. Oh, not in the way of some of these young women who appear on television from time to time, stroking each other's necks the way someone might twist a wedding ring when speaking. With Rebecca it's more of a discomfort she shows in male company. Even her choice of husband carries with it a hint of unease, like somebody toying with an image change, one which requires her to take a step too far. It is, of course, something which does not concern me and yet I keep on coming back to it – the endless testing out Rebecca and Wolfgang do on each other, a sort of protracted, academic probing. And they are at it again today over lunch.

Rebecca has been talking about her latest weekend course. Not that I can tell one from the other any more, they all seem so alike, attended exclusively by women engaged in rediscovering their selfhood as women. I want to ask her when it went missing, or how it happened, and if mine has been missing all my life without my realising it. But I don't ask for fear that I may not understand the answer. Now she is talking about a reinvention of self, as a goddess, I think she said. What a strange idea. But I didn't listen attentively and so I am not sure if this is someone in charge of the womanly self or perhaps some power figure who will tell us how to run our lives. It all sounds very mystical. Young women seem to have forgotten more about their essential selves than they actually know any more. At least, that is how it appears from what Rebecca says. The more she explores, the more she discovers has been mislaid along the way, although she never puts it in so many words. A few moments ago she was talking about unlocking the creative goddess in each of us and all I can think about is that brothel-pink tray I made in a craft class, all those years ago. I wonder what Rebecca's group would think about that, its inelegance, its crude materials and unsubtle colour. I suppose I could have piled it high with exotic fruits and carried it about on my head! This goddess of femininity. It's not the selfhood of women that has gone missing but their humanity. Too much looking into their shadowy side, and they forgot to lift their heads and see that the rest of us are still here, including the men.

But it is a nice idea, really, this goddess, all white drapery and long limbs and flowing tresses. Did I ever feel like a goddess? I can't remember a time when I did, perhaps never, unless I count that time with Tom. Poor Tom, all serious intent and clumsy chivalry without any style to carry it off, appearing eternally gauche, the subject of secret smiles and sidelong glances. Still, we did manage that weekend in Paris – a place so uncharacteristic of his temperament that I think the contrast struck even him. He was so determined to see everything, had worked out such a tight schedule for the weekend, it was at first irritating. But in the end, it was touching, the realisation that he had done all of this planning for me. And then he died, a week after our return home. His death was almost thoughtful – nice and tidy, at home, almost as if he had planned it. If I had been forewarned, I don't think I would have expected to be as devastated as I was. Perhaps I had an inkling then that it was probably the last time that a man would treat me as a goddess. But of course Rebecca would have a problem with that. She says we must discover our own goddess. I think that is what she has been saying. If only I can pay attention.

'But Rebecca, dear, you used to say that men were not taking you seriously because they treated you as a woman first and only later as a human being.'

Rebecca tries to convince us that this is not a return to the bad old days but more an attempt to interrogate ancient rituals, to resurrect best practices in becoming attuned to the rhythms of the earth.

Interrogate. Rebecca uses that word a lot now. Interrogate. I suppose she means to scrutinise something closely. But she makes it sound as if she intends intimidating someone who might hold different views to hers. There are times when unscrambling her language takes me away from her ideas, so that I feel that I am beating less and less egg in the bottom of a pot whose contents have slowly splashed over the edge and lie congealed across the top of the stove.

'You know, Rebecca, I used to like feminism. It used to

be about important things, like equality and fair play. Maybe when I was younger it had more relevance for me. But it was hopeful then. We thought everything was possible. I think that is what I liked about it most – that it was hopeful.'

My head has begun to ache and I realise that my afternoon nap is important in helping me manage my aches and tremors and I am missing it already, even though it is still early.

Wolfgang leans forward and is filling my wineglass. I take a sip and impale some peas on my fork, the green stark against the pale unpatterned plate. Wolfgang has remained silent for some time, appearing relaxed yet attentive. Rebecca looks at me, perplexed.

'But that was a long time ago, Rebecca, you were a child then.'

And we all laugh and express amazement that feminism has been around for so long. After a while she enquires if I have been making progress with the diaries.

'Nineteen fifteen, I think, yes, that's how far I've got – just after Papa's first home leave.'

And here we are, having slipped seamlessly back into the past again. Not for the first time, I wonder does she ever consider that these are my mother's diaries, that this re-discovery she pursues so urgently may be one that I do not wish to make. As a child, I wanted Mama to be in control, of us and of herself. I think that is still what I wish for, both for Mama as she was then and for myself now, looking back. It is simpler that way. I am too old for complications.

'I wonder if they had played their first friendly game of football with the enemy by then?' Wolfgang is tilting his large wineglass from side to side as he speaks.

'Football?' Rebecca's eyes are darting rapidly from side to side at each of us, as if she has misheard.

'Football. Engaging with the enemy. Interrogating the past, if you prefer.' Wolfgang smiles slightly at his reflection in the wineglass, a blown-up fish face smiling back at him. 'They played football together, the English and the Germans, on Christmas Day in no-man's-land.'

And suddenly I feel that is where I am, in no-man's-land, not knowing whether to go backward or forward.

'Oh yes, of course,' Rebecca mutters.

'The Germans won,' Wolfgang says, an afterthought.

Rebecca is perplexed again.

Wolfgang reaches forward with the wine bottle and fills her glass and I watch the wine-shadow lengthening on the white cloth beneath. Penumbra. Twilight zone. No-man's-land. I feel that I could go on stretching this thought out forever.

'The match,' he says then, 'not the war', as if he is speaking to himself. I remember Wolfgang telling me that we sometimes learn our lessons in concealment too well and feel a sudden rush of sympathy for him, this quiet, intense man, whose history has taught him not to look back.

'The diaries, Helena, what did Ally say? What was happening?' Rebecca seems not to have heard Wolfgang.

Vague, that is how I sound as I speak, vague, as I tell her reluctantly how nothing was clear then, that Mama was caught between anxiety and lack of information from Papa on the one hand, and the wives half-whispered horrors told to her on Thursdays on the other, so that she was afraid to believe anything that was hopeful, lest it might negate the nightmare that was his. And of course, she was pregnant by then. I feel exhaustion curdle through me like bile.

Rebecca joins in the fiddling with cutlery and glassware that has accompanied our lunch together, in a group displacement of tension. Wolfgang's eyes flicker momentarily in the direction of her stomach. The branch of the tree in their tiny courtyard scrapes against the window, a half-open hand scratching for entry. Even nature carries unease in our company.

'She is still talking about Shackleton in her diary – did I tell you about this before? She was fascinated by him, but by this time he had lost contact with the outside world and, as we now know, his ship was caught in the ice that would eventually cripple it. I believe that it was finally crushed at the time of Lucinda's birth in October. But Mama's diary then is full of ice and whiteness and light and crystals. Her whole being was fantasising about the expedition.'

'It makes sense, don't you think? An escape of sorts, from the horror that Richard was caught in.' Wolfgang sounds weary or bored, I can't decide. I too have become bored. I am skirting around the story, have even considered fabricating an episode that might distract Rebecca for a while, present it as a joke eventually, anything to arrest this relentless pursuit. Nothing comes to mind and I settle back into a restless waiting but change my mind.

'I suppose you're right, Wolfgang. But she had another escape, it seems. She mentions M.'

Rebecca springs to her feet, the muscles in her face taut, creating grey, irregular, uninteresting hollows unrelated to her bone structure, and I am absorbed trying to trace their origin. She knocks against the table as she moves away and the wine-shadow shifts, then steadies.

'What did she say about M?'

'But haven't you read these extracts, Rebecca?'

'No, Helena. I mean, yes. Well, no, not really. It didn't seem right to read them before you.'

No, of course it wouldn't be right. But I had read them already, years ago. I don't say this to Rebecca.

And we begin the dance once again, a series of veiled enticements and reluctances from Rebecca that are beginning to embarrass me in their transparency. And I play, out of boredom or habit, I'm not sure which.

'She didn't say much really, just a brief mention of the comfort she drew from M, the support, that sort of thing, nothing more.'

I hear the old woman in me, piqued by Rebecca's probings, raising another of my vague defences, feigning an indifference that I hope will serve to protect Mama, even at this late stage. The truth is that I want to keep her story for myself. It is the child in me that wants this, the child who burrowed into Ally's Chinese box and failed to understand what it was I found.

I hear myself proclaiming platitudes, all the things that Rebecca knows already but which will keep the dance moving along. Wolfgang switches on some side lamps as the light is suddenly fading and Rebecca starts at the sharp click of a switch and turns, as if intending to switch off the lamps again, but then sits back into her chair.

'We'll need a Mrs O of our own here soon,' Wolfgang says suddenly and I tell them how pleased I am for them both and how different it will be when the baby arrives and how it really will give them a new perspective on life. I wonder as I move through it all where such phrases come from and why I never acted on these beliefs in my own life and I sense the shadow of childlessness as it dilutes my words.

Rebecca is busy clearing away the dinner plates. She looks

fragile – but when does she not? – bending across the dinner table to reach the dishes.

'It will be difficult to find someone as dedicated as Mrs O. Do you think it will be necessary?' I say.

'Well, Rebecca travels a lot, as I do. If we continue to organise our lives as they are presently arranged, then yes, we shall need a superwoman on a par with Mrs O. But we haven't really talked much about it yet.' Wolfgang looks towards the kitchen before continuing. 'I do have a secret yearning, Helena, which I have not been able to air with Rebecca yet. What I would like to do is to move to the country, to a quiet rural area, close to a village, where the children could have their schooling when they are old enough, yet remain free of the worst influences of city living – you know, the endless visits to fast-food outlets, cinemas, even TV could be done without. They could concentrate on activities that nurture the soul, involve themselves with nature, animals, reading, music.'

Rebecca has re-entered the room carrying a large dish of tiramisu, saying apologetically that she knows this has become a culinary cliché but she likes it and it is easy to prepare. She has not heard what Wolfgang was saying.

'I've been telling Helena about some ideas I have about child-rearing while you were in the kitchen, Rebecca.' Wolfgang gives her an abridged version, watching idly as she dollops the dessert into bowls, placing one in front of me as he speaks. He beckons impatiently at Rebecca with his hand to signal that he wants a larger helping and then he begins to eat.

'It's the first time I have heard any of this, Wolfie. You mean, sell this house and move to the country?'

'Yes, that's about it. But it is really all about keeping

the worst influences of society at arm's length.'

'Oh, but it sounds like a hot-house existence. A social experiment almost.'

'That's not what I'm suggesting, Rebecca. Can you see what I'm driving at, Helena? '

'I think so, Wolfgang.' And I roll out the platitudes once more about what is best for the child and about setting one's personal requirements aside, and again that tiny chink is there, and beyond it the blot of childlessness.

'You think I'm too interested in being a good parent, is that it?'

'Goodness, it's way to early for that. I'm sure you'll be a very good parent.'

And a good European, I remember.

'I suppose I left home too early, Helena, too young to understand people and all their complexities. I was only sixteen.'

There is no place for my messy sympathies here and so I huddle into my chair, an old woman whose sensibilities have long been blunted and overtaken. I look down on sturdy, laced shoes and support stockings peeping from beneath my maroon plaid skirt and ponder when it was that I began to wear such things. Bindings. Mummies were bound too – in death. One great support stocking. What a good idea. That would hold all my sagging flesh in place. I hear that young women now have themselves wrapped like mummies, smearing seaweed and mud on their bodies first. Living mummies. And now Rebecca is about to become a mummy. I am thinking silly thoughts. It must be the wine.

'Helena, are you all right?'

I explain that the wine has made me a little drowsy and

Rebecca is immediately solicitous. She goes to get me some tea and Wolfgang smiles at me.

'I'm sorry about all of that. I have a very messy life, as Rebecca will agree.'

'Life is untidy, Wolfgang. The older we get, the more adept we become at keeping the raw edges tucked out of sight. I think that is why Mama kept a diary. It helped her tidy her life away into that battered Chinese box of hers.'

Wolfgang sits watching the untidy movement of the branch, jabbing erratically against the window. His chest rises and falls in a long, inaudible sigh.

A feeling of giddiness suddenly assails me and everything in the room is momentarily frozen, then begins to shudder and change shape and I think it is moving backwards, faster and faster, and I think that I am going to black out. All the time Wolfgang is standing to one side and at the same time is moving backwards faster and faster, is becoming younger and younger as he moves, his heels dragging on office carpet, on concrete pathways, on tarmacadam roads, across grassy embankments and unshorn meadows, through stubbled fields and snowy paths until I think I can see him faintly as a child, grey trousers and thick sweater, small and blond and large-eyed, as if afraid. I want to hug him and tell him there is nothing to be afraid of, absolutely nothing.

It is not clear if he has heard what I said. He sits staring ahead of him, unmoving, seeming not to notice Rebecca as she brings in tea things on a tray. And then suddenly he stands and takes the tray and places it on the table and Rebecca acknowledges the gesture with a tiny startled movement of her head.

We drink and talk, low, desultory murmurs that flow outwards into the shadows until Rebecca's tenacity takes us back once more to the subject of M.

'Don't you think it strange, Helena, that Ally does not identify this M by name, that she needs to mask the identity even from herself, for who else did she expect to read the diaries?'

'But of course she thought that someone might read them, otherwise why did she secrete them away? She would have destroyed them if she wanted to keep the contents secret. No, I think that she secretly hoped that some day – and perhaps she hoped that it would be after her death – that some day, someone would find them and make sense of it all.' I try to keep my voice from rising, yet hear an exasperation creeping in despite my effort.

'Rebecca, this may not be such a good idea. It is Helena's mother's story which you are asking her to read.'

'But she did not abbreviate anyone else's name, so it must be important.' Rebecca curves her right arm protectively across her stomach as she speaks. I watch as it slackens and loses its grip, sliding limply downwards to lie inert on her thigh.

The idea of M as Lucinda's father will not settle into place, into any place, in my mind. And Lucinda, always seeking approval through her ready smile and subtle manipulations, did she live so fecklessly because of a father denied her? Perhaps this is what Mama tried to avoid through her fixation with snow and ice, this great dark well of nothingness.

'I'm sorry, Helena, this is obviously exhausting for you,' says Rebecca.

'It's all right, Rebecca, really it is. This may seem strange, but since starting to read the diaries, I have tried to get inside Mama's mind. But the more I read, the more of a stranger she becomes to me. Of course I was a child then and could only know her as a child at the time she was writing. But there is a strangeness there. An other-worldliness that is inexplicable at this remove. Reading those jottings of a stranger, for that is what they are, has forced my mind to take great leaps of fancy, the sort of leap that reading a novel brings about for me, so that I find myself wondering about her pregnancy and, yes, may heaven forgive me, wondering about the father of her child, Lucinda. I even wondered if Bart might have been the father.' But I know that this is not what happened, it's my imagination, that's all. There's nothing more to it.

The memory of the two fragile blond heads bobbing together along the seafront in Queenstown, like marker buoys on the waves, comes to me and the boyish account of a farewell kiss that seemed to be more than that to a child. But the ludicrousness of the idea banishes the image and I turn to Wolfgang. 'But of course it is impossible. They cared too much for each other to jeopardise their lives in that way.'

'Lucinda was too dark, her hair was almost black.' Wolfgang gives a tight laugh, more of a grunt really, before he continues. 'Perhaps you two should give the diaries a rest for a time, your imaginations are becoming too lively. It's a good thing that Lucinda is not alive to hear this.'

'Oh, on the contrary, Wolfgang, she would have loved it, creating stories of endless excitement and possibilities. What a pity.'

Rebecca is aghast and does not look convinced by my attempt to lighten things. In seeking Lucinda's story, she is trying to clarify her own, perhaps even attempting to rewrite it. She wants a neatness of fit, a grandfather for her and a father for Lucinda, someone she can take along to her therapist and say, 'There, there he is, it was exactly as I told you, he was there in the diaries all along.' But she only dipped into the diaries, just enough to set her imagination to work. She does not have the whole picture. And I sit here tongue-tied, refusing to let her have this picture. I am afraid of what she will do with it.

We finish lunch and I tell them that I am tired and we travel back to the nursing home where life is simple, where I settle in with my companions who have joints that creak in similar places to my own, where James reassuringly tells me that if I eat oily fish three times a week it will ease my arthritic limbs and where May waits to dust Rebecca from my life for a brief period as she continues to tell me tales from the war zone that is her family life.

May has placed a crocheted rug over the armchair by the window, where it spreads like a garish cobweb across the faded tapestry figures of the hunter and the dairy-maid on the fabric beneath. Crochet is something she does in odd little moments of time. She gathers wool wherever it is available without any eye to colour or contrast, reaching into her wool bag for the next ball without a glance, feeding the end into the discontinued colour with a lick to her thumb and forefinger and a quick twist of the two strands until they become one. She continues, her left index finger poking into the air in the same way that I suspect she leaves it poking above her fork as she eats her dinner. I have become strangely fascinated by this lately, not by the crochet but by the stiff pointing finger. Sometimes I watch to see if she will bend it or even flex it a little for exercise. It is like watching someone who never blinks and my eyes begin to water at their effort. I secretly flex my fingers in an agony of suspension.

May produces her bag of wool from the strangest hiding places. She will whisk it from beneath my bed, from the bottom of her mop bucket or sometimes reach behind her and untie it from her apron strings, where it dangled unnoticed as she went about her work. She believes that there is an infinity of chairs and sofas all awaiting to be graced with one of her squares. May is moving around me now, settling me down, pretending she is indifferent to my arrival back from Rebecca's, talking about what I would like for my tea, ignoring my attempt to tell her that I have already eaten too much, that all I want is a cup of tea. Scones, crumpets, toast are all offered and offers withdrawn in quick succession and then she leaves me to fetch the tea, sighing as she goes.

The spring light is thinning the dusk beyond the window as the nursing home settles into its evening sounds. Doors quietly open and shut, television screens flash truncated traumas into the corridor and the occasional *squeak-squeak* of rubber-soled shoes moves off into the distance. I think about the residents around me, each of us poised to move towards a distant vanishing point. Sometimes I think it might be nice if I could haul on one strand of my life, like dragging a thick rope up out of the sand where it has lain buried for years and view the bubbles of subterranean moisture that come up clinging to it and prick each one. But first I would look inside, at each episode of my life caught there in miniature, exactly as it happened, free of memory and the falsity of memory, free of the duplicity of invention and re-invention that makes up a life.

'God, Helena, you look as miserable as a wet weekend.'

May bumps her bottom against the door, closing it with a resounding bang and places the tea-tray on the table. 'What on earth was Rebecca doing to you this afternoon to send you back to us looking like this?'

May is in ebullient form, starting to winkle news of my day from me, placing my cup of tea beside the window as she pulls and tweaks at me with questions as if I were a misshapen crochet square she was determined to reshape. And so I begin to tell her about the lunch and about Rebecca's pregnancy.

'I suppose she is still gallivanting off on those courses of hers. A load of rubbish, just a waste of time.' Her mouth turns down as she finishes.

'Oh, I don't know, May. There must be something in it that helps people make sense of their lives, otherwise why would so many people be attracted to it?'

'Ah, that's rubbish. Sure, I hear them in the staff rooms, the young ones anyway, talking a load of airy-fairy stuff, scraps of religions you never even heard of, the more exotic the better, taking out the bits that they like and stringing them together like a new set of rosary beads. It's all the fancy bits they like, you know the sort of stuff that lets them play-act for a while, make-believe in a way. You'd never find them singing the "Bells of the Angelus". Oh no, that would be too ordinary for them.'

I realise suddenly that May is feeling old, older than many of her colleagues, and that she is reacting as much to that as she is to Rebecca.

'I never thought that you felt strongly about religion, May.'

'Most of the time I don't. I just don't like people interfering with it, that's all.'

I sit waiting for her to continue. She pushes the teapot towards me but forgets to pour it. It is out of my reach.

'I'll tell you what Rebecca reminds me of, Helena. She reminds me of one of those flimsy looking blondes you see in those shampoo ads on television, you know them, the ones that run, or float more like it, across meadows, reaching to pluck at flowers as they go. Well, Rebecca reminds me of them, always plucking at something from the air on her way past. I can never see those ads without thinking of her.'

May's face has changed from sour to pensive and I realise with a shock that she feels sorry for Rebecca, that somehow in the midst of her coping with her warring brothers and her assortment of residents in the nursing home she has moved from dislike to pity without my noticing. But I am not sure that Rebecca would want to be pitied.

I reach awkwardly for my teacup, as yet unfilled, and the spoon falls to the floor. May has given me a china cup today, which I hate because the tea cools very quickly in its fragile shell. Also, it draws attention to the shake in my hand, as the cup makes a faint tinkling sound on the saucer like the shattering of a bird's egg. The shake seems more pronounced than usual this evening and I see that May is noticing. I give a little chuckle.

'It's as well that I don't smoke or I would never hold a light to the end of a cigarette with this shake in my hand.'

'It's a tremor, Helena, not a shake. You know that. The doctor says it's a tremor.' She appears briefly prim as she says this, which amuses me.

'He makes it sound like the forerunner to an earthquake. Call it what you like, it's certainly going at full strength on the Richter scale this evening.'

May is frowning and I am not sure if she has heard me. 'You're probably due for a check-up. When was it you last saw your doctor?'

'Oh, about three months ago, I think.'

'There, you see? We'll make an appointment for you tomorrow. You probably need to have your medication reviewed.'

I don't bother saying to May that there is a regular arrangement in place to see to all of that. Reviews and changes. Laying the rope along the surface of the sand for all to see the tiny bubbles shimmering and shivering, barely surviving the buffeting of the wind, yet vivid and bright. Each episode of my life is on the surface now, open to scrutiny in this place.

'And maybe you shouldn't be drinking so much tea in the evening.'

May whisks the tea things away without asking if I have finished and I watch her reflection in the window as she bumps backwards out the door. I look towards the darkening sky and the flat image of my room is reflected back at me. It will surely fit neatly into one of those bubbles, I grimace, before settling down to sleep.

22 June 1915

Today is Helena's tenth birthday, I almost forgot it. I shall speak to Mrs O. Perhaps she will bake some of her fruit scones and I think there is some of last year's damson jam left. Poor Helena, she doesn't understand my distraction, my tiredness, this endless, dragging tiredness that never leaves me.

This house is stifling me. Since Richard left, it seems to be closing in on us, this metal bowl with the sounds of voices bouncing around and around on metallic sides, louder and louder until I think I shall go mad. Everyone intent on talking, talk, talk, talk, yet it is impossible to understand what they are saying. They are trying to help, of course. 'Make sure the children eat well,' they say. 'Build them up for the winter,' they say. Build them up for what? 'You can't be too careful,' they say to no one in particular, as if we are all intent on living dangerously and need to be reminded to do otherwise. Life has become a series of petty anxieties, deadening weights that tear us ever downwards into pettiness.

Perhaps my condition has me exaggerating. I feel so much heavier this time. Mrs O says it is because it is my sixth child, that babies get larger with each pregnancy, but how can that be? I have managed to have my clothes altered sufficiently so far but soon I shall have to remain home from the wives' afternoons. It is unbearable to think of that. My only escape. Even M has been less helpful recently in the midst of all this anxiety and dreariness.

I have been having strange dreams – dislocated images of my family home in Dublin. The house is the same, leaning slightly into the curve in the road, the wall of the

Royal Hospital casting its crooked shadow over it, a spell long since cast. It looks exactly as I remember it, except that it quivers in my dream, as if the walls are insubstantial, moving slightly beyond my vision so that only a hint of the movement reaches me. And that's all there is, just this solid mass of brick and concrete and slate quivering, and I want to touch it, throw my arms out and steady it, yet I cannot, as my arms are too heavy, too heavy to lift, and anyway there is the tiredness. I am unsure which is preventing me from reaching out. And nobody appears in this dream. I look and look, expecting the quivering walls to change, to part or reshape themselves so that my mother will appear, or Bart. But nothing. The mirage-house remains intact. Nobody comes. I want to tell Bart about the child and wait and wait for him to come but he never does. And each time the dream repeats itself and I attempt to move beyond the walls in the hope of seeing my mother and Bart, yet I sense that she is being prevented from opening the door by my stepfather. And that is the point at which I emerge each time into the dawn and the damp cold of my bedroom, not able to sleep again.

Thoughts of Richard come flooding in then, his letters about parcels with Mrs O's fruit cake and newly knitted woollen socks and the awfulness of tinned beef and the flaring night sky full of noise and terror – but he doesn't speak of terror, just the light and the noise as if describing a fireworks display. He writes about the day he enlisted, underage, afraid to go home because he had taken his brother's bike, returning to announce that he was now a soldier, in the belief that this would save him from his father's wrath. Did he think then that this horror was

before him or was it all really a young boy's game? And
that is how it all appears now, this horror, a young boy's
game that went wrong. And now he knows that he is to
become a father once again. He says that he prays for the
child, for me, for himself. But how can he pray in the
midst of such chaos? He told me when he was home that
he could not. There is no sign of God in this war. We are
taught that He is visible in the flowers of the fields and the
beauty of the sky. But what happens when there is no
flower to be seen and only a sky filled with smoke and
fire?

Richard writes hopefully, tiny scraps of humour like
fluttering strips of cotton caught on a barb tucked into his
letters. But the wives tell of some of their men who are
not so careful about what they say, who let the horror
creep through. It is as though they resent this world of
ours that is orderly and mundane, a routine that is
exclusively ours, that picks us up in the early morning and
rocks us in its rhythms throughout the day, a succouring
movement that cannot be theirs. They resent this.
Sometimes Richard's letters pick over this routine,
savouring the familiarities of his days in Queenstown,
throwing the sash window upwards, inhaling the acrid
sourness of drying seaweed, laughing at my complaints as
the sea breeze rushes around the bedroom, threatening to
sweep everything onto the floor. Some of the wives have
spoken of other smells – the stench of death, of bodies
buried then uncovered in the endless rain.

My God, how long must this go on? How have we
come to this point where no movement forward seems
possible for any of us – Richard trapped by duty and me
trapped here between my children, my home and the

endless war effort – squeezing all hope from us, all the energy and vitality of life. And now there is another life to think of, a life to which Richard is clinging with a fixation that appears greater than that of preserving his own life. He is planning on a homecoming to see his child in the birth-month of October and yet I cannot bear to think of this event. It is too much now. It represents the opposite of hope for me. But of course I did not say this to Richard. And Bart – Bart, who does not yet know about the child. But by not telling him, it makes the event unreal, taking its place in a dream. And that is all I can do for now. Make it unreal. Perhaps I shall learn acceptance. That is all I can pray for now – acceptance. After that, perhaps there is hope. Hope comes now only from M – abiding warmth and comfort, the entering into another world where I so dearly want to remain more and more, where even the thought of my children recedes and I become someone special, soaring. And yet I regret that M has entered my life now, when my need is so great, when there is so little choice for me. Sometimes I think that now I must turn away, keep only what is required of me before me, refusing to enter this state which words cannot describe, this aliveness, setting all thoughts aside, feeling my body lightening, expanding as if it will tear itself asunder. And what if Mrs O were to read this and discover that the things that distract me are not always thoughts of Richard and the children and my coming confinement?

But M has made me whole again, fills the chasm my inside-outside life has left, even in my happiest moments, takes me to places that I never thought possible, before setting me down in a new place where everything is sparkling and bright, shimmering, like ice crystals. Shackleton's snow. He too escaped the darkness, into the whiteness of the southern oceans. He has not been heard of since December last. Not that he ever expected to be home by Christmas. The difficult part of his journey would only begin about then. But they are free, there by their own choosing, moving closer into that glistening whiteness. Movement towards something, movement that is hopeful. There is such a strangeness in that thought. Journeying into the unknown where anything is possible. Constant movement into brighter and brighter light, lighter, lightness, splintering light to the horizon. M has shown me. M can make the mud and noise and darkness recede, filling me with light that dazzles so that everything else becomes invisible and nothing exists but an endless expanse of light.

I try to introduce Richard into this light, alone, unadorned by uniform and kitbag, but I cannot. And I know that M cannot protect him or the children. I am the only one who can protect the children. Helena seems to understand this in the strange way she has of knowing something without asking. She is vigilant on behalf of the younger ones, as if sensing a new vulnerability in the house. She is once more becoming a confidante of William's, in a way that I could never be. She doesn't know that I am once more expecting a child, although I suspect that Mrs O may be preparing her in her own special way. And I saw her watching me the other day when I had the Chinese box on my lap. I must be careful, everything is blurred for me. Amelia told me that M would do that, blur everything. Distancing. She did not tell me that M would bring distant things closer, that I would find myself sinking without bidding into the whiteness of snow, into the shimmering blues of ice crystals and the green opacities of Antarctic waters all within seconds of each other so that for a brief time I am not haunted by absence, so that the great gap at the centre of my being is briefly covered over. Is that M's doing or is it my body reacting in some strange way to the child within? Perhaps my mind is slipping, becoming unhinged by the endless juggling and accommodations. I must conceal the Chinese box. The children can use the other three for their games of concealment.

What a strange thing gravity is. This morning while the nurse was attending to me I noticed the skin on my legs is slackening drastically and moving in a steady drift downwards, like crinkled wrapping paper. I haven't caught sight of my legs in quite a while, which is probably a mercy, given their condition. As I have been feeling a bit achy in recent days, they have decided to give me a break from the bath and wash me down on the bed instead. I can't say I liked it much. When I glanced down briefly at one point, it was a bit like looking on while someone was laying out a body in preparation for a burial, this slack mass of flesh, blue-pink and translucent. What grotesque things bodies are when they begin to break down. I mention this to May.

'Well, may God forgive you, Helena. You get a few aches in your legs and you have yourself dead and buried. You should be grateful that you still have the use of your limbs. There are those who are not as lucky.'

All that is missing is a loud harrumph. The strength of May's response is a measure of the seriousness with which she views my aches. That and her invocations to a higher power. And so I lower my head in anticipation of a shower of benedictions, sprayed at me like a scattering of seeds. Or pellets. That is what religion was for me – a series of tiny pellets shot into me by my teachers in religion classes all those years ago, which caused me to turn at an angle, slowly, without detection, until the tiny credos glanced off me, coming to rest somewhere else, far off, and God receded into the upper left-hand corner of my mind, to lodge there like a grey woolly mass, a silent admonition to my failures.

'When are you seeing the doctor? This afternoon, is it?' May says. 'Right. Just tell him everything. He'll probably say it's rheumatism or this awful humid weather and then you can stop worrying about it, OK?'

'I'm not worrying about it, May, merely trying to be realistic.'

And May, bless her, tidies my irritability away in her no-nonsense style, her apprehension assuaged for the moment. How well we have come to read each other. She banishes James's imaginary complaints with endless horror stories of neighbours' fatal conditions, yet takes my apprehensions into herself the way a mother takes a child's.

And suddenly it is there, this quiet way of old people as they slip into that cosy place from whence we came, the stifling hot-house of dependence and clammy protectiveness that wraps itself around the tiny kernel that is love. Must watch this tendency. It's tempting to sit back while others do my worrying, slipping unobtrusively into another quieter place. I have noticed how some of the older inhabitants' eyes seem endlessly to seek out distance, lingering on the horizon as if they might find something there, perhaps the minutiae of survival's requirements, avoiding the invasiveness of the close-up and personal. Beckett got it right when he said something about our ghosts forsaking us as we sink into mental havoc. Not that I want to read Beckett at this age, now that I have come into his time. But I think he knew. Perhaps it is our ghosts we seek along the horizon.

The morning is passing more slowly than usual. May left my door open by way of a distraction, although she did not say so. She has her little ways. Perhaps she knew that James was expecting his granddaughters, always good for entertainment value, as she likes to say. And sure enough, they arrived a few moments ago, like clockwork, just as James was getting his mid-morning coffee. Not good for the heart, the coffee, but a permissible treat because most of the damage is done by this age anyway. The granddaughters went into the small visitors' sitting room across the corridor and James followed, his slippers sounding a reluctant dragging movement along the polished timber floor. Strange how the sound has stayed in my head, a sibilant, convent sound that leaves me momentarily displaced, suddenly back in boarding school, in the nun's parlour, as they liked to call it, waiting to hear the swish of a long habit brushing the corridor wall and the wooden clonking of rosary beads knocking against each other. The high-ceilinged spaciousness and the deferential, subdued whispers that we used there are lost almost as soon as they come to me, as I hear James's granddaughters greeting him with their broken speech patterns and their self-conscious teenage giggling.

I know without seeing them that they are catching each other's glance from beneath stiff, black lashes in the intervals between their flirty jesting with James, who sits there, trying in his usual fashion to glimpse their lives. I don't need to see him doing this, it is what he always does. He asks vague, unfinished questions about school progress, their boyfriends' escapades, questions which fill them full of merriment, gasped-out responses exploding from them, beyond comprehending. As they double over and collapse backwards in their seats, they catch sight of me across the corridor, looking over the top of my crossword at the latest outburst and they pull faces at each other and laugh again.

A flash of light on the ponytail of the younger one reminds me of Rebecca as a teenager, whose hair was the same dark blond, and I wonder was she ever like this slinky, sinewy creature, loud, gauche, insensitive and compassionate in equal measure. But it eludes me. A wan face emerges with large eyes, opened wide as if trying to reveal her soul, or to reveal herself as someone without guile or malice, eager to please, a too-ready smile always on her lips. Lucinda's doing, surely. Not that it was her fault, for there was nobody there to show her that people were worthy of some consideration. Her child became someone for whom everyone was of great import. Poor Rebecca, worn down by her own burden of caring. She never got her chance to rebel.

I must have become very absorbed in my crossword, as I cannot remember hearing the granddaughters depart, and then suddenly it was lunchtime. I even gave in and had a nap after lunch and dreamt of a tree house, perched precariously in the birch outside my window. There were no obvious occupants, nothing appeared to be happening at all, just the anguished creaking of wood and then suddenly I was awakened and told the doctor was here to see me.

I wonder, do they have me in their sights now – me, as an old woman, do they have that in their sights? That is what I have been trying to recall, that is what was on my mind when I awoke. It was James's granddaughters I was dreaming about. It suddenly came back to me. They had been in the tree house and then vacated it, sliding down a rope, giggling and laughing. And that is when the thought came to me, that they had spotted me this morning and suddenly the picture of old age was there before them as they glanced at me across the corridor, frozen between the door frames like an elongated detail – me, sitting in my armchair, swollen ankles squeezed above my slipper-boots, sitting target for their mirth. They had me in their sights all right. They buoy up their vulnerability with their armour plates of laughter, sniping and jesting. But they mean no harm.

That sudden awakening from my nap has made me edgy. I wasn't feeling too steady when the nurse came to take me down to see the doctor. Pity, as I wanted to be ready for him. Steeled. But here I am and we work our way through the niceties that are habitual across the generations, at least between doctors and old women. He asks about my days and how I pass my time, although he must have heard what passes here hundreds of times. But we are accustomed to humouring each other and so I tell him about the bridge tournament and the table quizzes and he tells me about his latest tennis achievements and his awkward stepchildren, laughing uneasily as he does, whether because I have no children or because he expects me to be uncomfortable in the face of his second marriage, I cannot decide. And so we work our way slowly to his political fix, as May calls it, his insinuation of the latest bone on which he has been mentally gnawing on his long drive to the nursing home.

As is his custom, he begins to drop the pieces of his latest political preoccupation into place – the one-nation thing, the border thingummy, the consensus business – his vague, catch-all phrases blurring meaning so that I have to fetch around for something equally vague in response but nothing comes to mind. He studies his pen where he placed it on the windowsill with a strange, intense stare, as if expecting it to explode. I feel suddenly sleepy and struggle to concentrate.

And we have come finally to my real reason for seeing him.

'So, Helena, how is the tremor in your hand?' He smiles at me and sits into his chair, his eyes serious as he waits, his mouth continuing to smile as I talk and try to explain it away, noticing with annoyance that my voice has an unaccustomed waver in it. He questions me quietly and I answer but I have become disinterested, distracted, and I am not sure if he is enquiring about the tremor in my hand or the one that Papa noticed in Mama's hand and which he discussed with Mrs O during his leave. As Dr Brady talks, I can see Mama's hand emerging from a flimsy cuff of cream silk, like the blouse she wore in that christening photograph.

'The medication can be a little slow to act at your age.'

At my age. Tucking me into a woolly cocoon where things are not real, merely hints and touches of things, a surreal hernia protruding into an otherwise tidy world.

'We'll do a scan, that will tell us what progress we are making in reducing the tumour.'

And I sit here wondering who he means by 'we' and I think about the laughing skittish girls from this morning and their knowing looks and wonder how I became old without noticing it.

Time to bring out the Tokay. I can't remember if it was the romantic story told about the Hungarian prince who founded the house of Tokay or if it was that Hungarian holiday all those years ago that gave me a taste for this wine. Rebecca manages to get it for me with some difficulty. It has been overtaken by so many other more fashionable wines. But today I feel I have earned a glass, what with my trip down to the doctor and those ghastly staring granddaughters of James's. Perhaps May will join me for a glass before she leaves. Meantime there is just time to glance over Mama's diary again. But on second thoughts, perhaps not just yet.

John Philip Sousa – now that is what is missing. Some lively marching tunes. Not that they fit in with the atmosphere here. Too much animation. The rhythms might upset a few heartbeats. I'm sounding like Dr Brady now – all earnest concern and mental hand-patting. Still, the marching tunes take me back to the rituals of army life in Queenstown, all that triumphal drumming and piping of the army band, whipping up emotions into peaks, then leaving them adrift like stiff meringues skidding on ice. Brittle too. Crumbly, air-filled lives, all solid exteriors presented to the world, inviting crushing. Is that what we were secretly awaiting then, a crushing destruction? It is what awaited the insurgents at Easter 1916. We heard when Sean disappeared from Queenstown that he had gone to Dublin, but nobody really knew for sure, for they didn't talk about those matters. When the Rising occurred, everyone was certain that he had a part in it. The names of those who signed the proclamation declaring an Irish Republic, and later those of the dead and executed, were posted. Sean's name was sought diligently but to no avail. It was not until Esmee's funeral in Dublin, several years later, that he appeared briefly at Mrs O's side, an uneasy presence. He was thin and had the pallor of the jailhouse, as someone said. He was gone before the crowd began to disperse.

And there was Dr Brady talking this afternoon about consensus and one nation as if we had only recently opened a book and discovered these notions. I wonder what Sean would make of it all now as we stagger, dangerously wounded, towards the end of the century. 'Dangerously wounded' was how Papa's condition was described in a news release as he lay dying in a French field hospital.

But this is Rebecca again, intruding with her notions of our past as inescapable, pinioning us, indelibly marking us. Lucinda never cared about her past, seeing it as a road of sorts, featureless, dotted with brothers, like unremarkable telegraph poles along the margins – so many brothers, she liked to joke, that really she had no need to know about a father who died in her infancy. Or so she said. And perhaps she was right. She was happier than her daughter, on the surface anyway. Perhaps unhappiness was her legacy to Rebecca. Mama unhappy, Lucinda happy, Rebecca unhappy, her child happy. Swings and roundabouts, in and out, like figures on a cuckoo clock, turn and turn about. Where is the scope for choosing a life in all of that? Where are the corners in which we can conceal ourselves? Stepping out, into the next room – the comforting lines of bereavement poetry locate the dead for us so that we don't even have to stretch our imaginations. First you step in, then you step out again. A *danse macabre*.

I think that James is dying. Nothing to do with his slowing walk or his increasing confusion. It's something in the air, in the way staff are dealing with him in a more deliberate way, reminding themselves that he still matters, weighing each statement, checking it for hidden messages, attempting to deal simply and with clarity, sifting out the future, delivering a lived-in Buddhist present moment like sages bearing nuggets of wisdom. All this pared-down ministering to James serves to fix him in time, in the present, splaying him out like a figure strapped to one of those circular magician's boards that spin faster and faster while the magician throws knives that land precisely between arms, legs, fingers, yet never making contact with the person.

'Now James,' they say, 'today is a good day for a nice, long, relaxing bath, don't you think?'

He has a bath every day, and of course they know this.

'Your granddaughters are lively lassies. You'll enjoy them this afternoon,' they say, mentally ticking off his list of people to see, about whom he has no choice. They have taken to telling him how to view them in turn as they visit.

He has stopped responding to these statements, instead 'going with the flow', as May observed yesterday. 'He has got sense at last,' she said, 'he's going with the flow.'

Does she mean the rhythm in this place or the rhythm of his visitors or of his life, a river, a flood, a tide, ebb and flow, in and out?

'What do you mean, May?'

'Oh nothing, it's just a saying, that's all, just a saying to keep things moving along.'

Moving along. When will she begin moving me along? It must be the Tokay giving me these gloomy thoughts. No. It was Dr Brady and his talk of my tremor, as if he had just discovered some rare plant and had decided to give it a name. Probably something in my genes. Mama had a tremor too. Poor Ally. That's how she sometimes appears to me now – poor Ally. Removing the name 'Mother' or even 'Mama' is akin to removing a protective layer. And yet it is difficult to fix her in space and time. There is movement constantly, she keeps changing shape. I can't define her, too much paleness and translucence. A wisp of hair, a curling blondness above a collar, pearl pin on a dark jacket, narrow boniness emerging from a ruffed cuff, yet somehow never all coming together, never centred on a body that retains shape, colour, texture.

It is fortunate I never took a glass of wine in the afternoon until recently. It really is making my head muzzy. Perhaps that is the cause of the shake in my hand. I suppose that I should have mentioned it to Dr Brady. When I raise my hand before me and hold it there in order to watch the trembling, I can feel myself become a child briefly. Sitting at the evening meal in Queenstown, watching Mama's pale hand passing heaped plates around the table, my eyes are fixed on her frilled cuff, trying to discern whether it is the flickering of the gaslight that is playing tricks or if she really has taken to trembling at the same time each evening.

Rebecca told me once that I am like a bridge between the past and the future. That was a long time ago when the future seemed vast, especially to Rebecca, who was little more than a child at the time. Now it is the past that is vast and the future is growing narrower and narrower. There is a bridge I like on a river not far from here, low-slung, not very wide, but I like its proportions, the gentle rise and fall of its profile. I especially like it at night when it is lit from the bottom, so that its slender lines attain a depth it does not have in daylight, a subterfuge. Like the word 'Mother'. Like Ally.

My God, where did that thought spring from? *In vino veritas* – something I never believed in before. Sometimes I think that she stopped being a mother when Papa left in 1914. It seemed that she shed the whole burden of motherhood with a tiny shrug of her shoulders, dislodging the weight of responsibility in an imperceptible turning away, so slight as to leave hidden the immensity of what was cast aside. It was only after Esmee's death that Mama began to move to a central position in the family again. But by then we were adults, living in Dublin, the boys already leaving home. The lives that emanated from her, the sons who would go to war almost a quarter of a century later, the daughter who would marry and bear sons and a daughter, and the will to believe, to fight and to die that had sprung from her were all set aside in a sigh, a shrug in Queenstown. In that instant she was already, unknowingly, reaching for M. Ally the mother slowly ceasing to mother, leaving Lucinda unable to mother. At least that is what Rebecca would like to believe. And there lies the crux of this dilemma. Rebecca is afraid, afraid that when she has her child that she too will become the opposite of nurturing, just like her mother and her grandmother. Was I also afraid, perhaps? Is this why I never married?

What nonsense this is. Listening to Rebecca has made me think that life is simple, full of solutions to problems if only we can pose the right questions. But I want things to be simple at this stage of my life. I'm too old to deal with complexity.

How my encounter with the doctor this afternoon could have lead to all this, I can't imagine. I must let Mama speak for herself. But where did I put the diaries?

Ally, my love,

This is a rushed note, as I am thinking of you and wanted
to let you know, even though it is 4.00 in the morning. I
am surrounded by inky blackness with only the flickering
of one small paraffin lantern to light the gloom. It is
difficult to sleep here, with camp beds that are too narrow
and the snoring of men close by. But I manage.

You asked me in your last letter to tell you a little
about France. Ally, believe me, there is no news or at least
none that I could possibly share with you from France, for
there is too much gloom abroad here and I'm afraid that
if I put words on it I too shall become infected with it.
The melancholia that besets men here is worse than most
other things that might befall us, for it gets in the way of
doing the job we are here to do, preventing us taking the
best possible care of ourselves and each other, making men
careless, almost as if defying death. But sometimes, Ally, I
think I understand it. And underneath it all is this huge
longing for home, for our loved ones. I think of you,
often, and of the children, especially in the quiet times.
But it is an indulgence which I cannot allow myself for
long and so I can only dwell there briefly with you and
then move on.

That is what I seem to do here more than anything else
– move on. In my thoughts, my words, my hopes. I
cannot believe that where we are and what we are doing
is real and so I play this little game where I constantly
rearrange where I am, what I am doing, so that I can

believe, even briefly, that this has passed, that I am
somewhere in the future. But, of course, we physically
move on too, every few weeks, but where we move to I
cannot tell you, because this letter, like all my letters, will
be censored. We have moved a little way south now,
although we still remain close to the capital. And in our
own way we have organised what could be loosely
described as a daily routine, so that we have quickly come
to accept it as normal, from one hour to the next, until,
that is, something happens to show us the sheer,
outrageous abnormality of it all. And beneath the routine
that unites us all in this godforsaken place, there is a layer
that marks us out as Irishmen and Englishmen, Ulstermen
and Orangemen, and who knows how many others, and
beneath that layer again we are all men, alone, struggling
to survive. And when the truly horrible fact of war
intervenes without warning, that is what is revealed, that
single uniting thread. Believe me, Ally, the humanity that
lies hidden within is what I try to hold on to, to retain the
flashes of it I see around me in this sea of inhumanity.

   You can tell from what I have written that it is the
hour before dawn, the hour when we lose our bearings,
when we begin to drift. It is not my usual style, you'll
admit, Ally dear. And I started out to try to cheer you up,
as you sounded in your last letter as if that is what you
needed. And I truly understand how difficult it must be to
keep the children fed and clothed and happy and that my
salary does not always arrive on the expected date. But the
children sound happy and healthy. You said that William
has forsaken the boats for the local drama group. What a
strange volte-face that is for him. But perhaps not. You
said he is involved in a Yeats play. Yeats can be

dangerous, full of transformations and death. Dangerous sentiments, Ally, requiring careful watching where William is concerned. It has always been difficult to know what goes on in his head. How is my funny, sensitive, wise-before-her-time Helena? I hope all is well with her.

You did not speak about your health. I hope you are taking good care of yourself, especially in these last few months, and that you take any opportunity you can to rest. You are fortunate to have Mrs O'Sullivan there with you. She is truly a gift. Please give her my regards. The thought of a new baby coming to bless our home is something I think about in the quietness of the night. And I think then back to those brief January days when we were last together, such a long time ago it seems, such a different world to the one we occupy now, apart.

This letter has wandered a little and is not the cheerful note that I set out to write. Please take care of yourself and the children. I think of you all with a great yearning.

> With my eternal love,
> Richard

That was Papa's last letter to Mama. Well, it was probably not his last letter to Mama – for he lived through the horror for another twenty-one months, until May 1917 – but it was the last remaining letter in the box. Heaven alone knows what happened to the rest of them. It was also the last letter remaining before Lucinda was born. And of course the absence leaves a gap that is hugely significant for Rebecca.

'Perhaps she told him about M in one of her letters. It is possible that she was so overwrought that she could not contain herself and unburdened herself to him at that late stage in the pregnancy.' Rebecca herself was sounding seriously overwrought as she spoke.

And in trying to placate her, I wondered why the irony did not strike her. Dear me, how confusing life has become. But I am relieved in a way that there are no further letters, for, truly, I do not want to know any more. The waif-like creature that was Mama for me was someone I loved dearly even as I strived to know her. And that was fine by me. Still is. But to accept her now as someone who stepped outside her own time, who stepped so far outside it as to conceive a child by her stepbrother, is not fine by me at all. There are some things that even at this advanced stage of my life I cannot be asked to contemplate. And Rebecca of all people should understand that.

And yet it has all been deeply frustrating for Rebecca as she twists and turns in her efforts to work out what transpired between them, about the unreality of the situation for Mama that was pushing her towards a disclosure. Poor Rebecca, so close and yet so far. In her agonising over this, she displays the imagination of a serial fiction writer of romantic melodrama. She has conveniently shelved her objectivity in her rush to wrap up the story, tie up the ends. I want to tell her that life is messy, snarled and tangled on barbs, but instead I leave her to her headlong flight to shape and reshape her imprint. Perhaps she will come to her senses when her own pregnancy is over. Meantime, I shall leave her to it. I am far too tired to begin another chapter in her project.

But what I did expect her to ask me, and what she has bypassed with a constancy that is breathtaking, is the event of Lucinda's birth. Fatherhood, or the specific father, is of the essence for Rebecca in Lucinda's story, so that her arrival and the actuality of her early years is of no interest to her at all. But I made up my mind to tell her, slipping little details into her consciousness at unlikely moments, or even likely moments, until Lucinda's arrival became a reality for her.

'She was such a joyful little baby, Rebecca, forever

squealing as if at some baby joke, her little arms and legs jigging up and down in rhythm with her exuberance.'

Rebecca would look away as I told her these snippets, never saying a word or indicating that she had heard what I said. But I am continuing to drip-feed her these inconsequential pictures of her mother's early life, a picture unburdened by M or questions of her origin, merely the tiny rhythms of an emerging life in stuttering, shuddering bursts, while Mama struggled, with Mrs O in the background, in an incessant battle with her demons.

Not that I remember much about Lucinda's arrival. Except, that is, for her birth, which is still marked for me by the plaintive sound of Mama's voice drifting like fine ether from her bedroom. One day Lucinda was not there and the next day she was. Mrs O kept us firmly at arm's length in the last few weeks, insisting that Mama needed her rest, that we must remain playing quietly out of doors whenever possible. And yet it seems that Lucinda was always there. Our lives were arranged around her for so many weeks and months prior to her birth that she had long become a tangible presence. She existed somewhere between the bottom of the stairs and the inner reaches of Mama's room, a small, elusive bubble that seemed to bounce slightly ahead of Mrs O, as she shooed us out to play, waving her hand like a large white plate in the direction of the stairs, as if directing the bubble upwards to the specially reserved space above.

And when she finally arrived, things were pretty much as they had been for a long time now, with the same whispers and stifled sighs, the resting periods allotted to Mama by Mrs O and the long period of subdued murmurings behind the closed bedroom door. And sometimes when I caught a glimpse of Mama without her noticing, she appeared to shake and shudder, sometimes her arms, sometimes her whole body, with Mrs O constantly in attendance, trying to restrain her by wrapping her shawl tightly around her, and I was reminded of a binding cloth that swaddled the baby in the Christmas crib.

And the anecdotes that I fed and continue to feed to Rebecca are embellished or invented for the most part, setting normality against her fantasies – that is all that I am doing, really, rewriting the story a little to offset her needs and expectations, which are way beyond my knowledge or understanding. And I have not told her of my glimpses of Mama, pale and shaking, or reclining on the sofa when she eventually reappeared downstairs, looking as if she had no bones in her body, as if her flesh was taking up the shape of the sofa, seeming to flow over its edge and droop towards the floor in a languid sweep that made me wonder what held her, preventing her from sliding those last few inches. Yet sometimes I have wanted to shake Rebecca, reveal Mama's suffering to her in one great gasp, tell her to drop her silly theories about Mama's life and her needs and satisfactions and see it all as one bleak, individual struggle that we can never really know. But I don't do this. Instead, I have left her to move deeper into the quagmire she has chosen and shaped for herself, in the belief that she will tire of the project, or because I am a coward and want to avoid the confrontation. And deep down there is the hope that her pregnancy will generate some affinity with Mama and Lucinda. But that may be the naive hope of an old woman who never once carried a child.

17 August 1915

I wrote to Mother today and reminded her that our new
baby is due in October. It is such a long time since last she
wrote but I expect she is very busy with her family.
Perhaps she has someone to help her in the house but she
has never told me. She tells me so little in her infrequent
letters. But I do hope that she has someone like Mrs O,
who is such a staunch helper and friend, especially since
Richard returned to France. Mother would like her, I'm
sure, and appreciate her sincerity and caring nature.

I asked her to come to Queenstown soon to visit.
Perhaps it will cause her to worry, but I told her how
lonely it is here as we contemplate our second winter
without Richard. But of course she will understand this,
coming as it does from the heart. It is not easy to relate
much of what is in my heart in a letter to her. I wish that
we could sit by the fire together and talk once more, the
way we did when I was a child. It all seems such a long
time ago.

If she can manage a visit, she would get to know the
children. I know she would love them, with all their
funny little ways, even William's increasing awkwardness.
I asked after Bart — as well as the rest of the family. One
short letter is all I have had from him since I wrote telling
him about my condition. I do hope that all is well with
him. But I expect that he too is busy with his work.

Perhaps Mother will come to Queenstown in October.
Sometimes the thought of another child overwhelms me
but it will pass. It is this exhaustion which is making me
disconsolate. A good night's sleep may help.

My dear Ally,

It was so good of you to write – but such a strange letter.
You sound a little down in yourself, dear. You must cheer
up, at least for the sake of the new baby.

I am afraid a trip to Queenstown is out of the question
at present and indeed for the forseeable future. Charles is
involved in some scheme to establish a residency associated
with a new school in the midlands which takes up large
amounts of his spare time. It's a scheme to allow the heads
of departments to live alongside the school. I don't really
understand why they can't have homes of their own. He
does not complain, of course. He has always been happy
to give generously of his time for worthy causes. As a
member of the Board of Governors, he meets interesting
and useful people.

Bart told me that you were pale and tired during his
visit in January. He was also concerned about a slight
tremor which he detected in your hand. I hope that it was
merely tiredness and that you are not succumbing to some
nervous condition. There has been no history of nervous
complaints in this family. I do hope that Bart imagined it.
Besides, Bart may have been confusing things, as he has
not referred to the fact that you are with child. I was
unsure if you had told him in your letter and so I have
said nothing. But he has been away from home in recent
months, travelling to rural towns in the course of his
work and when he is home he seems tired and distracted.
Goodness, everyone around me seems tired and strained

these days. Perhaps it is the weather and anxiety about this awful war.

Please take good care of yourself, Ally, and give my love to the children. They sound like such dears, but do be firm with them. They miss a father's hand you know.

Mother

Mrs O took me with her to the grocer's shop on the corner, below the Admiralty building. Deep carmine paint was laid thickly on all of the outside timberwork, with the name of the owner painted above the window in bold gilt lettering, the Gaelic script outlining the name, one that Mama could not read but whose baroque curliques she had always admired.

Inside the shop the high mahogany counters made comfortable armrests for the shopowner, popularly known as Thady, although Thaddaeus was the name above the window. Mrs O had placed her basket to one side of her as she leaned on the counter, slightly breathless after the short walk, her broad rump protruding as she bent forward.

'It was this day a year ago that poor Pope Pius died, may he rest in peace.'

'In the name of God, woman, what made you think of that right now?' said Thady.

'Well, it happened the day after Sean's birthday. I suppose I'll always remember it, the two of them coming so close together.'

Thady gave her a long look and then winked openly at me as I began to move slowly around the shop, past tall timber shelves stacked with jars and boxes, the faded blues and greens and yellows and reds of their labels receding into the shadows. Tall sweet jars stood at either end of the shelves and in between lay the short squat glass containers full of hard-boiled sweets, their jewel colours belying their nondescript tastes. Behind me, Mrs O and Thady talked on about the Pope's death and the war, their tones lowering out of deference to me, whose father was fighting in France. I was accustomed to this by then, expected it as my due somehow. It filled me with a vague sense of self-importance, set me apart – this covert attention paid to me over the past year by the adults beyond my home.

'It's a year since they left, a whole year. Hard to imagine. And who would have thought that it would last this long? And they're looking for more volunteers.' Mrs O frowned as she spoke.

'Ah, sure you'd have to be mad to volunteer for that.' Thady drew Mrs O's basket towards him as he spoke and I watched, wondering would he slip his arm through the handle the way Mrs O did, as if it were part of her dressing routine.

'Oh, I don't know. My son Sean said that it might be time for people to get their experience at someone else's expense and then come back here and secure a future for this country.'

'And what might be meaning by that, Mrs O'Sullivan?'

Mrs O shifted her bulk away from the counter before continuing, her voice suddenly wavering and unsure. 'I suppose it is something to do with running our own affairs, Thady.'

'And you know what comes before that, don't you?' he replied. 'Securing our freedom, that's what. And are we prepared to do what is required of us, that's what I'd like to know? We are all talk in this country, always have been. And we should know by now how cheap talk is.'

Mrs O grasped the handle of her basket and I thought for a moment that she was going to take it and leave the shop.

'Well, you had better let me have the eggs then, Thady, and I'll leave you with this list. Maybe you could send the boy over this afternoon with the rest of the goods.'

With a hint of a smile, he took the list and stood reading it slowly, so slowly that I understood that he was letting her know that they were both in the business of serving others, that he would do her bidding in his own time. He raised his head then and looked to where I was standing at the end of the counter, turning over some balls of wool in a large, unplaned timber box.

'Mrs Galvin isn't too good today,' Mrs O whispered to Thady. 'A bit down in herself, so I don't want to be away for too long. You know how it is.' She sounded deferential, had understood his smile. Out of the corner of my eye I watched her withdraw again, tugging her dark navy and green shawl up further on her shoulders, shrugging as she did so.

'It must be an endless worry for the poor woman,' Thady said stiffly, 'but then, that is the side she chose to be on, isn't it?'

And Mrs O remained silent. Then catching sight of me as I fingered the wools, she asked gruffly if I would like some wool and without waiting for an answer she took up two balls, one red and one blue and said, 'We'll take these. You can put them on the bill.' She dropped them into her basket and almost in the same movement she grasped my arm and steered me quickly towards the door.

'Mind how you go now, Mrs O'Sullivan,' Thady called out in his ringing lilt as the door swung to, the dull heavy clang of the bell sounding behind us.

'I suppose he thought I should buy a white ball of wool as well,' she said angrily into the air as she reached blindly downwards for my hand.

She was right of course about Mama. She was not herself. And Thady's remark about her choosing the side she was on was not fully comprehensible to me and yet I had a sense of what he meant and that it had something to do with both Papa and Sean. Local women, whose sons, but not many of whose husbands, had volunteered, whose plight on the face of it was similar to Mama's, lived a life like hers, reduced to an ever-narrowing focus on inaccurate war reports, an escaped breath as the postman passed by or when a knock at the door was of no import and their heart rate slowly returned to normal, until the cycle began again. These were the women who should have huddled together with her on the street corners and in their kitchens in their common anguish, consoled each other with each day that passed, leaving them unscathed. But instead they bade Mama the time of day, weathery comments hurriedly exchanged, a flickering glance across her face in a shadowy scrutiny of her condition, of her ability to contain this, as if she had been granted a wisdom not available to them. A momentary communion of hearts that had moved them beyond words receded and they closed in on themselves once more. In this way she was reminded daily that she belonged with the others, with the professional army families, with the Thursday wives.

'It's very confusing, Mrs O,' Mama said one day. 'People seem to have closed off from me. Do you think perhaps that I am imagining it?'

She had come in from her walk along the seafront, her usually pale cheeks whipped a pink that was tinged with blue towards her temples, her nose looking narrower than usual.

'I don't really know, ma'am. Why would they want to do that?'

And Mrs O herself seemed to shrink, her large arms clasped across her chest, drawing herself in, closing herself off.

'I think they believe that in some vague way I am to blame for their grief and their loneliness. Do you know, Mrs O, sometimes they look at me as if they hate me.'

Mama looked distractedly across the kitchen at us, scattered at various activities around the room, seeing us as if we were somehow out of place there, then switched her gaze back to Mrs O. She was beyond caring about what she discussed in front of us by then and Mrs O, in her urge to support Mama, had begun to ease back in her concern to protect us from what we might overhear.

'Hardly that, ma'am. It's probably more to do with confusion. They don't understand the war, you see, no more than I do myself. They think that the likes of your husband – begging your pardon, ma'am, your husband being a full-time soldier and all, joining up of his own

accord when he wasn't really required to all those years ago
— they think that's odd, they think that soldiers like him
wanted this war, in a way. They think that this is what
their lives were all about all these years, that it is what
they have trained for all this time. And they know it was
different for their sons, that they were caught up in
something they did not understand, something that has
nothing to do with them. I think that they might be a bit
afraid, ma'am.' Mrs O's face had coloured with the exertion
of her explanation, appearing faintly surprised at the extent
of her insight.

'Afraid? You mean afraid for their sons.'

'Well, yes, but they fear for themselves too. It's the
Home-Rulers, you see.' And this time Mrs O lowered her
voice and looked towards where we played in the corner of
the kitchen. Then she rearranged a chair noisily beneath the
kitchen table so that the legs rasped and scraped across the
uneven tiles, as if this might obliterate what she had said or
hide what Mama might say next.

'I see. And do you believe that is how it is, Mrs O?'

'I'm a bit confused, ma'am, if the truth be known. We
don't talk about it much at home, with Sean having such
strong feelings about things. And I don't want to cause any
upset. I shouldn't even be mentioning this to you. I'm sorry,
ma'am.'

'I'm glad you did, Mrs O. I would really like to hear more
about Sean and what he thinks about what is happening.'

'No, you wouldn't really, ma'am. Sean is a bit difficult,
always has been. If his father had taken a firmer hand with
him, it might have been different. But we let him get away
from us, if you know what I mean, and now it is too late.
But ma'am, you must be careful. Sean fills young William's

head with a lot of nonsense, with things that I don't understand. That's all I will say, ma'am. I'm sorry.'

Mist shifts slowly across the harbour, adrift in its own energy. No wind, nothing but this murky veil. Mama is associated for me now with veils, opacity, when I conjure up that period of her life.

Her pregnancy seemed incidental to her existence. She drifted aimlessly, moving through her days thoughtlessly, Mrs O occasionally realigning her, like a watchful guide dog. She never seemed to notice, steadying herself through her days around her walks along the seafront and her Thursday trips uphill to meet the wives. As Benjie seldom came to visit now, I had nobody to accompany me and so I had stopped following her in that purposeful way that Benjie and I had developed over the previous year. But I had become cleverer. I would watch from the window as she bent into the wind, the sea spray threatening to drench her as she moved resolutely along by the rail, past the bandstand, unused since the army band had moved out with the troops, its ornate dome congealed with the droppings of seabirds as they crisscrossed in a crazed flight pattern, distracting my watchful gaze. And when I could see her no more, I turned towards her room, for this was where I believed I could reach her, now that she was beyond all reaching. But this was not a childish hunt for evidence that might tell me something about her, for I knew that nothing material could help me there. It was her very essence that I sought but could not put into childish words. And I knew it lay there, somewhere in her room, in the air, in the scent that lingered on her clothes, in the slightly damp sea smell that crept in under the casement window, the acrid stinging sensation that rose at me from the base of the wardrobe, the scent of camphor from her blanket chest brought from the East by Papa's father. They combined into a tangible presence that I believed I could see as a faint haze that came and went in the prevailing draughts in the room, that I had come to believe was a living wraith that had swept out of Mama as she distanced herself from us and had settled itself in this room like the good genie in my childhood storybook.

And each time when she returned from her walk, revitalised, it seemed to me, I thought, now it will happen, now the spirit will re-enter her, now she will become whole again. And on her re-entry from her walk or from her Thursday meeting, she was more upright, walked lightly, floating almost, going immediately to her room. And each time as I watched I thought, now, now it will happen, if she goes now to her room, if she goes quickly now to her room, if she remains there a little while, long enough, it will happen, if she is willing, then the wraith, the essence, the genie, will re-enter her and she will be our own dear Mama again.

Mrs O watched on these occasions too. Sometimes she followed Mama upstairs and I knew then that this was one of the bad days, because I knew it would not happen, and I thought that Mrs O was interfering and would upset the wraith, get in the way of its re-entry, in a way I could not clearly define. These were the only occasions when I came close to being angry with Mrs O. But Mrs O seemed propelled by a mission of her own, speaking behind the closed bedroom door to Mama, low urgent tones reaching the door but inaudible beyond it, urging, pleading tones from Mrs O. And there was an occasional brief response from Mama that sounded to me like a closing-of-a-door sort of sound, so that she was on one side and Mrs O on the other. And on those days I knew that the wraith was nowhere to be seen, that it had become separated into its individual strands, was now only a collection of smells lurking in separate corners of the room, awaiting the first opening of the window to dispel them. On those days there was nothing, nothing.

There was something else that I began to notice then. Mama began to talk strangely, as if her thoughts had become scrambled. She developed little fixations which we children found amusing, in the insensitive way that children do. She became fascinated by shapes, seeing shapes in the most unlikely places, constantly drawing our attention to them, wanting to talk to us about them. Sometimes she would approach complete strangers in the street and embark on a lengthy discussion of the qualities of a spreading shadow across the path or the shape of a leafless tree silhouetted against the sky. She considered the shapes and the density of shadows, whether it was possible to see through them, how they became lighter the further out from the object the eye moved and how the shadow became more or less elongated depending on the direction of the light. She loved to reach out and touch an object whose shape had fixed her gaze, testing as if to see if it existed in space or was a figment of her imagination, withdrawing her hand quickly in wonder as she encountered solidity, texture, coldness. Once, as her fingers slid down the bulbous shape of a glass bud vase, she looked upset and muttered, 'Just like a tear, its shape is just like a tear.'

After a while, we children became bored by this behaviour, once we had learnt to cope with the embarrassment. We learnt quickly how to detect the onset of her latest, newest fixation, the sudden alighting of her gaze on an object or a shadow, a relaxation in her stance as she gave it her attention, as she began leaving us again, her lips apart in tiny inaudible murmurings we were never intended to hear and yet I never gave up in my effort to detect a clue as to that place to which she had drifted.

But even then, I suspected that the clue to her condition lay in the big Chinese box, among the letters and diaries and jottings of an occasional journal. It was this tangible jumble that seemed to concentrate her thoughts and came to be the focus of mine. And I know that Mrs O too held the contents of the box in some special regard and it became the subject of urgings and pleadings that seeped their way beneath the closed bedroom door.

But it is not quite true to say that I never followed her again to the wives' meeting on Thursdays. True, Benjie and I had moved apart but there was one occasion when I did follow her. It was early September, a misty Thursday, late in the afternoon, and her last outing before her confinement. The sight of her moving awkwardly into the mist gave me a pang of anxiety. Without pausing to consider, I rushed out of the house and up the steep hill to the houses that looked more precariously balanced than ever in the mist, which deprived them of any obvious supports of steps or railings. This time it was not curiosity that held me there but the need to protect her. Nothing, I believed, could happen to her as long as I waited and watched. The mist lay like a veil before the house, the blinds had not been pulled down nor the curtains drawn, as if the occupants believed they were already screened by the mist beyond the window. There was a mantle of droplets on every surface and as I leaned against the lamppost I felt the moisture penetrate my clothes. It settled on my hair, and around me it muffled sound and stopped the very air from moving. I tried to breathe with my mouth closed, remembering Mrs O's admonitions to me about vapours and chills.

And then I looked up and saw them dancing, two or three of them to begin, waving their bodies slowly from side to side, shadows undulating on the wall behind them as they waved fragile fabrics above their heads, russets and pale golds, ochres and burgundies, glinting in the candlelight. I watched, enthralled as more figures arose from the edges of the room and joined in the weaving sensuous motion, passing the scarves from one to the other, heads back, eyes closed. I tried to see Mama but could not, yet I knew that she was in there somewhere. The room became more charged with colour that whirled streaks of warmth at me through the mist. And still I could not see her, stretching upwards as far as possible on toes stiffened with the damp cold. Then suddenly she was there to one side of the dancers, her ungainly pregnant shape standing awkwardly beside the mantelpiece, one arm supporting her, the other hand resting lightly beside the Chinese box, which lay on a side table against the wall. The box was open and as one of her friends danced gaily past her she threw her head back and said something over her shoulder to Mama, a laughing, coaxing, foxy look on her face, as she gesticulated with her hands entwined in a scarf towards the box. Lucinda's inheritance. Poor Lucinda, not yet born, yet present at the exotic scene in this Aladdin's cave. Even then I understood

that these bereft women, who could not grasp the chaotic
times in which they found themselves, were managing
their grief and loneliness in the one way that allowed them
to forget.

They sent for Mrs O shortly after Mama dropped from my
sight and the window was filled once more with colour and
movement, no longer fluid, but jerky, twisting and
bending, then sudden straightening, like puppets whose
strings had suddenly been pulled too taut by a vengeful
puppet master. I saw them place her in an armchair, aware
that my watching had been insufficient to protect her, that
perhaps my attention had wandered at some point, so that
she had slipped down beneath my view, like a naughty
child evading a parent.

Mrs O emerged into the mist with Mama, upright, stiff,
staring at the roofline of the houses further down the hill,
like a naval pilot taking a bearing from a star. I fell into step
behind them as they moved slowly down the hill, Mrs O
casting a quick glance behind her, nodding to me, then
moving ahead, her hand firmly placed beneath Mama's
elbow as they walked.

Without turning her head, Mama began to talk in a clear,
low voice, her unusual accent, which had always placed my
friends in awe of her, floating its cadences back to me like
summer grass on the wind. 'Pigs! Pigs! Pigs! Pigs for
consignment to this place and that place. Half a page in the
paper yesterday, half a page, addressed exclusively to pig
feeders in this country, to pig feeders and pig men! Going
to war on bacon. Is that it, then? And how, pray tell, do
they intend satisfying their thirst? Bacon and cabbage. Do

they never tire of it? And here's one for you. Last week there was an item making the case for allowing pigs to graze on open spaces, stating that the pig is by nature a grazing animal. Are we to have them wandering abroad like Indian sacred cows?'

Mrs O looked back bleakly at me once or twice during this tirade, while Mama looked directly ahead.

'What use will bacon and cabbage be to any of them? The women's emergency committee is stretched to the limit preparing supplies of bandages, arranging nursing classes, needlework groups, opening subscription lists. That is what we need. Not pigs. Definitely not pigs.'

It was this episode which marked Mama's confinement, enforced, I believe, by Mrs O. She lay on the green chaise longue beneath the window in the drawing room, where Mrs O had arranged it at a slight angle to the window so that she could see the comings and goings along the seafront and across the harbour. It was as if her last energy had been expended on that walk downhill and all her distracted talk of pigs and bacon. She lay there without talking, barely discernible in the shadowy autumn light that stirred occasionally above the harbour, casting damp pools on the granite sill beyond the window. When we enquired of Mrs O why she lay there all the time, why she didn't speak to us or even notice us, Mrs O would place her fingers on her lips and say, 'Sssh, 'twill be her time soon, that's all, 'twill be her time soon.' And the sun, which was moving further into the southeast each evening, seeming to bend the horizon in an ever tautening bow, sent a shimmer across the dark timber of the table and flared briefly in the large mirror on the wall so that Mama looked, in her reflection, like a firefly, her body bathed in flames, her pale blond head as if newly carved in ice. It was then I knew how she felt when she danced with the wives on Thursdays. I also knew then, although I could not put a name to it, that she was addicted to M.

30 September 1915

My head is full of colour now. So much colour, the colours of India. Perhaps I can write it out of me, it is too much to contain.

My father died in India, not really in India, but on his way home from there. He left all those rich colours behind, all those russets and golds and ochres and burgundies – spice colours – he left them behind him in India and then he died. Buried among exotic fish in a far-off ocean, in a box that sank like a stone, Asian hardwood and heavy at that. Not like this box. Chinese lacquer, light as a feather, balsawood, the wood of the peasants, so light it would float. Like me now. Floating. Its contents keep me afloat. Like my friends this afternoon. They too were floating. But they are not earth-bound like me, heavy, gourd-like, giant spice-pod ready to split open. Yet I do not smell of spice. M carries no smell but an exotic sensation that causes me to inhale as if I cannot have enough, snuffing desperately for this indefinable scent of hard Asian woods, jungle foliage, burning rainforest smells of rot and decay rising from a forest floor. Dancing birds, wings spreading around them, brushing past me, anchored in this place while they soar. The colours of heat. A non-white. No white of snow or blue of ice here. No frozen ridges capable of holding sledges and dogs and boats and men locked fast or falling backwards in their own tracks as they struggle for a toehold. It seems that Shackleton has been caught up in one long attempt to gain a hold in the ice since the year of my marriage. The first year of the century. Bright, hopeful dawning, all glorious promise and sparkling new life. Off with the old. No more falling

backwards, only an endless march forward, as Richard
says. Always forward. White mud. Black ice.
Boots. Toeholds. Falling backwards once more. Like me.
'Staggering from pillar to post', as Mrs O might say of a
local drunk. Pillar to post. Richard, Bart, M. One post
too many. Fallen, lying instead as a crossbeam, jamming
the door, keeping me prisoner within. Like my child.
Prisoner within, kicking, weighing me down, oppressing,
pushing ever downwards, unbearable weight, so that my
knees have become like melting ice or rigid stalactites that
have dripped away from beneath me, icy ripples that bend
and arch, pillars of ice, and me, like an icicle at the mouth
of Scheherezade's cave, dripping into non-existence
in this . . .

This is becoming a habit, not taking my coffee with the others, pretending fatigue – such a vague, wimpish excuse – remaining here at my window, watching the mountains through the flickering birch leaves. Like tiny emeralds spraying outwards from a broken necklace. Rebecca was right to insist on this room for me. I can sit here for hours, seeing and yet not seeing, the glassy flash of canal, the tall, cylindrical shapes of apartment blocks, oblong windows wedged throughout their length and the occasional drooping clothesline draping a balcony. Distant roofs are visible in greys and slate blue, as if a painter, wanting to create distance, had slathered a mixture of smoky blues indiscriminately, so that they might blend into the foothills beyond. Here, in this room, I have begun to replace the soft furnishings in my mind with starker pieces, against my newly encroaching germ-free future – metallic finishes whose wipe-clean surfaces gleam dully, visible spaces beneath betraying any lurking dust. 'Slut's wool', May continues to call it, even though I have long since ceased to laugh, yet still I conjure up a picture of a diminutive unwashed woman, spinning and knitting frantically beneath the bed. It is, after all, the sort of furniture that one associates with clinics and patients.

'You're not a patient, Helena, you're a resident. And stop feeling sorry for yourself. The doctor said that you can go once every couple of weeks for your chemotherapy to the hospital and then you can come back here immediately. Sure this is a great place for a rest. And that's what he said you will need after each session, a few days of good rest. And can't we all make sure that you get that at least? If we can't do that here, what good are we?'

This is different to the way she used to handle James's complaints and hypochondria, before he became really ill. There are no epic stories of illness and death to be told now. May knows better than that and I can tell that she is upset, the way she continues talking and sweeping at the same time, not using conversation as an excuse to sit down as she usually does. Suddenly all those acquaintances of hers who succumbed to a variety of tumours are crowding at the window behind her, jostling to remind her of their presence. But May is moving forwards fast, into some place she has not yet formulated, some tight narrow ledge that needs to provide some space for us both, that will somehow prevent us from looking backwards or downwards towards those beckoning stories. But I have already moved ahead of her, continuing to redesign my space. I have even begun to furnish it with sounds. The sibilant sliding of metal on metal, the finite clink of a side-rail clicking into place on a bed-frame, locking into its groove the better to contain a patient. I am perilously close to imagining death agonies here. Better watch it. May's doing. I am jumping the gun, as she might say.

'This does not have to be a terminal condition,' Dr Brady had said a few hours earlier. 'The chemotherapy will already have begun to reduce the tumour and may well eliminate it altogether. Let's be optimistic here, Helena, OK?'

And of course I said that I was optimistic, played along, smiled in acquiescence. He knew all about playing along, a rugby player until injury forced him onto the tennis court. But he is still good at assessing a situation at speed, adept at keeping the big picture in his head – positions, tactics, how to duck and dodge and weave. But beneath that tough exterior, how did he accommodate the uncertainties of living? From what I know about his life, he was confused by it. Confused not so much by his own life as by the act of living a life. Sometimes I thought I could see it coming at him like a rugby ball, hurtling unexpectedly from a strange angle, knocking the wind out of him before bouncing back into play. Every so often life seemed to catch him unawares, losing him his first wife to a rugby-playing lawyer, shedding his ambition for a private consultancy, letting it slip away from him like a gradual hair loss, waking up one day to discover it was irretrievably gone.

'Pain, doctor. It is a well-kept secret, but I am a hopeless coward where physical pain is concerned.'

'Now why would you want to talk about pain, Helena?'

And I fought down the usual terror, the child's voice that I fear and have always feared, the one that might escape and protest in its high tremor of petulance that it wants the pain to go away, please make it go away. It is the voice I heard from Mama's room when she was giving birth to Lucinda and which Mrs O tried to quell with sounds of water clattering into delft bowls and coals thrown into the small October fire in her bedroom. And I heard my adult voice speaking and it had a tremor that I could not control.

'I must be realistic, doctor, that is why I am telling you what a coward I am. I need to prepare for all eventualities.'

'I see. Yes, of course. Well normally I would not be talking about this with a patient at this early stage, but if you insist, Helena . . .'

'Yes, I do.'

He smiled at me, a tiny amused smile that says at once 'trust me', that says he is very comfortable with all this, that he is on familiar ground, that he will somehow enjoy hearing himself soothe me with his talk.

'Well, pain management is very sophisticated now, you know. And it is possible for a patient to self-administer pain-killing drugs at the push of a little switch.'

I heard him say 'a little switch', as if I were eavesdropping in the next room and he was talking to an electrician about some useful device that will raise the temperature of the heating system or turn on a fan when the room becomes stuffy.

'Did you say a switch, doctor?'

'Yes, a little hand-held device that allows you take control of your medication yourself.'

As if taking control is a good idea, as if taking control is something he has just thought up himself for the first time. At least he did not use the word 'empower', although he might have done if Rebecca were here. A small mercy. And he looked pleased.

'What sort of medication are you talking about?'

'Oh, morphine, probably. It's nearly always morphine now.'

It's nearly always morphine. Always morphine. Yes, of course. Morphine, opium derivative, what the addicts used to call snow, the languidity of snow birds, blown off course, caught up in an alien flock, separating out to follow strange ships aimlessly in a southern ocean. Snow. Always snow.

'You look puzzled, Helena, is there something else on your mind?'

'No, doctor, I was just thinking about snow birds, that's all.' I smiled and he was unsure if I was deliberately trying to mislead or lighten things or if he had perhaps misheard me. And then I sighed deeply, the better to dispel the iciness of the image. 'It all seems so strange, all this new technology that I never knew was there.'

'Think yourself lucky, that you never needed it before now. Just be glad it's there now that you need it.'

And he continued to talk about his plans for me as if he were planning a holiday, one which he was having to work hard at in order to get me to enthuse over, as he plotted later scans to check on the progress of my tumour, as if it were travelling overland to some far-flung place to join me there at some later date.

'Have you any further questions, Helena?'

I heard him dimly and said no, not for the moment. An overwhelming tiredness swept over me and I wanted to be alone. I was unable to sleep after he left but slipped eventually into a fitful doze that did nothing to refresh me. And God knows, I need to be bright and breezy when Rebecca arrives. I'll have to bring her up to date on all of this, before she notices May's heightened sense of vigilance on my behalf. Things are strained enough between them without letting May feel that she has the edge over Rebecca for a few hours of hogging information to herself.

Everything is taking on the sense of being second-hand. I feel as if my life has moved into some new place, lodged between truth and fiction, like a photograph. No doubt that has something to do with all this talk about X-rays and scans. Rebecca is due to have a scan any day now. She told me but I have forgotten when. Such a different experience to mine, thankfully, yet each of our images caught in the same innocuous black and white. Black and white. Non-colours of chic style. And what has style got to do with birth and death? Imprints of an entry and an exit.

Perhaps style is relevant after all. Sepia. Now there's a tint with style if ever there was one. Bart's photograph of himself which he sent to Mama shortly after his visit. Was it faded when he sent it or did that happen over time? I have always presumed that those old photos were always sepia, that somehow the chemicals were inadequate to the job. But perhaps they were adequate after all, pushing us rightly into that second-hand view of things, where everything is filtered down the years, letting us know gently that this was closer to our imaginings of events than we might like to believe, the closest we would ever get. Rebecca must have seen that photograph of Bart, the one on which he wrote, 'Please, for my sake, give up M'. But she is overdue: I have lost all track of time.

And now she is here, looking paler than usual, talking rapidly about the traffic and rude drivers as we move into our settling-in ritual, taking us through the early minutes in a series of neat sidesteps, quietly taking stock of each other's vulnerabilities, which seem to mount with each passing year.

'Helena, I have just now been talking with Dr Brady.'

I detect an admonition in her voice, as I resist feeling that she has found me out in something.

'Really? He is a kind man. He was here a couple of hours ago.' I begin my deflection, light-hearted, breezy, talking him out of the picture.

'Yes, I know, he told me. He told me everything.'

Everything. The admonitory tone is gone now, replaced by a tiny waver and I wonder if her chin is quivering as I watch doggedly the shadows of the leaves on the windowsill moving gracefully into their own autumn. Suddenly the shadows vanish as the sky clears and I remember the garden in the sanatorium further south, on the outskirts of a coastal town. Not so much a garden, more a long, narrow wedge, surrounded by high, pebble-dashed walls, almost black with the grime of years. Huge unkempt shrubs of dubious origin were dotted along at the base of the walls, darkest greens retreating into blackness at their base, as if chosen to harmonise with the cankered walls. Standing in contrast to the murky shade that pervaded the place was a stripling of a beech tree, planted close to the old house, which had thrown out ethereal salmon-pink leaves the first time I visited Esmee. She was lying on the verandah along with about eight other patients, their beds positioned immediately before the french windows, so that they could be quickly withdrawn into the ward at the first hint of rain. They lay there, propped up in a semi-upright position, their upper bodies bloated by a variety of overcoats and dressing gowns and scarves, the beds high under blankets neatly tucked in beneath their tartan Foxfords, as they called their over-blankets, after the woollen mill in the west of the country where they were woven. I can remember sitting with Esmee, watching her pale face with its tiny blotches of heightened colour on the cheeks, her eyes over-bright, seeing her anxious look sidewise as one or other of the people lying alongside her began a fit of coughing and spitting and I tried to keep my eyes on the fluttering pink beech leaves that reminded me of babies' tongues, steeling myself not to think about the colour of the tongues of the tubercular patients beside her.

'You are miles away, Helena. You have not heard a thing I have said, have you? What on earth has you so preoccupied?'

'Babies' tongues, Rebecca. Oh, don't pay any attention to me. It's just the wanderings of an old woman. Speaking of babies, did you tell me that you were due to have a scan about now?'

'Oh, that's been arranged for next week. But never mind that now, it's you that I want to talk about. The doctor says that all of this can be dealt with, reduced, perhaps eliminated completely.'

I don't want to talk about this. Neither does Rebecca. She cannot even bring herself to mention the word tumour.

'Yes, yes, I know all that and I'm not concerned about it, really I'm not. It is all manageable, even the pain is manageable it seems. Or it will be when it comes.'

I deliberately remind her about the pain, a sneaky sense of gratification flickering briefly before me as she struggles to obliterate the reminder.

'But you might never reach that stage, Helena. The tumour may be reduced to something completely insignificant.'

'Perhaps. Did you know that there are these little button things that allow people to administer their own pain-killers? The doctor told me all about it this morning.

Morphine. It's morphine they use. It's what she used, you know.'

And I cannot pluck it from the air before me. Cannot bury it back in the box with the diaries and letters. It carries a maroon sound in it, it hovers there like a great kite or a billowing sail, the dried-blood colour of a Galway hooker, sailing to Atlantic islands with turf and sheep and mail and flour, dark canvas arrangements preventing rolling in the swell. And I want to reach up into the air and steady my utterance, prevent it rolling to and fro between us, knowing it will settle down eventually, but not yet, not yet.

'I don't understand, Helena. Who used morphine?'

'Mama. She used morphine. It was what some of the wives used on those Thursday afternoons. She wrote about it all the time. That was her secret love, M, the one you thought was Lucinda's father. And in a way, perhaps you were right. M may well have been a sort of father.'

There is so much more I need to say, so much that I should say to Rebecca and yet I cannot. I have known this for so long that I cannot make it more tangible than the shadow it has been for me for years.

Rebecca is looking at me with incredulity, and I see the child she was once gazing at me as if I am a magician pulling something unexpected from a hat, watching an endless stream of garish colours unfurl, waiting for the white handkerchief she gave the magician to reappear so that she can return the small white square to her pocket, out of sight, for her own ordinary use. Return to the ordinary. But there is so much here for her to take in and I am suddenly fearful that this shock may not be good for a pregnant woman. And this thought is replaced by a kaleidoscope of images. Well, perhaps more like the disintegration of a kaleidoscope, a collapsing downward of shapes, like grains of sand slipping silkily down the side of a dune. Slipping downward before me are a series of transparent shapes, bulbous, like misshapen balloons, the X-rays of lungs and kidneys and skulls and embryos slipping downwards into an amorphous heap. And I can't help wondering if this is Rebecca's imprint, her personal template encapsulating the essentials of her life, a template which has fallen into disarray, is suddenly no more. Was it really as simple as this, was this all it took to destroy her version of Mama's story and ultimately her own story, a simple rejigging of events, a tiny tug here, a tweak there and lo! Then suddenly fluttering into place on top of them is Bart's photo, sent to Mama with its cryptic message on the back, a plea to turn from M. It lies there inert, a tiny image released into the world for us to make of it what we will. And sure enough we do. M may well be morphine but that is all I truly know.

'How do you know this, Helena? When did you discover it? Surely you must be mistaken.' Rebecca is talking to me, yet not expecting a response, beyond hearing a denial, if it were to come, and so I move relentlessly on.

'I found the equipment she used years ago, before I knew what it was. It was in her Chinese box. There were a few photos and postcards in the box and a false bottom. I found everything else beneath that.'

Everything else! I cannot name the things I found. To name them is to make them real. Even now I cannot do that, the naming of things.

Rebecca clutches at her sweater, a grey fluffy thing which I suspect is too warm for indoor wear and yet she manages to look cold. She begins to question me again, a quick-fire succession of darting sounds – when did Ally first mention M, the context, what exactly she said – turning it over and over, refusing my suggestion that she might read the diary entries herself, preferring a steady inquisition which is making me dizzy. Her questions are without direction, as if the inquisition has become the point, and I answer thoughtlessly and we move further and further apart.

In a sense we have always talked different languages, Rebecca and I. She has all that therapy and introspection at her back, which she hauls around like an armadillo. There it is again; I cannot think of it as anything else, try as I might, seeing this clumpy creature endlessly trundling to and fro along the horizon whenever she reaches back into her theories for an explanation. Everything seems to come down to language in the end. Or God. Or both. Sometimes, when she talks about her colleagues in her therapy group, they sound like they are clad in lead-weighted boots, attempting to fly, yet held down by choices they made a long time ago, choices long forgotten. They ditched things they now need but don't know how to recover them. And I can see this as she talks about her paradigms and holistic theories of human behaviour, none of which I pretend to understand, except the bit where she assumes that everbody and every action fits neatly into these boxes. But nobody seems to agree about the boxes, always squabbling, redefining, as if things or people never existed before they began to describe them. Back to language again. And God. In the beginning was the Word. Playing God is what they are at and what is worse is that I think they know it.

But for now, Rebecca has lost her way. Language has slipped away from her, as she tries to reach for certitude. I think she liked the idea that Lucinda's father was an unknown quantity for them both. As an unknown, she could play around with the possibilities, shape him in whatever likeness she chose. And Lucinda played along. It was always a game to her, her 'army orphan status', as she liked to call it. 'I was packed off to boarding school at six, you know – paid for by the British army and left to the mercy of those horrible nuns.' She enjoyed telling this story, embellishing it with each telling, so that her escapades in the hut at the end of the nuns' garden, where she helped in the making of wafer-thin bread for later consecration as communion hosts, piling it into sterile steel buckets and feeding the leftover dough to the cows, was a story she used to shock and amuse, a subtle revenge on the nuns she loathed. She forgot in the excitement of the story that I had been at that school too. But our time together had been brief, the period of overlap short. Rebecca was more comfortable with all that than she is now that there is some clarity. She was also comfortable with her idea of an imprint hanging over her. In a strange way it gave shape to her life, something she could pull against, while at the same time believing it was her destiny to fulfil its every tenet. And suddenly she discovers that she misread things, the imprint was not as she thought it was. And anyway, is there a difference between her notion of things fixed for us by our history and the idea of a divine plan? I wonder. But of course, Rebecca would not consider things in these terms. Too woolly for science. Too woolly for old women, at least for this old woman.

'You look tired, Helena. This must have come as a huge shock for you. I'm sorry, I should have realised that earlier. It just does not seem credible.'

Rebecca is sitting upright and stiff, which makes her look more pregnant. She listens intently as I tell her that I am not shocked, that it has all made great sense to me really.

'Mama never seemed mad to me, Rebecca. Not mad, you see, but sensible.'

'Sensible? Don't be ridiculous, Helena, how could taking morphine ever be sensible?'

'Action leading to escape, if only momentarily, appears eminently sensible to me. It's what I'll be opting for in a few months' time.'

'You almost sound as if you are looking forward to it.'

Rebecca retains her stiff, upright posture and I resist looking towards her to check if there is a hoist or a pulley anchored above her, about to drag her up out of her seat. Her eyes flicker briefly towards me as she waits for me to say something, but I am sinking into tiredness, into this new ague that has crept into my bones without my noticing in recent weeks, a surprise guest who outstays a welcome.

'I'll phone Anthony and talk over the test results with him if you don't mind, Helena. He may be able to offer advice.'

The realisation that my body is about to be appropriated as a project, to be passed around between these siblings for comment and analysis, accompanied by head-nodding and head-shaking and quiet reverential voices, so that I will resemble wine at a wine tasting, amuses me slightly until I remember the spitting and discarding.

'Yes, as you wish, Rebecca.'

I can hear my disinterest, but there it is. Protecting Rebecca from my indifference is not something I feel inclined to do right now. And talking about test results and phoning Anthony gives her something to do, so that she does not have to think beyond that. But given time she will and then she will come back to me and want to talk about Bart's photo and his message about M written on the back. But what I want most is for her to leave and let things settle around me. I want to lie back on my bed and listen to the sounds of this place and smell its evening smells. My place. I want to discover these things anew, commit them to memory against a time when memory is all there is left to me. I want to use these things to escape into the present. The past has me all used up.

Rain streamed down the window of Rebecca's kitchen yesterday. Long, slim slivers of silver moisture, as if sprayed on for effect, in keeping with a mood. Right as rain. When was rain ever right? Strange notion. It can only have come from somewhere that never had rain as frequently as we have it on this island.

Wolfgang was what I can only describe as light-hearted. He moved so briskly about the kitchen that I expected him to break into a skip or to start singing at any moment. Rebecca seemed puzzled by it and sat back, at his bidding, on a narrow bench running along the wall beside the table, watching him at the lunch preparations. Languid, I suppose, it might have been in someone other than Rebecca but it is not a word I can associate with her. Her pregnancy is quite noticeable now, yet she still sits bolt upright in what appears as an attempt to minimise the bulk of her profile. But every so often she slumps in a betrayal of tiredness, and then she looks like a wayward child with bad posture and I have to resist the temptation to pull her shoulders back.

Rebecca had a scan last week and came away with a photo of her baby son. I didn't admit it, but I could not make out much from the image – too blurry for my tired old eyes.

Wolfgang is planning a trip to his father's home, his 'Heimat', as he likes to call his village. It has been such a long time since he last saw his father. Surely the old man will forgive him his long absence and warm to his grandson.

But here I am writing his story before he has written it for himself. The privilege of old age, perhaps, sitting here in my room as if I am sitting inside a huge telescope that only permits me to look inwards, never outwards. Alice through the looking glass; Helena through the glass tube spiralling ever downwards, round and round. Dizzy. Chaos. Havoc. That's what it is, old age in all its unforeseen havoc. And nobody warned me!

There was an occasion a long time ago when I thought I stood inside a telescope. There was a particular street in the city which I can still recall vividly, which stretched in a long, straight line to a vanishing point that lay, it seemed to me then, beyond the curve of the horizon. The street was grey, anonymous, lined by dank, pebble-dashed walls, broken by patches that were almost black in their darkness where the surface dressing had fallen away. At intervals parked cars and delivery trucks huddled along the kerbside, but what mesmerised me was the distance to the horizon at the street's end, which ran on and on uninterrupted by any crossing or by the bending sky. And the sky was clear, not blue but a sort of washed-out faded colour, suffusing the street with an ethereal glow. I stood at the end of the nondescript street transfixed. It seemed to me that if I walked along this street, if I walked down its narrow length, on and on towards the horizon, that I would eventually reach the sea, of this I was absolutely sure. And a lifetime later the strength of that belief is still palpable, the light curving the dank walls inwards so that I believed the long glistening tunnel was mine alone. And for a long time afterwards, whenever I passed this street on my traverses through the city, I always paused to take a quick look along its length. And always I felt sure that the sea lay at its end.

Those trips to the city were with Mama, after we had left Queenstown and come back to the place of her birth. To be near her parents, she had told us children. So much grief and so much hope was vested in her return. But it came to naught. They had steeled themselves, steeled themselves against her marriage to Papa and again on his death. For them, his death had come too late. There were, after all, his children. All six of us. They could not bring themselves to confront us. Except, that is, for Bart.

'Do you remember learning about your father's death?' Rebecca asked me yesterday. She is no longer carefully turning up the edges of things, discreetly peeping beneath the corners, but has taken to asking me pointedly whatever is on her mind. Her pregnancy appears to have collapsed life and death issues into each other, so that she needs answers to everything now.

'No, I don't think that I remember.'

She'll have to make do with that. It's the words that elude me. There are pictures in my head, yet I don't know if they are imagined or if they have been placed there as a result of conversations over the years. One picture that has remained unchanged is that of Mama, sitting alone in the drawing room, in the subdued light of an early summer's day, the gas mantles not yet lit. She is composed, looking at the opposite wall as if she is seeing through it, and I know that she has sat like this on many occasions, waiting for whatever it is she finally sees before her. This is how I believe that she must have sat when the news of Papa's wounding was brought to her. 'Dangerously wounded' were the words used to inform her. What an odd way to put it. William whispered it to me in disbelief. 'The man said he is dangerously wounded.' And he thought that he would live but I know that Mama knew that he would not. He survived in a field hospital for two days before succumbing. Shot in a small French wood, on a slight incline, an innocuous, pastoral place, and he died after making the short journey down the hill to the field hospital. And it has been well recorded that a golden madonna atop a spire in the town of Albert was visible to the troops for miles around. But the incline was not significant, so he may not have had the benefit of such a comfort at the end. He died in one of the many tiny French villages which raised a monument to its dead sons and which never bore his name. Instead he lies among thousands of war dead in serried limestone rows of inscribed tablets, uniform dispatch cards that ticked them off one by one across the fields of France.

At least their names were displayed near the places where they fell. Here in their homeland it took us years to clean up a park dedicated to their memory and even then we locked the names into stone mausoleums lest they might be revealed. But there was a safety of sorts in that concealment for families like ours. And all those thousands of families had to learn the art of secrecy. It was as if their men had never died. Papa said about the leaders of the 1916 Rising that they got one thing right – they managed to die on their own soil. But that letter was lost too. Perhaps Mama could not bear the bitterness of his view, which was evident even as she related it to me years later. But men like Papa, she said, were scattered along the borders of an outdated map.

Almost three years of struggling to survive a descent into hell and we can never know what it involved for Papa, only the final act of annihilation. Lucinda was a year and a half by then. And this is what really causes Rebecca to focus on Papa's death. A child without a father, someone whose father, she believes, is unknown. It's like a pendulum there in the background, moving ponderously between the known and the unknown. But Papa was lost to us all in 1917. And in a way, so too was Mama. And yet her picture is more tangible in that period than it was either before or since. The clarity of her figure sitting there, looking straight ahead, eyes boring through the wall and beyond that, beyond the house to a place that was green or the blue-white of ice or the greeny grey of congealed mud – that image holds the picture of Richard as father in it. Whether he was a father for Lucinda too will probably never be known.

And it was after that initial period of shock and grief that Mama fell away from us completely, not into the flickering absences that resulted from her Thursday afternoons with the officers' wives. This falling away was more profound. This was a shocking withdrawal which left us with a daily encounter with a shell, which Mrs O placed carefully sitting where she could watch her and where we could play within her sight and hearing. I think that Mrs O hoped we might somehow manage to force Mama back into an existence of sorts in the present by dint of noise and boisterous play.

Then suddenly one day Mama began to pack things –
anything she could lay her hands on, placing them in any
container she could find. The hall slowly filled up with
trunks and baskets and canvas bags and boxes, all
precariously placed on top of each other, sometimes falling
over with a loud crash into the centre of the hallway, to lie
there until her next foray with another container, when she
would begin again to heave things back against the walls
while Mrs O watched helplessly. And somehow in the
midst of this desperate activity she decided that not only
were we leaving Queenstown but we were going to travel
to Dublin, where we would live close to her family. And
once more it was William who told me this, who told me
how Mama was up in her bedroom shaking uncontrollably,
'Not crying,' he said, 'just shaking', while Mrs O tried to
wrap her tightly in her shawl, saying to her that of course
she could not return to Dublin, sure hadn't her family
disowned her when she married and what use had they
ever been to her up to now?

Sometimes I dream about this pathetic shivering creature,
who appears always as a wraith with no resemblance to
Mama except in her upright posture, staring straight ahead.
And in the dream Mrs O is still attempting to wrap her in
her enormous green and navy woollen shawl but the wispy
trails of vapour from the wraith-like creature escape
constantly from her ministering arms and float upwards
and along the walls as if seeking some tiny crack in the
plasterwork through which to escape.

Last night I had this dream again but the green and navy
shawl seemed much bigger than in the past, the squares
much larger than I recall. And Mrs O kept shaking the
shawl over and over, as if trying to dislodge something,

when suddenly a baby came tumbling from within the plaid folds, sliding in slow motion down the thick creases, the small plump limbs curled upwards as if braced for a landing. And neither Mrs O nor Mama noticed the baby, as they each remained immersed in Mama's needs. In these dreams she has almost become the opium itself, the snow, flaky, white, translucent, as if another shake of the shawl might send her scattered to the corners of the room. And at the same time the dream was filled with refracted light and colour and tactile sensations that I can still sense now.

Perhaps this is what awaits me when all the chemicals are exhausted and I am too wasted to resist floating off on morphine to this other sensual place and I will not want to return to the edgy reality that I have fetched up in here. Not that Mama ever hinted to any of us what it was like in those days. Perhaps she suggested to Mrs O the release that her Thursdays brought, as she struggled with loneliness and anxiety and the searing demands of children and pregnancy. I don't remember. I don't remember and yet even as I think about it there is a familiarity about it all, a stirring in the back of my mind that is more than William's whispered reports, more than words overheard from Mrs O as she tried to placate Mama. It's a mental shiver, an anticipation of something dreaded, yet longed for. This perhaps is what it was like for Papa as he moved, unknowing, into the final months of his life. Perhaps noise was the only difference between his torment and Mama's at the end. But his letters are missing, destroyed by her or lost in the move to Dublin. Stories of a war, his life diminished and finally snuffed out, floating as ashes before a wind or stirred by Mrs O as she rattled the range in the back kitchen in Queenstown.

'We can't take too much with us to Dublin, Mrs O.'

Poor Ally. She thought that by leaving things behind she could also leave memories.

But the echoes of course hung around in one form or another. Her Chinese box travelled with us anyway, whether in oversight or in a final reluctance to leave so many memories, I shall never know. And hidden beneath the false bottom was her bong, tucked into a tightly woven hessian bag with a drawstring top. It may have been a decorative prop, something that gave a glamorous edge to the Thursday activities. It is something I have tried not to dwell on for long. The box came to the city with Mama, even though she was now adrift from the Thursday afternoons and the wives. And the bong surfaced once when the Chinese box fell at her feet and burst open in front of Gerald, who quickly leaped to retrieve it, placing it in his mouth and pushing out his chest, strutting up and down with mock puffing gestures like a miniature grandfather figure. His thin legs were bent with the effort of his performance and I can almost see the shadow in those strutting limbs of the debilitating polio that was to shrivel one of his legs in his teens and deprive him of his ambition to follow his father into the army.

'There's all sorts of diseases up there in the city,' Mrs O had whispered fearfully to Mama, 'tuberculosis, polio-myelitis, even some of that 'flu the papers have been talking about,' she said, as if too loud a mention might bring about a visitation of one of these horrors. It was a last, faint attempt by Mrs O to dissuade her from leaving for the city.

I suppose that Mrs O suspected that we might be forced to leave Queenstown. But perhaps not, for she did not understand the workings of the military, the need for them to keep a garrison up to strength, to move along the dependants of the military in order to free up accommodation for their replacements. And she did not understand how our position as a family was indissolubly linked to Papa's military status and how his removal to war had left us flapping in the wind like the coloured strips of bunting at the West Cork regatta a lifetime ago. But whatever she understood in advance, when Mama decided to leave, it seemed to strike Mrs O 'like a bolt from the blue', as she said to me one afternoon while Mama was resting. And it was only then that I realised that departing from Queenstown meant leaving Mrs O behind.

'It'll only be for a little while. And it will be good for your mother to see her family again. She surely needs them at this dreadful time, God help her. Sure you'll be back here in no time.'

And we pretended, all of us, throughout the preparations and the departure, that, yes, we would be back. But we children were not to know, nor I suspect, did Mrs O, that our departure would be to a smaller house, inadequate for a large family, close to our grandmother and to military accommodation, yet so far removed from the support and contact with either as to be irrelevant.

But this tidying up and tying of strings in Queenstown has no appeal for Rebecca as she moves lugubriously into her pregnancy. She doesn't expect to find anything more of use there. Instead she has her sights set now on the details of childbirth – she has decided to go for the natural approach, as far as safety will allow. She still dips into Mama's story from time to time but she has begun treating it like a story that she wishes to continue indefinitely, as if it is a tale that will help me rather than her, so that she poses questions that she would like me to ponder, little exercises she devises for me in quiet moments.

'I wonder what it was like for Ally returning to the city with six children whom her mother and stepfather had never met, coming to live so close to them, yet never being invited beyond their hall door?'

But she does not expect an answer and I never attempt to speculate on one. After all, what would be the point? We could muse together or separately on why this happened, on why Mama's mother permitted her husband, Mama's stepfather, to dominate the household in this way. They were such different times. But right now I don't want to deflect Rebecca's thoughts, couldn't bear to hear her pushing and pulling at the edges of this story in an attempt to secure a neat fit. Right now all I want for her is to concentrate on herself.

My only concern now, according to May, is to take plenty of rest in between my sessions of chemotherapy and eat well to build up my strength. Such neat, simple solutions. Complexity laid bare, like a flayed skeleton, deceptively simple at first glance. Outside in the corridor I hear the seductive sucking sound of the rubber-wheeled trolley on the non-stick floor. May is coming with tea to deliver me into the ways of regular nourishment. I lie back and wait for the door to yield to the push of the trolley. Beyond the window, the mountains appear to have been rolled back to make way for the lowering clouds and a violet haze begins its descent on the city.

THE
THIRTEENTH ROOM

Siobhán Parkinson

•

**'You remind me of somebody, but I can't think who.'
This part was quite untrue. Elise knew perfectly well
who it was that Niamh reminded her of . . .**

It has been nine years since the death of a young girl on the Taggart farm near the quiet Irish village of Dromadden. But memories of the tragedy are powerfully called up when Niamh comes to Planten to nurse the dying Taggart. Niamh quickly becomes embroiled in the manipulations and deceptions of the Taggart family, but her questions about Miriam's death meet with silence from both the family and the villagers. As Niamh uncovers the truth, it becomes apparent that her own fate is bound up with that of Miriam. Retelling the age-old story of the fall from innocence into experience, this original novel by acclaimed Irish writer Siobhán Parkinson is a complex exploration of the often precarious nature of women's lives that resonates far beyond its Irish context.

'An original and beautifully written novel'
ÉILÍS NÍ DHUIBHNE

'This absorbing story, lyrical and blackly comic, is an intriguing exploration of past deceptions and hurt. An impressive Big House novel with a difference.'
NIALL MacMONAGLE

A thought-provoking novel, elegant and enigmaatic, with a lyrical style to be savoured slowly
Irish Independent

0-85640-745-3
£6.99

CALL MY
BROTHER BACK

Michael McLaverty

•

**'His tact and pacing, in the individual sentence
and the overall story, are beautiful . . . McLaverty's
place in our literature is secure.'**

It is 1918 and thirteen-year-old Colm MacNeill is living
happily on the idyllic island of Rathlin when his security
is suddenly shattered by the death of his father. The loss of
the family breadwinner forces the MacNeills to leave their
island home to make a life for themselves in the city. On the
streets of Belfast Colm and his brothers enjoy a different kind
of freedom – childhood adventures that run late into the
evening, games that last for days and friendly tussles make life
in the city a new kind of liberation. This sense of freedom is,
however, short-lived. As sectarian violence erupts in Belfast,
the MacNeills become unavoidably caught up in the conflict
and tensions around them . . .

PRAISE FOR *Call My Brother Back*

'A truly great novel, and the best novel out of the North, or
for that matter, perhaps out of Ireland, in modern times.'
Irish News

'a book of decided quality' *Observer*

'a new milestone on the road of Anglo–Irish literature'
Irish Independent

0-85640-746-1
£6.99

COLLECTED
SHORT STORIES

Michael McLaverty

•

M ichael McLaverty, one of Ireland's most distinguished short story writers, paints with acute precision and intensity the landscape of Northern Ireland, its remote hill farms, rough island terrain and the terraced back streets of Belfast. His stories evoke moments of passion, wonder or disenchantment in the lives of people living in environments that are often hostile and cruel. These small dramas are depicted with remarkable compassion and perception, and a breadth of vision and purity of language which is nothing short of masterly.

This collection is a fitting celebration of the life of a writer whose achievements have been compared to both Joyce and Chekhov.

'It is quite easy to equate McLaverty with
the perfection of the short story form.'
Irish Independent

'McLaverty's work is mesmerising'
Sunday Business Post

0-85640-727-5
£14.99